DEAD
HEAT

Also by Sabine Durrant

Having It and Eating It
The Great Indoors
Under Your Skin
Remember Me This Way
Lie With Me
Take Me In
Finders, Keepers
Sun Damage

DEAD
SABINE DURRANT
HEAT

C
CENTURY

CENTURY

UK | USA | Canada | Ireland | Australia
India | New Zealand | South Africa

Century is part of the Penguin Random House group of companies whose addresses can be found at global.penguinrandomhouse.com

Penguin Random House UK,
One Embassy Gardens, 8 Viaduct Gardens, London SW11 7BW

penguin.co.uk

First published 2026
001

Copyright © Sabine Durrant, 2026

The moral right of the author has been asserted

Penguin Random House values and supports copyright. Copyright fuels creativity, encourages diverse voices, promotes freedom of expression and supports a vibrant culture. Thank you for purchasing an authorised edition of this book and for respecting intellectual property laws by not reproducing, scanning or distributing any part of it by any means without permission. You are supporting authors and enabling Penguin Random House to continue to publish books for everyone. No part of this book may be used or reproduced in any manner for the purpose of training artificial intelligence technologies or systems. In accordance with Article 4(3) of the DSM Directive 2019/790, Penguin Random House expressly reserves this work from the text and data mining exception.

Typeset in 12.5/17.38pt Times New Roman by Six Red Marbles UK, Thetford, Norfolk
Printed and bound in Great Britain by Clays Ltd, Elcograf S.p.A.

The authorised representative in the EEA is Penguin Random House Ireland,
Morrison Chambers, 32 Nassau Street, Dublin D02 YH68

A CIP catalogue record for this book is available from the British Library

ISBN: 978–1–529–95294–0 (hardback)
ISBN: 978–1–529–95295–7 (trade paperback)

Penguin Random House is committed to a sustainable future for our business, our readers and our planet. This book is made from Forest Stewardship Council® certified paper.

For Giles

The Court of First Instance

Sparta
February 2025
2.10 p.m.

He looks thinner, as he shuffles in, than at the trial. Four weeks in high security at Korydallos will do that, I guess. He's holding his left elbow through the sleeve of his orange boiler suit and I wonder if it's damaged, but he could just be squeezing a mosquito bite.

    A backlog and an ill judge have delayed sentencing. It's February now and most people have left. I see him scan the rows, notice me, keep going. He's searching for her, of course, instinctively. Or for any of the old gang. Sorry, mate, they've all gone. His eyes return reluctantly to me. I remember something nice Celia had said once: that I was dependable, you could see it in my face – like an old station clock. I adjust the strap of my watch – bloody hot in here – and shrug apologetically. Just me, I'm afraid: nobody.

They tell him to sit, and I see the shackles on his wrists. Interesting. No more special treatment, then.

An official stands and starts to talk. Some of it's translated; a lot isn't. I slightly zone out. A woman in the corridor told me this judge 'gives out years like chickpeas'. But it could still go either way, even at this stage. All that money, the best lawyers, his public standing, that house – it might yet count in his favour. He's still watching me, I eventually realise. I try to read his expression. Gratitude? Sparta's not the easiest place to get to. Or remorse? I have a horrible feeling it's defiance.

I think about the old Maniot flag and its motto: 'With it or on it' – the cry of Spartan women as they handed departing warriors their shields. What did people fight for then? Honour? Really? Didn't it always come down to something less grand – resentment, betrayal, envy? Sex? The newspaper I used to work for called this 'a crime of passion'.

Celia was better off without either of them. I could have told her that from the start.

And now the judge is speaking and the moment of reckoning is upon us. I unstrap my watch and lay it on the adjacent empty chair. Very soon we'll know how this ends.

PART ONE

1

The summer I turned fifty-one and realised I was a failure, I went to the Mani to lick my wounds. Old friends had a house there (it had been in the family for generations) and, knowing I'd been let go both by the paper and my girlfriend, they told me the stone cottage in the grounds was mine for as long as I wanted, or needed, or both.

I landed late and missed the last bus, so hitched a ride out of Kalamata with a Dutch structural engineer – not much given to conversation – who dropped me in the lee of the mountain up on the road a mile or so beyond the village of Kardamos. The southernmost point of mainland Europe (the middle finger of the Peloponnese), the Mani is famously hot, harsh and unwelcoming; its inhabitants, apparently descended from the Spartans, are said never to forgive a grudge. ('Victory or

Death'.) But it had good associations for me. Takara and I had made a pleasant visit several years ago and, despite my Celtic skin, I like the sun. After a morning's writing, I'd lie in it, sleep in it, soak it up like a basking shark. As I used the torch on my phone to find the track that ran past the high wall of Villa Mimosa, my friends' house, and steeply on, down between rustling olives, I felt optimistic for the first time in weeks.

The cottage, which emerged out of a small clearing, was a simple whitewashed building, single storey with a high, pitched roof. Celia had mentioned trying to 'send in her housekeeper', and I assumed it was she who'd left the ill-fitting door unlocked. It was musty, airless, inside and the light switch didn't seem to work, but I dumped my suitcase in the doorway, unzipped it, and dug out my trunks. I'd been dreaming of my swim since Gatwick. In the jostle of the queue at Pret, I'd imagined the silence and the darkness, the stroke of inky water against skin; longed for it on the cramped flight. I promised myself I'd go in whatever time I arrived. It would be cleansing, purgative, the first step towards a fresh start.

The cottage was in the last hollow of tree-covered terrain before the land ran down to the sea, and I followed the uneven path, avoiding cacti and prickly pears, and scrambled over rocks towards what I remembered to be a small inlet, a tiny pebbly beach, the last bite-mark in a much bitten wider bay. The air smelt of oregano and thyme. A few shapes – bats, I guessed – darted above my head. The low moon threw flickering shadows, layers of grey shade, and I felt the early wallow of a not unenjoyable self-pity. It would be several days until

Celia and Adam joined me and, under that huge expanse of navy sky, I fancied myself very much alone. It wasn't immediate, more of a slow dawning as I reached the water that what I'd felt beneath my feet had not been the pounding of waves but the thump of dance music, and that I was anything but.

Dividing this bay from the small harbour of Kardamos was a low craggy promontory; there'd been an abandoned building on this site for years – a folly, built in the 1980s by an Athenian shipping magnate, who'd neglected to secure access to water and electricity. What I remembered as an uninhabited ghost house, its weathered walls almost indistinguishable from the bedrock, was now ablaze with light, a fairground ride, a liner on gala night. It had doubled in size, produced protuberances – the flank of a pool, the finger of a jetty, beyond which, further out, a huge white yacht was anchored. Music was throbbing, the lyrics clear across the empty stretch, each word reverberating, and, on the top terrace, figures were dancing, arms punching, as they all loudly longed to live like common people. All the windows were lit and some sort of multi-coloured strobe-effect pulsed across the bay. Nothing was black, all was ignited; the sea and sky beating, thrumming, vibrating.

In a recent interview – to promote his latest cultural/travel documentary – Adam appointed the Mani as his 'spiritual home' (though of course it was Celia's long before his). He bemoaned the various pockets of development along the coast but described this spot, where they'd inherited 'a tiny house' (Villa Mimosa actually had six bedrooms), as remote and undiscovered. I thought about this as I changed behind a rock, putting my watch inside a shoe for safety. So much for his 'secret patch of heaven'.

The water stretched in front of me like an iridescent cone, stripped with coloured light. Not ink, but petrol. I stepped blindly in. The song changed. Someone across the water screamed in delight, and I slipped. There'd been moments when I'd felt pretty irrelevant over the previous months – losing my column, discovering Takara's infidelity. The agony of treading on a sea urchin was, in comparison, almost exquisite.

It's not important. I only mention it because that juxtaposition – one person's pleasure, another's pain – seems pertinent, a reprisal of past events and a presentiment of the terrible things that were to come.

2

I found it hard to sleep that night – my foot throbbed, the sheets smelt stale and there was only one pillow, which wasn't great for my acid reflux. I woke abruptly at one point, convinced I'd heard someone outside: the rattle of dislodged stones, the crack of twigs snapping. I thought I saw a shadow pass across the window, but when I pushed aside the blind, no face loomed, just trees flickering in the darkness.

In the morning, as the sun shafted in, I told myself I'd been stupid. I was in Greece, in the middle of nowhere. Most likely I'd been terrorised by a goat.

The cottage, in daylight, was simply decorated, with white walls, wooden beams across a spider-webby ceiling, sisal rugs on a rough stone floor. Aside from my bedroom there was an open plan kitchen/living room – a sofa and a couple of chairs – and a lean-to bathroom which you accessed from outside. It was perfect, aside from the underlying mess: the housekeeper clearly hadn't been in after all. Adam and Celia's kids – a boy, my godson, and a daughter – who'd been using it as a den, were clearly accustomed to people clearing up after them. This, I set about, scrubbing the crumby table and worktop, washing the dirty cups, throwing away the toothbrush and the old milk, and putting various scattered items of clothing – including discarded underwear – in a plastic bag to give to my hosts when they arrived. It amused me, actually, how teenage it all was: the cigarette filters above the fridge; the packet of Durex under the bed; the lump of hash wrapped in cling film in the coffee jar.

Once that was done, I had a fiddle about with my foot – using tweezers to remove a couple of spines – and then wrote myself a shopping list. By the time I set off for Kardamos, the nearest village, it was late morning; the sun – it was early July – was already strong. Sweat quickly gathered in my hairline and, as I reached the main road, long trousers already felt like a mistake. But the day was rich with possibility: small birds darted and soared; cicadas hissed; bees hummed. It was quiet. A couple of pick-up trucks trundled past on a burst of radio, and a girl on a quad bike – long dark hair, bare brown legs, no helmet (a catalogue of potential disasters) – buzzed towards me and away. The sky was blue, white clouds slipped from the top of the mountain in an orderly line, and at certain points the bend in the road revealed a sudden gleaming expanse of Messenian Gulf.

Dead Heat

I was about halfway to Kardamos when I passed a sign: a large slab of slate inscribed 'ARCADIA' in a rather naff Greek-style font and a stretch of newly tarmacked drive disappearing towards the promontory. On one of the rather vulgar white pillars was pinned a poster for a missing person: 'HAVE YOU SEEN MARC ASHLEY?' printed in big capitals above the photo of a man: grinning, helmet under arm, astride a large motorbike. There was writing in various languages underneath but in English I read he was Marc, 38, brown-haired and of medium build, and that he had last been seen, wearing navy Nike joggers and a red baseball cap, on 9 June. The phone number was for a police station in the nearby town of Aetolia.

I counted six identical notices along the main road into Kardamos and a further one in the window of a small grocery/hardware store I found in a back street. Paying for my provisions, I pointed to the poster and, using the Greek dictionary I'd brought with me, asked the shopkeeper, a middle-aged woman with a wide, open face, if she knew anything about it. She shook her head. 'What about the big new house? That's all changed,' I said, partly to let her know I wasn't just a casual tourist, that I had a history with the place. In good English, she replied that the new owner brought a lot of business to local shops and bars, so . . . I gave up on the phrase book and said, 'I thought the problem about that house was you couldn't get planning for water and electricity?' and this time she brushed her thumb back and forth along the underside of her fingers to suggest a backhander. 'Oh,' I said knowingly.

I told her I was here for the summer, staying over at Villa

Mimosa in a cottage in the grounds, which she seemed to know of (the '*spitaki*' she called it, which translated, she said, as 'little house'). I told her my name and she told me hers – Andrea – and we shook hands. It's always good to establish a rapport with locals; if nothing else it gives one a sense of belonging.

After that, I went down to the small harbour and sat on the wall beyond a few parked cars and ate a custard pastry – flaky and still warm. The new house, Arcadia, was hidden by cypress trees, though I could still see the yacht, a great white monstrosity piled high with satellites, jet skis strapped to its rear. It looked out of place in this sleepy environment. Swallows twittered and swooped from crumbly nests; halyards clattered. On the jetty, a man in a vest top sat cross-legged, cleaning squid in a bucket.

I'd got used to the change in my situation, to keeping emotion at bay, but I had a sucker-punch memory of the last time I'd been here: in the taverna filing a late piece of copy while Takara sat on the wall with her sketchbook, drawing maybe even the very same fisherman.

I'd been part of a couple then. Now I wasn't.

I thought again about the afternoon I'd arrived home unexpected. Rick of all people: the head architect at her firm, *twice* divorced, who, when he came to dinner that time, kept saying how much he loved Japanese culture, and Takara of course meant 'Treasure' and would we be eating on a tatami? He was, as I told Celia, such an *arse*.

Celia had laughed and said, 'You're too nice, that's your

problem.' I'd asked her if it was really true that women liked nastiness? It surprised me she would admit to it, even taking Adam out of the equation, because she was such a spiritual person. And she'd been silent for a while and finally murmured, 'No, not really,' but not in a way that convinced.

I stared down at the water, yellows and blues and pinks, reflections of boats and buildings splitting into wobbly squares, but heard a shout and looked up to see a speedboat churning messily in past the harbour arm, and then, with a loud cranking of gears, heading towards an empty space on the jetty. The sea slapped against the wall. The fisherman in the vest top leapt over and ran down to catch a rope. The engine cut, and six or seven people clambered out. They stood for a minute, smoothing hair, tucking in tops, rearranging skirts, then picked up their suitcases and wheeled them, rattling, up to the triangle of parked cars.

They stopped a few feet from where I was sitting. The men were in linen shirts and shorts; the women in maxi-dresses and leather sandals, what Takara would call 'Me+Em-style luxe'. One of the men looked vaguely familiar – did he run a famous media company? One of the women yawned, tapping her fist against her mouth, as a black SUV came around the corner. The doors slid open and more people emerged – three women, two men. The two groups stood awkwardly next to each other. One of the new women brandished a bottle: 'Tequila with a worm in it!' she said. 'For the man who has everything.' The others laughed politely.

The driver took the new bags out of the boot and put the old ones in and, finally, the people who had got off the boat got in the car and the people who had got out of the car headed towards the boat. The car did a complicated several-point turn, causing people who were passing to stand out of the way, and purred off. The speedboat, when I turned back to look, was already whizzing out across the water towards Arcadia.

When I went up to Islington to collect the key to the cottage, and while Celia was searching for it in a series of over-stuffed kitchen drawers, Adam gripped my shoulder and said, '*Do* something. *Use* the time. *Write* the bloody screenplay.' It stung a bit – I can still remember when I was the success and he was the ne'er-do-well – but I had downloaded the software 'Final Draft' and that afternoon, on a small metal table in the shade, I did my best to follow his instructions.

I had a notebook of ideas, one of which I was quite keen on. The year before, when the paper was finding things for me to do, I'd interviewed a couple in Iowa who'd invented a sonar machine that could find dead bodies in water. It struck me as rich ground for a thriller. The cottage had surprisingly good Wi-Fi – I guess Celia and Adam's kids had insisted – and I spent several hours researching such pleasant topics as false conclusions regarding accidental death and the effect of bacteria on bloat. It was quite enjoyable, and after a while I felt I'd done a good day's work. Solitude and isolation do strange things to time and I was surprised, when I closed my laptop, to see it was only 3 p.m.

I washed and tidied up, and looked at my new home from

various angles, wondering if it might once have been a chapel, with its small windows, its high pitch – might that even be a cross buried in the ivy? It was an apt, comforting thought, good for my long-lapsed soul to be kipping in a place of God. I watched a lizard and a couple of small beige doves who were nesting in the roof and I downloaded Duolingo and signed on for Greek. Later, I soaked my sore foot in vinegar, which was a hot tip online, and I had another swim – wearing the pair of turquoise neoprene 'aqua shoes' I'd bought in the village. I found a sock on the beach I must have dropped the night before and was glad to have it back. Everything needs its pair.

I gazed across at the new house on the headland. If you went on the evidence of his visitors, the owner wasn't a Russian oligarch as I'd imagined, but English and male and about my age. Connected, maybe; if I'd been right about the media owner. Also *showy*, using the boat to transport his guests when he had perfectly good road access. I expected the new arrivals would be settling in now. I imagined them handing the worm-ridden tequila to their host, trying out their beds, dipping their toes in the pool, but not yet ready to plunge. Shy, as guests sometimes are, even with old friends.

For now, across that short stretch of water, all was quiet.

3

I had drawn up a budget and supper out was not part of that night's plan. But as darkness fell, and the electric rattle of cicadas dropped to a gas hiss, I felt such an acute need for the presence of other people, I decided to treat myself, and make cuts somewhere else along the way.

Arriving back in the harbour, I was surprised to find it much busier than in the morning, positively sparkly and bustling, smelling deliciously of grilled meat and charcoaled fish. I remembered Adam insisting Dimitri's, the taverna at the far end, was the best ('They're all the same,' Celia had mouthed as he'd stalked ahead), so I headed straight for that, eschewing Alonissos, which looked very similar, and Roxi's Place, a white-and-gold-themed cocktail bar. At Dimitri's, fairy lights danced along the roof, and 'Zorba's Dance' was playing softly on the sound system. The chairs were blue-backed and rush-seated and my table had a rustic wobbliness; I put a napkin under one leg to secure it.

The waiter, intimidatingly sideburned and open-shirted, had the air, as he slapped down the menu, of having more important things to attend to. I felt under pressure to order quickly and remembering Adam talking about '*horta*', a green vegetable loved by the locals, asked for a portion of that. There was a fish Adam said one had to eat, horse-something, but the waiter wasn't helpful, so I panic-plumped for deep-fried calamari, which would be a) frozen and b) bad for my cholesterol but c) reliably delicious. I ordered a semi-carafe of retsina because it was cheap.

As I swilled my glass and took the first throat-scraping swig, I noticed the woman at a table by the water. She was younger than me – in her early forties, I guessed – with chin-length dark hair and large eyes, dressed casually and maybe too warmly in jeans and an oversized grey hoody. She looked up while I was watching her and, in the spotlight of her gaze, I felt a familiar heat, an animal stir of interest, immediately quashed by the memory of my own dark bedroom, Takara's small high breasts as she leapt to one side, Rick's long white limbs. Embarrassed, I spun my head, pretending to be seeking the arrival of my food. Next to me an elderly couple were gamely tackling a fish in a violently red sauce. Further away, a muscular man in a dark-blue uniform was standing at the bar, gun at his hip.

When I turned back, the woman had risen lightly from her chair and was moving towards me. I managed to pull myself together when she said, 'Are you English?'

I asked jauntily if it was the phrase book or the panama hat that had given me away and she smiled and said did she catch an accent? I told her I was originally from Manchester, though I'd long lived in the softy south, and after that she said she hoped she wasn't disturbing me?

Still trying to suppress the image of Rick's penis lolling, semi-tumescent, against his pale thigh, I said, 'Not at all. Please,' and, leaping to my feet, I pulled out an empty chair.

Her eyes brushed over me as she shook her head. She bent to rummage in her bag. The police officer had noticed and was already walking towards us as she brought out a sheaf of paper and handed the top piece to me. Still flustered, I frowned, pretending to be reading it carefully. It was another flyer about the missing man, with different photos and more writing, new details about a reward.

'My brother, Marc,' she said.

'Oh gosh,' I said gauchely. 'I saw the posters. He's your *brother*,' stupidly as if it were an amusing coincidence.

An expression skimmed her features, more weary than irritated. 'He's been missing for four weeks. Tomorrow there's another fingertip search and we're looking for volunteers.'

The police officer was standing protectively at her shoulder now, legs apart, thick hands on sturdy hips. She glanced up at him. 'Christos and his team have been brilliant, obviously, and they've thrown everything they've got at it. We just think it's worth widening the net as the season is building. Particularly now there's an incentive.'

'An incentive?'

'The reward. A kind benefactor has just put up some money. We're hoping it'll make all the difference.'

I looked back at the flyer. Fifty thousand euros. 'Oh, I see.'

'I appreciate you're probably on holiday, but if you could spare a couple of hours, we're meeting at nine a.m. tomorrow on the path up to the ravine – you know it's off the main road as it goes south? But all the info's on the sheet. Anyway.'

Her cheeks suffused with pink and her shoulders sprang together in a shudder, or a shiver. Beneath the bulky clothes, I could see there was something delicate about her. I realised she was warmly dressed because she *was* cold; grief does that – I remembered my mother in our front room after my father died wrapped in a blanket – and I wanted to put my arm around her, to express some kind of comfort. Maybe if it hadn't been for the initial sexual attraction, I might have done so. But it was too late; she was already turning towards the older couple on the next table.

Realising Christos, the police officer, was about to follow, I asked him quickly if he knew what her brother had been doing out here?

He looked at me consideringly. 'He had come for a party,' he said. He gestured towards the headland.

'You mean he was staying at the new house when he disappeared?' I said. 'At Arcadia?'

He moved his chin from side to side, and eventually nodded. 'On the Sunday morning, he went for a run and never came back. It is a very sad occurrence.'

His chin vanished into his thick neck as if he regretted saying even that much.

'What do you think *happened*?'

He sighed. 'I have told Sara many times, the landscape here is not to be treated lightly. It is harsh and unforgiving. The mountains are not a playground for tourists. If you leave the path, you can be lost, and never found.'

I lowered my voice. 'So you don't think her brother's coming back?'

Maybe he didn't hear because he'd already turned away.

I was halfway home, just past the drive up to Arcadia, trying to keep the weight off my sore foot. There was a fullish moon; the stretch of sky was a deep blue and the mountain, looming to the left, a bleak black, but the road itself was stippled with lacy pale grey ribbons of light and, in my semi-inebriated haze, I imagined the creature weaving towards me to be a Nereid, a sea nymph, who are said to come ashore on this coast. Only when she was up close did I recognise her as the girl with the long black hair I'd seen that morning – dangerously *sans* helmet – on a quad bike. Seemingly unaware of my presence, she sank on to the low wall by the side of the road, and put her head between her knees.

I assumed she was even drunker than I was and, as she was quite scantily dressed in shorts and a corset-like top, I felt quite uncomfortable. I didn't want to abandon a damsel in distress but if I were *her*, being addressed by *me* – middle-aged, which is to say old but not reassuringly old – in the dark, in the middle of nowhere, I might assume the worst.

So, approaching gingerly, I perched on the edge of the

brickwork several feet away, and waited a few minutes before I said, 'Are you OK? Can I do anything to help?'

She looked up then and for a fleeting moment I thought I saw a flash of calculation, but immediately discounted it because her mouth was downturned, and her eyes, dark brown and heavily lashed, brimmed suddenly with tears.

I said, 'Oh no. Don't cry. Please.'

'It's all pointless. I've come all this way and it's all for nothing.'

I asked whether she had far to go, and she said no, she was staying nearby. 'No thanks to him.'

'And are you OK getting home on your own?'

'I am. I've just hurt my fucking foot.'

'Oh, me too,' I said.

She frowned, and I lifted my knee, dangling my brogued appendage, and said, 'I trod on a sea urchin. I think it's infected.'

'A sea urchin?'

'In the sea. I know. Stupid of me.'

'Aren't you supposed to piss on it or something?'

'I think that's jellyfish.'

'Oh yeah.'

She smiled, revealing a neat row of small white teeth, and I felt a moment of camaraderie which, to be honest, I'd missed recently – having a woman to joke with – though, of course, she was far too young.

She turned her own foot towards me, and I shuffled along the wall to examine it. She was wearing flip-flops and blood seeped from a flap of skin on her rather grubby big toe. I bound it with my clean hanky and told her to wash it carefully when she got home. Maybe apply Savlon if she had some.

'Savlon? What's Savlon?'

'An antiseptic cream. When I was young, it was all we had.'

She asked if I was a priest, which took me by surprise – maybe it was the grey shirt and trousers. Or the St Christopher, which always hangs around my neck.

'Who is he?' she asked, pointing at it.

She wouldn't know, I realised, being of different ethnicity and also just *young*.

'He's a saint but wearing it doesn't mean I'm a priest. It's just a symbol – a gimmick, really. He's supposed to provide safe travel and protection, to help you, you know, overcome adversity, follow your destiny.'

'So like a superstition? A lucky charm?'

'Something like that.'

'Maybe I'll get one. I sodding well need a bit of help overcoming adversity.'

I laughed first this time and she joined in.

I double-checked she was OK getting home and said I ought to head off myself – that it was a bit dark and creepy at night in the cottage where I was staying. She looked interested then, and asked where it was. I told her and then I explained how Andrea in the local shop called it a *spitaki*.

'A *spitaki*?' the girl said.

'A small house. A cottage.'

And that was it. That was all there was. Afterwards, we bid each other goodnight and staggered off in opposite directions.

I must have accidentally left a window open, and a battalion of mosquitoes had got in. I leapt from side to side, trying to slap them in the air, or catch them against the side of the fridge, so it was a few minutes before I was calm enough to sit down at the table. The connection that linked my laptop with the lead was dodgy and earlier, leaving it to charge, I'd created a balancing arrangement with a book and a mug to keep everything in place. The lead was now lying on the ground, detached from the computer. Combined with the open window, it freaked me out a bit, and I became convinced someone had been here while I was out. Was my bag where I'd left it? Had there been more beer in the fridge?

For a mad moment I imagined Marc Ashley had been hiding here; that it was his presence I'd felt. I put the thought out of my head. Isolation, I told myself, was driving me mad.

Notes from my notebook

A cadaver in the water starts to sink as soon as the air in its lungs is replaced with water. Once submerged, the body stays underwater until the bacteria in the gut and chest cavity produce enough gas – methane, hydrogen sulphide and carbon dioxide – to float it to the surface like a balloon. (The build-up of methane, hydrogen sulphide, etc. can take days or weeks, depending on a number of factors.) At first not all parts of the body inflate the same amount. The torso, which contains the most bacteria, bloats more than the head and limbs. The most buoyant body parts rise first, leaving the head and limbs to drag behind the chest and abdomen. Since arms, legs and the head can only drape forward from the body, corpses tend to rotate so that the torso floats face down, with arms and legs hanging beneath it.

Whether a drowned body floats face up or face down depends more on scientific and forensic factors than the sex of the deceased. The majority of drowned bodies initially float face down. However, people with excess fat in the breasts or stomach may float face up – making it more likely that women will float face up than men.

Water-related deaths are often prematurely and subconsciously labelled as accidental drownings. This presumption can hinder timely recognition of indicators of foul play and other important clues present around the death scene – particularly challenging due to inherent characteristics of an environment that is constantly changing. This in turn may ultimately lead to false conclusions regarding cause and manner of death, and hamper further investigation including interviews with persons of interest. A study in the US found only 12 out of 2,617 homicides were a result of drowning.

Need to find out:

Floating patterns – whether alive or dead when body hit the water?

Floating patterns – whether enter the water face first or legs first?

4

I didn't join the search the next day. I felt terrible about it, but my foot seemed to be properly infected and I'd have been no good to anyone.

That was the headline at least; the body text was, of course, more complicated. I'd thought about the missing man's sister a great deal in the night. I remembered how she'd flushed when she was upset, and how she'd controlled the emotion with crisp physical movements – a hand pressed against her face or stuffed into the back pocket of her jeans. I thought how I'd found myself willing the people she approached to smile kindly, and how I'd bridled when anyone was offhand. (The two German girls, for example, who'd backed away as if she were asking for money.) In the early hours, I thought about the moment she'd have received that phone call – both parents must be dead, I decided – and imagined every step of her awful journey out here. When it dawned on me, actually around dawn, that the outsized hoody would have belonged to her brother, I felt engulfed by such an all-encompassing desire to find Marc – carry him home alive, victorious, on my shoulders – I almost got up then and there and marched up to the path to straddle Mount Taygetus like a colossus.

In the morning, as I limped from bed to kettle, I knew I could no more fingertip-search alongside the mighty Christos than take Sara to bed, which I understood, in my shameful heart, this was really about. Better by far to hide away down here, never see her again. I set up a Google alert in case there was news (there wasn't). I didn't even get dressed, and spent the entire day in my pyjamas.

Over the next few days, I kept myself to myself. Breakfast (Greek yoghurt with honey), and coffee, followed by Duolingo and a small amount of creative work – more research, more planning – a swim and a nap or read in the shade (it was too hot after all to lie in the sun). For lunch I'd have salad with half a tin of fish. Once or twice I was joined by a gaunt black and white cat, haunches prominently bony. It wouldn't let me touch it, but I gave it my leftovers, which it ate greedily before slinking away. In the afternoon, more work, more Duolingo, more swimming, and for dinner I'd make myself what I called 'my mush', a mash-up of various stewed vegetables, with either rice or pasta. Consistency suits me. People, in my opinion, make too much of variety.

Dead Heat

I was conscious of life at Arcadia most of the time. Activity ebbed and flowed; noise burst and dissipated. The guests had their own rhythm: periods of somnolence followed by frantic amounts of fun. In the afternoons, a breeze (the famous 'meltemi' wind) wafted shrieks right up to my table; quite often pair of bright yellow jet skis leapt and thrusted out there in the bay, buzzing back and forth like annoying drones. At night, I'd feel the vibrations of music in my trackpad. Under certain meteorological conditions, it could seem as if a party to which I was not invited were taking place under my very roof. But as I felt no sense of ownership – *nothing* here belonged to me; even the 'holiday' was borrowed – I told myself I had no right to take it personally. Maybe I should have googled, but I think I was trying to detach myself. When that poor woman Sara crossed my mind, I wondered what the high, jet-skiing spirits might look, sound, *feel* like to her, but they were dark, unhappy thoughts and I did my best to squash them.

One day, I went into Kardamos to do some shopping and arrived in the harbour to a flurry of activity – two police cars, onlookers and a motorboat with several people on it bobbing a little way out beyond the main jetty. A mild-looking Englishman told me fishermen had spotted something floating out there and called it in. I searched the crowd for Sara, but there was no sign of her. When the boat finally docked, it turned out it was a poor dead porpoise they'd found, killed by a ship strike.

'Anyone know what kind of ship?' I asked my fellow onlooker.

He shook his head.

'I bet it was a jet ski.' I pointed out to the bay where one had just whooshed around the corner, driven by a half-naked man. 'Look, they're out there *even now*.'

He shrugged again.

'In Ancient Greece,' I told him, 'killing a dolphin was a crime punishable by death.'

He smiled and jutted his chin. 'I'm not sure anyone's told them,' he said.

One afternoon, after extensive googling, I caught a bus inland to Aetolia, the nearest big town, where a pharmacist painstakingly, and painfully, removed the sea urchin spines and sold me a course of antibiotics. Recovering, I sat outside a bar under some plane trees where moustachioed old men were playing backgammon and eating cheese with toothpicks. I drank a small sweet Greek coffee and fell into conversation with a fleshy woman, somewhat older than me, who was drinking ouzo at the next table. She was down from Athens to visit an ancient relative – mother or aunt: I forget the precise detail. She had a daughter who worked in London and lived in Wood Green. Her son was a doctor in Thessaloniki. Did I have children? She said she was sorry when I shook my head. It turned out we were waiting for the same bus, so I helped her on with her heavy bags and we sat together. As we rattled and swung along the switchback road, the conversation drifted into darker waters. The hand she rested on my arm was yellow, sprinkled with age spots. She'd been one of two, she said, but now she was an only.

Dead Heat

She bent her head so close, I smelt the aniseed on her breath. Had I heard of Ekaterini Dimetrea? No? Well, she was the poisoner of the Mani, a serial killer, the last woman to be executed under the death penalty in Greece and she – my companion tapped her chest several times – was this woman's *niece*.

Now I find it hard to separate what the woman told me then from what I later read online, but in essence: Dimetrea, a single mother who lived in poverty close to where we were talking, successfully murdered several members of her family – her mother, one cousin, one brother – with a variety of foodstuffs (spaghetti, coffee, eggs respectively) laced with parathion. Each death was attributed to natural causes until Dimetrea went a step too far and killed her five-year-old nephew with a piece of *loukoumia,* the Greek version of Turkish delight. The boy having no underlying health issues, suspicions were finally raised.

At her arrest, Dimetrea claimed she had acted out of spite; her family and the village had shunned and mistreated her. It transpired she had also tried to kill her sister-in-law and her niece by proffering a lethally laced pomegranate – they'd refused – and had even planned to poison the entire village at her brother's funeral.

Before her trial she underwent psychiatric evaluation – this I did find on Wikipedia – which concluded she was below average intelligence but not insane. She suffered, however, from a neurological disorder that caused partial hemiparesis and led to her left arm and leg being weaker than the right. The prosecutor described her as a 'hyena of hell' and on 10 April 1965, after being found guilty, she was executed by firing squad at the shooting range in Goudi.

'So,' my new friend said, clasping her pale hands together on her lap. 'I am lucky to be alive.'

'Goodness,' I said. 'Oh, I see. Yes. So you mean you're the surviving niece. Gosh. Yes, you *are* lucky, but I'm sorry to hear about your close relatives. That's very tough. Family is important. I lost my own father young, and my mother more recently. I'm grateful I've still got a sister.'

She turned to look out of the window. The vehicle clattered and swayed. I thought she was taking a moment to compose herself, and we sat in silence for a while. The view was dramatic: the hunched shoulders of mountain, the glittering triangles of sea.

She dug me with her elbow. 'She was a foolish woman. She got carried away. At first, it was perfect – her mother had a weak heart; her cousin hit her head; her brother had issues with his gall bladder. In each case there was the perfect cover, like for a magician, a distraction. But that poor little boy: *that* was a mistake.'

The vehicle clattered and swayed for a bit and then continued straight. Our conversation dried up. I couldn't think of anything to follow her revelations. We sat in awkward silence until we reached a bus stop on the main road behind Kardamos. A handful of passengers disembarked with a burst of diesel and heat, but my companion didn't move and, as the engine started up, her mouth engaged damply with my ear.

'You know about the rich man on the headland, don't you?' she whispered.

I slid sideways so she would receive the full force of my Interested Expression.

'I know about the missing house guest,' I said. 'Who went for a run in the morning and never came back.'

'*Did* he go for a run?' she said. 'Did anyone see him?' She tapped her finger against her nose, her tongue clicking.

'Tell me,' I said, journalistic faculties fully engaged. 'What do you think happened?'

'My daughter told me it is not right with that man. The rich one who built the new house. His business . . .' She wrinkled her nose and shook her head. 'Terrible, terrible.' She made a gesture, clasping her right finger and thumb together and poking them under her left bicep, which I took to be another mime for bribery.

And then she put her finger to her lips.

The bus was approaching the entrance to Villa Mimosa, and I had to alert the driver to drop me, so there was no time to ask more and only a few seconds in the end to say goodbye. Standing on the dusty road, watching the bus trundle south into the Deep Mani, I felt uneasy, as if somewhere, on a deeply human level, I'd failed.

Celia, when I told her all this, said the woman was obviously a fantasist. According to Wikipedia, there *was* a small niece – four years old at the time – who had indeed turned her nose up at a pomegranate. Her name had been Anthoula Thomea and she'd have been in her mid-sixties now, but still, it just didn't make sense to Celia. Would the real Anthoula Thomea recount her history to a stranger with such obvious relish? Surely it would be the subject of deep trauma (she had lost three close family members, for goodness' sake). She wouldn't idly recount the story, complete with what sounded like a very odd commentary, to a stranger on a bus.

Playfully, I parried that maybe it was the deep connection between us that had caused her to confide, and Celia said goodness, how hopelessly susceptible men were to female wiles, to which I'd looked gnomically at her over my glasses and said, 'Apropos of nothing,' even putting aside the age difference, it was not my impression that pomegranates, or for that matter any form of fruit, featured particularly prominently in the woman's diet, and we got a bit giggly as we sometimes do.

When we'd recovered, I repeated what she'd said about the rich owner of Arcadia, and Celia replied, 'Well, there you go. Exactly.'

5

But I am getting ahead of myself. The bus trip took place on the Saturday, and it wasn't until the following Wednesday that Adam and Celia arrived. They were already in Greece but had delayed their arrival at the house for a small cultural tour of the Peloponnese. Their daughter, Lydia, was studying 'Class Civ' for A level and they were taking her and a friend around various sites – Epidaurus, Olympia and Mycenae (theatre, sport, war: covering the bases) – in an attempt, as Adam put it, 'to spark a bit of fucking enthusiasm'.

On Wednesday morning, he texted to say they were aiming to arrive, 'though it's hard to predict with girls', by mid-afternoon. I was on edge from lunchtime. From 3 p.m. onwards, I threw myself into various attitudes – reclined on a rug in the shade, or hunched, absorbed over Duolingo, at the laptop, or energetically doing my crunches. Any minute, I thought they'll burst in on me and I'll get to my feet as if I'd almost forgotten they were coming.

I'd met Adam Murphy at work in the early 1990s. I was working on the arts pages – 'the youngest arts editor on Fleet Street' (entirely conceptual by then; we were out at Canary Wharf); Adam knew someone vaguely who worked on 'Business & City' who'd asked if I'd 'give him a go'. I still remember the moment I saw him in reception. He was leaning against the desk, chatting to Sonya (later I discovered he'd got her number), wearing a cream poncho-thing he'd bought in Peru, his hair long and sun-kissed from island-hopping. He'd pushed away from the desk almost reluctantly, greeting me with one hand in the air, like someone hailing a taxi. Oh God, I thought. He won't last a second.

I'd been wrong. His attention to detail was shocking (he once passed a page with 'Rembrant' in a 70-pt headline), but he was clearly bright, with good ideas, and most importantly had a boundless, if unfocused, energy, as happy to get cuts out of our trickiest contributors as he was to attend daily conference (which, a year into the post, I still found intimidating). Even then, looking back, he was wriggling out of things he didn't want to do (the coffee percolator, for example, didn't 'play to his strengths'), but he was such good company – full of tales of the previous night's exploits, always the first to suggest a post-work drink – he was easy to forgive. At the end of a month's work experience, he'd graduated to a paid role as sub-editor, and when several months later my deputy Harriet

Owen went off on maternity leave, he slipped seamlessly into her shoes.

He didn't have a grand background at all, though you wouldn't have known it. I remember being surprised to discover, after listening to him josh in the lift with the op-ed editor about England's 'batting collapse' at Headingley, that he hadn't attended public school. The media in those days, if it isn't still, was a place of privilege. It was student papers and night shifts at the *Northern Echo* and articles 'on spec' that had got me in. Adam had done none of that, hadn't even finished university. 'I'm a wastrel,' he told me once, 'a natural arsehole,' but the fact he admitted it was charming in itself. He was a chameleon; he had a sort of protean ability to adapt. With no beliefs or convictions of his own, he could be what people wanted. It's how he was accepted so quickly, I think. His feet were under the table before anyone noticed.

It was a period when television was keen on 'Culture', enjoying the novelty of mixing high and low, and one day, when a late-night arts programme invited me on to a panel, Adam ended up going along in my stead. He claims I lost my nerve. I remember it differently: that he begged me and, as a favour, I rang the producer and asked him to use Adam instead of me. That night's show – I remember it clearly – contained a discussion of Jim Carrey in *The Mask*, a new sitcom called *Friends*, and 'The Glory of Venice' at the Royal Academy, for which I had provided Adam with extensive notes. He was good at it, offering the perfect combination of film-star looks and 'bloke in pub' accessibility. Pretty soon it became a regular gig, and eventually he came to me, very sadly, and said they were offering 'quite a hefty whack' to present 'the whole shebang' and he 'didn't have the bandwidth' to do both jobs and I'd understand, wouldn't I; and of course I did.

The other thing to say is that it was on his very first appearance – the one that should have been me! – that he met Celia. She was the researcher on the show, and it was up to her to show him the green room and get him a fizzy water and check the microphone was correctly pinned to his collar. Her surname is one you'd recognise, a name that's so attached to a hugely profitable corporate entity it's a surprise to discover there's a real family behind it. Not that you'd guess to meet her. She wasn't made aware of her personal wealth until she was eighteen, and ever since she has been . . . not exactly embarrassed – she's too composed – but *guarded* maybe in her attitude to it. Adam less so! (Can I put it like that?) At the very least, you could say the cushion of her money gave him space to be creative – which is not to say he hasn't deserved his success: the presenting jobs and the travel documentaries and the podcasts and the books, all of which are clever and glib and immensely popular.

The hours passed. Mid-afternoon became late afternoon. Late afternoon became evening. Mosquitoes began to bite. Had Adam and Celia already arrived at their house? Could I go up to check? Should I have left a care package – milk? tea? bread? Takara would have known; she had such a clear notion of how these things worked. I felt a fresh spasm of loss. I gave up on being unexpectedly 'surprised' and lay face down on a patch of yellow grass, inhaling the prickly straw-scent, ants tickling. I'd been alone for over a week – or five months, depending how you looked at it. I seemed to have lost my social bearings.

It was dusk and I was perched on the edge of my bed, looking out of the window, when lights flickered through the olives: flashes of limbs, skin, the crunch of stones and within seconds, they were both at the door, torches in hand. Adam was saying, 'Fuck, man, you made it,' and Celia, her hair a halo, was hugging me. I breathed in the scent of her neck before she was holding me at arm's length: 'Let me look at you. I promised Takara I'd let her know you were OK.' (She'd seen her? Of course she had!) Her fingers left my skin, and she swung away to sit at the little table, elbows pressing into her knees, still searching my face intently. 'Has everything been OK? Are you eating? Are you *happy*?'

I plonked down on the stool next to her, instinctively smiling because she was so intensely anxious, so sweetly invested, and told her I'd had the most marvellous week; I didn't know what I could do to thank them. I was forever in their debt. This darling cottage, I said, with the little bit of camp I knew she enjoyed, had saved my life. Happy? I said. I'm *delirious*.

Adam was prowling the room, picking things up, putting them down: my glasses case, some mosquito spray, a tube of anti-itch cream. He looked at my book – Patrick Leigh Fermor's *Mani* – read the back jacket and cast it aside. Adam seemed oblivious to any space he inhabited, only conscious of his own presence within it; he was like a cat leaving its scent. He'd certainly become more leonine with age – wild eyebrows and full lips, wide-set brown eyes, crooked bottom teeth; his hair still shaggy; receding a little at the temples, but long enough to tuck behind his ears. His body had filled out – he was self-conscious enough to tap the mound of his belly now and then, breathing in sharply, but he did twice-weekly Pilates and was very proud of his basement gym; the rowing machine, he'd told me more than once, was 'key'.

He and Celia were not an obvious match; while he always seemed brightly multi-hued, she was almost colourless, with her straight hair, her bag-like skirts and tops, her old-fashioned mannerisms. News of their engagement had led to raised eyebrows. (As one of his college friends said at his stag, 'So what first attracted you to the millionaire Celia M—?') It seemed irrelevant to me. Celia was always very *herself* and, to my eyes, had anyway got prettier with age. Her neutral colouring had resisted the lurch to grey. She'd lost a bit of weight around the hips because, like me, she struggled with her cholesterol, and I noticed she'd caught the sun. Freckles scattered her nose and cheeks and a pink triangle gaped on her chest below the crucifix. The top two buttons of her shirt were undone. I glimpsed the off-white lacy top of her bra and quickly looked away.

Adam picked up my laptop, opened it, and balanced it theatrically on one palm. 'How've you got on?' he said, pretending to inspect the screen. 'How's the masterpiece?'

'Oh, don't interrogate the poor chap,' Celia said. 'Not yet at least.'

Dead Heat

Her fingers went to her breastbone and noticing the gape, she fumbled, flushing sightly, to do up the lower button.

'Nice nails,' I said.

'The girls took me to a nail bar. Gels. Can you believe it? Neon orange! At my age.' She laughed lightly. 'I'm trying to stop biting them.'

I craned forward and stroked the little orange nail. It was very shiny and felt like plastic. 'Well, it's clearly working.'

She laughed lightly and moved away. 'Right, I need a drink. And food. You haven't eaten, have you, Matt? Please tell me you haven't eaten. I'm starvarama.'

I said I hadn't, I was starvarama myself, and went into the bedroom to get the box of chocolates I'd bought her from the bottom of my suitcase. When I came back out, Adam was trying to squirt her neck with the mosquito spray, and she was laughing and pushing him away. 'Idiot,' she was saying. 'Utter moron. *Child.*'

The fact was, she adored him.

As I handed the chocolates over, I searched her face. They were artisanal, her favourites. Before flying out, I'd made a special, not inconvenient, pilgrimage to Selfridges for them. She didn't look as thrilled as I'd hoped. 'You're an angel, Matt, an absolute brick,' she said, but she added, 'Let's put them in the fridge for now.' It's true, they were a bit melted.

Before we left, I looked for the bag of teenage clothes I'd gathered up when I'd arrived, partly to make a point, but it wasn't under the table where I was sure I'd left it. Or in the cupboard with the Hoover. As Adam was getting restless – 'Pull yourself together, man, stop fussing' – I forgot all about it.

We drove into Kardamos not in the hire car – due to be collected the following day – but in 'Daisy', the convertible Beetle they kept out there all year to use in the summer. It was pale blue and a little battered, a vehicle that announced its owners as low-key, but fun – a red plastic gerbera bounced in a special vial on the dashboard. Inside, it was dusty but clean, unlike the Volvo they drove at home, which was littered with old exercise kit and sweet wrappers and stank of sweat and off milk. I sat in the back, peering between the front seats, face and hair blasted by warm thyme-flavoured air. I'd been careful not to bring up Arcadia, and we passed the end of the drive mercifully fast – Adam hunched at the wheel, like Mr Toad. I hadn't mentioned the missing person either – another blot on their perfect landscape – but we parked by one of the posters, not that either of them seemed interested. 'Oh, English,' Celia said, as if that was the only thing worth mentioning.

We headed straight to Dimitri's, naturally, and all went perfectly well at first: lots of back-slappings and jubilant greetings from Dimitri, a tall thin man with a neat beard and a practised charm. It was only when we were sitting at Adam's 'special table' on a platform over the water that it all went wrong.

Adam stretched expansively, arms crossed behind his neck, looking around at all the other holidaymakers not fortunate enough to be on first name terms with the owner. His T-shirt had come untucked from his shorts, revealing his round paunch and an arrowhead of abundant black hairs. When the waitress arrived, he waved her menus away. 'We know what we're having,' he said. 'Starting with *horta*. My kingdom for some *horta*!'

The waitress bent forwards – revealing an elaborate feather tattoo on her collarbone – and said she was sorry, but *horta* was not tonight available, and he said, 'Don't be ridiculous. It's always available. I'm a regular.' He stood up and shouted, 'Dimitri!'

Dimitri came back over, wiping his hands on his white apron, and explained jovially, that there was indeed no *horta* left; it had all gone. Adam let out a mock cry of horror. 'All gone. The *horta*? No *horta* with my *safridia*. What will I do? How will I survive?'

Dimitri clasped his hands together and smiling, added, as if amusement was the only way forward, 'No *safridia* either, my friend,' he said. 'We have moussaka, or red mullet, which is very good today.'

'No *safridia*? What's happened, Dimitri?' Adam said. 'You've let your standards slip!'

'I'm so sorry, Mr Murphy. This week there is such a big group at Arcadia and we've been privileged to have been asked to cater and—'

'Arcadia. What do you mean: Arcadia?'

'You know.' Dimitri waved vaguely in the direction of the headland.

Adam turned to look to where he'd pointed but from here all you could see was the harbour, the sea flecked with light, the spiky masts of yachts. 'What do you mean, you've been privileged to cater – you're doing takeaways? For *boats*?'

Dimitri stood on his dignity (or got on his high *horta* as I planned to repeat to Celia later) and said *safridia* – which is to say, horse mackerel – and *horta* were both Ray's favourites, but he apologised. Maybe next time, if Adam let him know he was coming, he could set some aside.

'*Ray?*' Adam said. 'Who's Ray?'

Dimitri smiled again, letting out a small laugh, as if the question were rhetorical, raised his hands genially and escaped to talk to someone on the other side of the terrace. The young woman with the feather tattoo was still standing next to the table with her notepad. Celia muttered a few words to her: 'Greek salad, tzatziki, lamb chops,' I assume, because that's what later arrived. 'And wine, Ad, don't you think, lots of wine?'

'Ray?' he repeated. 'Who's Ray? And what does he mean: Arcadia?'

I told him the little I knew – the changes to the house on the headland, and the guests who came and went. I was mindful of Celia really; the area was still properly wild when she came as a child, her father and her grandfather had hung out with Leigh Fermor ('Paddy' as she called him). Her expression was steady; it was Adam whose eyes winced, whose face scrunched.

'Ray?' he said again when I'd finished. 'As in sunshine?'

'I guess so.'

'Ray who?' A muscle pulsed in his cheek.

'I don't know. It's the first time I've heard a name.'

'And he's bought that monstrosity? And renovated it? Electricity and everything?'

'Yup. I guess if you have enough money, you can do whatever you like.'

'And he's *there*.'

'Very much so.'

'Oh dear,' Celia said at last. 'Will we be able to see it from the house?'

I winced.

'And is it very ugly?'

'Well, it's bigger than it was,' I said.

She held my gaze and nodded slightly.

The wine arrived and then bread and eventually gnarled bits of roasted meat, saucers of garlicky yoghurt and piles of feta-dotted salad. I tried to distract Adam as we ate with cheering gossip about mutual friends – a divorce, a bankruptcy, a terrible review in the *Observer* – and he did his best to respond, but it was clear his heart wasn't in it.

After a while, he pushed his chair back and stood up. 'Give me a minute,' he said.

'Oh dear,' Celia sighed again after he'd gone. She was silent for a bit, and then she said, 'He takes things personally. He always has.'

'The Mani's changed a lot,' I said, sounding apologetic.

'We've always thought we might be safe from any developments because of having no proper beach.' She shrugged. A few seconds later, almost laughing, she added, 'I guess we don't actually *own* Greece.'

'It would be quite a lot of responsibility if you did.'

'And so much extra work.' She wrinkled her nose, as if it were something seriously under consideration, and I laughed.

She had her back to the restaurant, but I could see Adam just inside, talking to the waitress.

Celia, leaning across the table, clasped both my hands. 'Anyway. *Enough.* How are *you*? *In yourself?*' It was a construction we often used faux ironically with each other. I told her I was fine, all the better for seeing her, and she said: 'Are you really? Really, really?'

I knew where this was going – *she'd seen Takara* – and to deflect, I said, 'Yes, tickety-boo; how about you?'

Oh, Celia herself, she said, had been 'madly busy': she'd had a lot of commissions (she was a florist: weddings, etc.) and they'd resurfaced the tennis court in Norfolk, which had ended up being 'quite a palaver'. She had a habit of closing her eyes whenever she spoke at length, as if the world, for someone with as much on their mind as her, was too much of a distraction. It gave me the opportunity to gaze at her uninterrupted. Oh, she added, she'd also just taken some of 'her oldies' to Lourdes, which was always uplifting. I asked if any of the trips had been successful, trying to keep my tone neutral, and she said, with a small smile, 'Belief is an amazing thing.'

'Yes, I'm sure.' And then I laughed. 'I remember.'

A beat passed. 'Do you miss it?' she said lightly.

I sighed heavily to illustrate a weight of thought. 'Miss what? That enormous piece of moth-eaten tapestry or whatever it was Larkin called it?'

She smiled briefly both to acknowledge and dismiss my literary pretension. Then she looked serious again. 'Really, though. Are you lost to us for good?'

It was a subject we returned to often – the subject itself a reassuring old friend: her way of referencing the heart attack and death of my father when I was fifteen, the crisis that had led to my loss of faith; her way of letting me know she loved me anyway.

'I miss feeling that someone was looking out for me. And I miss having an object of worship.' I gave the table a little drum roll in preparation for a joke: 'Or am I talking about Takara?'

She smiled gently and we sat in silence for a bit and then she said quietly, 'Oh my God, Matt, I've been having such a nightmare with my tooth.' She'd had an abscess and had had a front one taken out; she was getting an implant, but for now she had an actual false tooth. At night, she had to put it in a glass of water. You can't tell, I told her, which was true. She pressed the tips of her fingers against her top lip and breathed in sharply, almost but not quite laughing. 'Promise you won't tell anyone. No one knows, not even Adam – he'd *die*.' Apparently, he'd woken up before her the other morning and she'd had to talk with her mouth only a crack open until she could get into the bathroom, and recently she'd been in Peter Jones and she'd tried on a lipstick at Estée Lauder and then wandered around a bit, and when she held a dress up against herself in a mirror, she realised the lipstick was all over the tooth. 'Because it's plastic and it had sort of clung.'

'What colour?'

'Red. Bold Desires.'

I laughed a lot then, and gratifyingly she joined in. I checked to see if Adam was watching. He had moved to the back of the restaurant now, and was standing by the door to the kitchen, still talking to the girl with the feather tattoo. He was propped against the wall by his elbows, and this thing happened that gave me a bad feeling. He said something softly in the girl's ear and she bent, chin to neck, shook her head without looking at him, and he reared back in mock outrage.

Celia looked as if she might be about to turn to see what I was looking at, so I said quickly, 'So no luck at Lourdes? With the tooth, I mean?' and she said, 'Oh Matt. Really. You know it doesn't work like that.'

I said, 'Isn't that the nature of a miracle?'

'Not for a tooth.'

We were riffing on this – what ailments did God consider worthy of his time: a broken leg, yes; what about nasal drip? – when Adam was once again standing over us. He said, 'What's so funny?'

'Oh nothing.' Celia said. 'Matt just being Matt.'

Adam rolled his eyes. 'You won't believe it,' he said. 'Rey, the bloke who's bought the house. It's Reynash de Souza. You know, fucking Reynash from my school? I mean.' He'd been addressing Celia but he turned to me. 'Didn't you think to find out his name? He's not Ray as in fucking sunshine. He's Rey as in . . . I don't know . . . fucking *Rey*.'

'Who exactly *is* Rey then?' I said.

'He *was* nothing,' he said, still gripping the chair. 'A nobody.'

And then he had one of those sudden changes of humour that made him such unnerving company. He collapsed into his seat, his features caved in and he laughed, genuinely laughed. The sound came from deep in his chest and his skin crinkled, his eyes disappearing into the crumple of his face; he looked at me as though the whole world were a joke we shared.

'He sold his company for more than a billion pounds,' he said. '*A billion.* Can you believe it, Matt?' He opened his mouth and let it hang like a silent scream. I remember a reviewer of one of his cultural/travel shows once said, 'The thing about Murphy is he has no pretence, no filter,' and it was utterly true. In that moment, he looked ugly and very human. He knew his own reactions were off, he was behaving badly and that the joke was on him. I loved that about him.

Celia and I were both laughing now – impossible not to – and she was getting out her phone and looking Reynash up: he'd invented some piece of tech, it turned out, a business model based on 'adaptive behavioural analytics'.

' "Developed at breakneck speed," ' she read, ' "AdVent was released in 2016 and had extraordinarily quick market penetration, crashing overnight when it was first launched." It says here it was listed as one of fifty smartest tech companies by *Newsweek* in 2020, and was sold to Google at the beginning of last year.'

I found a profile of Reynash in *Wired* that said, after attending a south London comprehensive for his GCSEs, he was home-schooled for A levels, going on to study Natural Sciences at Cambridge before doing research in adaptive pattern recognition at MIT. A piece in the *Financial Times* described him as 'driven and single-minded' and concluded that 'early tragedy' – the death of his sister – had 'incited' him to succeed.

Celia and I tried to find out how much he was worth, but all the websites said different figures. One and a half billion. Two. What was the difference?

'Luck,' Adam said. 'Just bloody luck.'

'I don't know.' Celia was still reading. 'It's a search technology that stops ads popping up for one-off purchases, like beds or fridges, you've already just bought. I can see that's quite smart.'

'Fridges,' Adam said, missing the point on purpose. 'I mean, who wants to work with *fridges*?'

'This him?' Celia held out her phone. A man with dark hair in a white shirt, giving a talk on stage.

Adam's nose crinkled. 'Yeah. See: *nobody*.'

6

I woke up on Thursday morning, lonelier than I'd felt all week. Until then, anticipating Celia and Adam's arrival had given shape and meaning to the days. Now they were *here*, I had nothing to wait for. I was highly conscious of them up there in Villa Mimosa and me down here on my own. The night before, as I'd set off down the path to the cottage, Celia had called out after me, 'Use the pool any time, won't you?' and I knew I could – I *should* – but I worried she hadn't meant it. It was a long summer that stretched ahead and I didn't want to be in the way.

The cat was joining me for breakfast now, apparently partial to a saucer of Greek yoghurt, and he collapsed on his side a few feet away, watching me as I ate. I'd give him a name, I decided, even if our relationship was likely to be temporary. I went to the bookshelf for inspiration. It contained several of Adam's books – glossy tie-ins to his cultural documentaries, most of them involving travel. I pulled out *The Medicis*, with its jacket photo of Adam standing in the middle of the Ponte Vecchio; and then flicked through *The Brontës* (Adam striding across the Yorkshire moors). The chapter entitled 'Failure Brother' was written in his usual chatty, slapdash style (I noticed a dangling modifier the editor had missed), but covered the bases: the disappointments, the lack of talent, the resentment. Branwell, I decided: a good name for a cat. That would do.

Maria, the couples therapist whom, on Takara's urging, I'd continued to see on my own, told me I 'ruminated', that I worried obsessively about small things. That morning, in no particular order, I worried about the chocolates, now white-furred in the fridge, and whether in fact I'd got the wrong kind. I worried whether when Adam had referred to my 'masterpiece' he was being facetious or (worse) sarcastic. At dinner he'd said, 'It's all in the idea, mate, all in the idea,' and I worried I didn't have one. I worried about when and where Celia had seen Takara. I worried about the mortgage I was still paying on a flat I didn't live in. I worried I would be alone for the rest of my life.

An insect in my ear. A blade of grass. The scent of guava, iris, sweat.

I brushed the spittle from the corner of my mouth and dragged my eyelids open. Celia's face was up close. 'We're going down to the cove,' she said softly. I could see the velvet fur of her cheek, smell the tannin tang of fresh tea on her breath. 'We've got a picnic. Will you come or are we disturbing you?'

I sat up quickly. Her legs and arms were bare. The sun was hitting the side of her face. Adam was behind her. The girls, too, their daughter Lydia and a friend: two long, leggy creatures. 'I'll come. I'm awake,' I said, though my voice sounded croaky. Adam sniggered.

I got to my feet, felt the world settle. They were all prepared for the sea – flip-flops, striped bags, straw mats, towels. Celia's navy costume was baggy and worn, the elastic in the straps wrinkled. Adam's trunks by contrast were expensively geometric, a pattern of various blues: 'Orlebar Brown, mate,' he said, seeing me look. He gave the swelling of flesh above the waistband a playful pinch. Without clothes, his heavy body seemed bold and uninhibited. A thick silver chain nestled in the dark squiggles of fur on his chest. It seemed a bit vulgar even for him.

'Interesting chain decision,' I said doubtfully. 'Is it new?'

He nodded, ignoring the doubt. 'Yeah, it is. Thanks.'

He went ahead with the girls while Celia waited for me to get my things together. As we walked down to the cove, she told me Lydia's friend was called Jasmine; they were at school together at Camden Girls (both the Murphy kids went private until sixth form; then state 'to better their university chances'). They'd scooped her up for the summer because her 'utter cad of a dad' had left her mother for a younger woman. Jasmine, 'a darling', was an only child, very close to her poor mum, and had taken it hard. 'Everyone thinks as soon as kids are teenagers it doesn't matter,' she said. 'But split the family unit and you're pulling their life apart.' She shuddered. 'People can be so selfish.'

I made a noise, one I hoped was both sympathetic and non-committal. Takara, who didn't believe in marriage (or, at any rate, marriage with *me*), had got on to the subject of divorce with Celia once and it hadn't gone well. 'So, Adam could do anything,' Takara had said. 'Anything at all? Even murder?' I'd felt a wrench of pity for Celia, believing her cornered, but she'd gritted her teeth and said, 'For children, divorce is as *bad* as murder.'

'Poor old Jasmine,' I said now. 'How lucky she is to be here with you.'

She smiled gratefully. 'We do what we can.'

At the cove, Adam was sitting cross-legged on a rolled out mat under an olive tree. He was sipping from the lid of a red thermos – coffee, he liked it strong – gazing out to sea. Lydia and Jasmine were lying on their fronts in the shallows, all long hair and shoulder bones, the light glinting on their foreheads and cheeks. Lydia, like her mother, was fine and pale, with an upward tilt to her nose and a sprinkling of spots on her forehead. Her friend Jasmine was curvier, larger lipped, heavier browed. She had a stud in her nose and an elaborate tattoo – ivy, or maybe Cyrillic letters – curled up the back of her right arm.

I called out to them to be careful – the spot they'd chosen was close to my lethal sea urchin. But they looked up only briefly and didn't move, as if my words didn't quite make sense, as if I were a puff of cloud crossing the sun.

Dead Heat

Celia unpacked the food: hard-boiled eggs, with salt and pepper in twists of clingfilm; cold floppy pittas; a carton of ready-made hummus; cellophane-wrapped slices of pre-prepared cheese. Her catering was always, as Takara used to say, 'Very loaves and fishes without the miracle.' Love her as I did, the heart never soared at the prospect of 'a bite to eat' in Islington: usually watery soup and some sort of beige stew. In Norfolk, I always pushed for supper in the pub.

Adam stood up and went a few steps closer to the water. It was gleaming, the sun like droplets on the water, dazzling. But there was activity out there now – a small motorboat piled with people was heading towards the moored yacht. You could hear cries of laughter above the buzzing of the motor.

'He's got such a fucking nerve,' he said.

I laughed. 'Having fun. How dare he?'

'It's not even a proper yacht. No sails. It's all just engine.' He gestured to Arcadia itself, the great grey concrete slab of it. 'And the house itself is far too big. It's ridiculous. We're under siege.'

He looked at me expectantly. It was our routine: he'd say something outrageous; I'd lobby a rebuke.

'It's a holiday house, Adam,' I said dutifully. 'Not Stalingrad.'

We watched as the tender reached the yacht and a ladder was released. Adam waited until they were all aboard, the tender hoisted and the yacht beginning to pull away, before he sat down. 'I've made a few calls,' he told me then. 'Spoke to this bloke I was at school with. Steve. He said Rey took him and his wife skiing in Morzine in January, all expenses paid. Apparently, Rey doesn't even ski. Last summer he rented a twenty-four-bedroom riad in the Moroccan desert, fully staffed, balloon rides and whatnot. He invited newspaper editors, even politicians. And before that was Glasto – full luxe – bell tents, feather duvets, helicopters in and out. Elton John played. Rey didn't see him; was busy with calls. I mean – *why*?' He laughed bitterly.

'"Wealth may come and go, but influence lasts forever,"' I said. 'I heard someone very charming say that recently on an excellent television series about the Medicis, which, if I am not mistaken, was shortlisted for a Bafta.'

Adam grunted something about it not having actually *won*, but Celia threw me a grateful look. 'Exactly.' She polished a tomato on the edge of a towel and handed it to him.

He took it. 'I just don't believe it.'

He stared at the skin gloomily, then picked off the stalk and laid it on a stone where it sat, curled, like a spider. When he bit into the tomato, seeds dribbled down his chin.

'Dweeby little Gaynash.'

I thought about one occasion I'd picked Adam up from his childhood home – we were on our way to a festival the paper was sponsoring – and his father, whom I knew had been laid off from work, opened the door. While we waited for Adam, he said, 'So you're the arts editor then?' and he did a thing with his wrist, a sort of limp flop, a statement on the sexual orientation of the people he assumed worked in my chosen field.

'*Rey*nash,' I repeated to his son, carefully.

Adam let a noise out from the back of his throat. 'Yeah. I know. Yeah. Whatever.'

I can't remember whose idea it was to swim across the bay. It must have been Adam's. I doubt it was Celia's. Definitely not mine. But the idea, once mooted, got into our heads. 'Rey doesn't own that beach,' Adam said. 'There are no private beaches in Greece.' He stood, brushing pitta crumbs from his crotch. 'You and me,' he said, re-energised. 'All of us. He can build what he likes. We all own that beach.'

'It's too far,' Lydia cried from the flat bit of rock where she and her friend were sunbathing. 'And we want to tan, don't we, Jas?'

Jas agreed.

Celia said, 'OK, darling girls, be good then,' and Adam jumped to his feet and pranced towards them, shoulders rounded like a bear, growling, 'Yes, you two. Be good. If you can manage that.'

They both squealed.

'Right, I'm entering the water in my usual way,' he said, sucking air in through his teeth. 'Matt? Joining me?'

'Fuck off I am,' I said.

Celia sighed. 'Please don't.' And then, covering her ears as if that would help, 'Honestly, Matt, I can't bear it.'

Adam, ignoring her, clambered up to the top of the closest rock. He looked down at us. 'See you on the other side,' he called, and disappeared around the edge to a point where the sea was deep immediately below and, if you were very careful, you could dive in.

Celia and I waded in the conventional way, slowly, enjoying the feel against our feet, ankles, knees. You had to be careful not to slip on the stones, or worse, but it was bath-warm, small fish flickering at our toes. We heard Adam behind us: the blood-curdling whoop, the loud splash, a triumphant shout. 'He'd prefer to have had an audience,' Celia said, rolling her eyes. 'He'd have liked us to have stood in a row at the top, watching.'

'Hurry up!' Adam shouted. He had already swum further than us. 'What's keeping you?'

I was about to launch myself properly in when I realised I was still wearing my watch. It was my father's: an old Omega, brown strap, cream face, wind up. I'd worn it every day since he died. I asked them to wait a minute and was wading back, but Adam swam back towards me, 'God's sake, man. Can't watch you do that again,' and he took my wrist, undid the strap and hurled it, recklessly, in the direction of our towels.

I watched it land. I felt a flush of resentment. He was so careless with other people's possessions. If you complained, he accused you of being uptight. A few months ago, Takara had said, 'Adam's right: you're such a fusspot.' *When* had he said that to her? *Why?*

'Come on, slowcoach.' Celia was waiting for me, a few metres out, and, crouching, I threw myself in and started swimming. I found it easier to relax as soon as I was out of my depth.

When I reached her, I said something about the sea urchin and she said, 'Yes, yes, but it's better now, isn't it?'

Adam had surged ahead, and I happily swam alongside her – a careful breaststroke, slow but steady. I turned on to my back, just kicking my legs, so I could keep at her pace. Looking up into the blue of the sky, I was aware of the endless space above and the untapped depths beneath, and maybe it was proximity to her, but I felt a surge of well-being that was almost spiritual. She had asked me the night before if I missed my faith and I'd answered facetiously. But actually, I did. I yearned for the certainties of my upbringing, for the high after confession, the repletion from Sunday communion – the relief both were over. Occasionally I felt the promise of belief as if it were waiting for me to find it again. For now, it was just good to be here, in the middle of the bay, the cool water lapping my head, my ears, occasionally my face.

'Oh goodness, I'm a bit unfit,' Celia said. 'Too many croissants.'

I told her she was fitter than me: the last proper exercise I'd done was for that series for the paper.

'I *miss* your pieces,' she said.

'Thank you.' I turned back on to my front. 'I'm not sure anyone else does.'

My column was supposed to have connected with people, to link personal experiences to bigger themes. I told her it had become increasingly obvious it didn't speak to anyone.

'It spoke to me.'

'Well, that's nice.'

Adam was halfway across the bay now; he had clambered on to a buoy, but as soon as he had our attention, he flung himself back into the water and kept going, if anything swimming faster than before.

I was hoping Celia might say more about my writing, but she was briefly silent and then she said, 'I'm a bit . . . worried about . . . Adam.'

She was tired now, speaking in spurts.

'Are you?'

'I think . . . something's up. Will you . . . talk to him?'

'Of course, though I hadn't noticed.'

I'd always suspected she knew about his affairs. She'd never asked me directly, though once, a couple of years before, when he'd been filming a documentary about the Beat Poets in California, she'd rung wondering if I'd heard from him and then got a bit tearful, saying she hadn't. Perhaps I should have let her talk, but I knew too much, couldn't bear her to guess that, so I'd carefully changed the subject.

'He's just . . . on edge,' she said now, her breathing still heavy. 'He always . . . takes up a lot of space, but . . . he seems very restless. I don't know.'

'I mean, he's obviously incensed about that.' I raised my chin to Arcadia.

She swam a few more strokes. 'Will you talk to him? See what's up? He always listens to you.'

'Of course,' I said again.

The beach was closer now, beginning to take shape. It looked smart and manicured. Umbrellas with coconut-thatched roofs protected a run of white-cushioned sunbeds and wooden crates filled to the brim with neatly rolled navy blue towels. A path disappeared into the trees.

Adam was standing on the jetty waiting for us – chest puffed, hands on hips, like a child pretending to be a pirate. 'What took you?' he said as we threw ourselves down on to the sand – neatly raked, imported (presumably) from the Sahara. The foam at our feet slid softly away and dissolved. Celia flicked a piece of seaweed with her orange-tipped toes and I flicked it back. I was aware of the sound of her breathing and of the worn, thin Lycra of her swimsuit. It was so translucent, I could see her nipples.

One weekend when I was staying with them in Norfolk, I passed Celia and Adam's bedroom door on the way to the bathroom. It was open a crack and I caught sight of Celia on the bed, moving backwards and forwards, her shoulders scooped with tan-lines, her buttocks pale beneath Adam's clenched hands. Takara was always silent, self-contained in her pleasure, and I'm embarrassed to say, as I lay there, Celia's small noises, the sudden 'Fuck', so out of character, came back to me.

A thump at my head, sand in my mouth, as Adam leapt off the jetty and landed next to us.

'Come on, you two.'

'I'm tired,' I said.

'Don't be such an old woman.'

'Language like that,' Celia said, 'and you'll be cancelled.'

'God, how I'd love to be cancelled. You have to retire from

public life for a bit until the dust or whatever settles. I'd love that.'

'You'd hate it,' I said.

'Yeah, maybe.' He laughed and nudged me with his foot. 'Come on. Let's find the house.'

I said, 'I don't think that's a very good idea.'

He reached down for Celia's arms but she rolled away. 'Don't be stupid.'

'Let's explore. We know they've all gone out on the yacht.' He started tiptoeing away, shoulders hunched, knees lifted high, miming the cartoon walk of a cat burglar.

We both laughed then – impossible not to.

'All right then,' Celia said, getting to her feet. She stretched out her hands to pull me up and I took them. 'We're all quite mad,' she said as I stumbled up.

How easily he had won us both over.

The path turned out to be made of shells laid side to side – slipper limpets, Celia said – silvery and smooth underfoot. Adam was already ahead of us in the trees. She sped up to catch him, and I followed. The path became steeper and then doubled back on itself. It was much hotter away from the water. The vegetation changed: less spiky, softer shrubs with flowers. The glint of pool, the hiss of an irrigation system. We passed a small humming structure, solar panels on its roof, one of those giant pool net-scoops leaning against the wall. At a crossroads, wooden arrows on a signpost read 'Jetty', 'Beach', 'Pavilion' and 'House'. We continued a few feet up the main path and then I stopped, and said, 'This is ridiculous.

What if someone stayed behind? We can't keep going. Not like *this*.'

They seemed to take in the sight of me, my over-long trunks and my turquoise neoprene aqua shoes, my sunburnt, under-exercised torso, the ridiculous, puny, balding figure that I make, and Adam shook his head, almost sadly, and I could see him trying not to laugh and then suddenly all three of us were laughing – because it wasn't just me. It was Celia in her see-through scrap of fabric and Adam with his chest hair and ridiculous rap-artist necklace. We were shaking our heads and holding our hands to our mouths, and I for one had rocked against the wall and slipped, wordlessly, to the ground. It's a difficult memory, and it's made me cry a bit writing this down, but it's important to remember. Nothing, no one, is ever all bad.

Celia suddenly stopped laughing and let out a yelp, and Adam said, 'Oh shit.'

I turned my head. A heavily bearded man was standing a few feet away, biceps bulging, what looked like a gun tucked into his belt. I stood up quickly, raising my hands, as he fired a barrage of Greek at us. I desperately tried to remember what I'd learnt on Duolingo and I said sorry and good afternoon and please and thank you and sorry again.

'*You! Hey, you!*'

A woman was leaning over the wall above us. Upside down, her face was distorted, half concealed by long wet hair, but there was something in the tone of her voice when she said, 'What the fuck,' both amused and outraged, and I recognised her then as the helmetless woman on the quad bike, the one I'd met on the road later that night, nursing her bleeding toe.

'Oh God,' I said. 'We must stop meeting like this.' To Adam and Celia, I said, 'We know each other. We met the other night.' And to her, well, I can't remember exactly what I said, but something about how we'd swum over – sort of by accident, gone out a bit further than we'd intended – and that my friend Adam had been at school with Reynash . . . I know I turned to point at him, my friend Adam, but he had already slipped past me and was standing further down the track. *Chicken*, I thought. *What a wuss.*

Celia said, with her disarming honesty, 'We were just curious to see the house.'

The girl said, 'You can come up if you like. I'm alone. The others have gone to Diros to look at the caves.'

Celia's hand was on my arm and I felt her reluctance so I said, 'No, don't worry,' but the girl said, 'You can all have a drink; there's everything,' and Celia looked at me then, and shrugged.

We looked for Adam but he had disappeared. 'His loss,' Celia whispered.

At the top of the path, we turned a corner and suddenly there was the house: a rising slab of beige concrete, acres of glass reflecting nothing but sky, a huge glistening pool. I turned my head: sea, and more sea. Blue, blue, blue. This is what I would buy if I were rich, I thought. Not the house, or the yacht, or the jet skis. Not friends. Or women. Or Elton John at Glastonbury. This. This view. This light.

The girl was walking towards us across the terrace, barefoot, dark prints on the flagstones. She was wearing tracksuit bottoms and a pale blue T-shirt, the wet lines of her bikini showing through. She pulled at a piece of lavender from the top of a big terracotta pot, rubbed it between her fingers and held it to her nose. There was a sway to her walk; she was aware of her sexuality and her youth.

'I'm glad to see your foot is better,' I said, when she reached us.

She frowned, apparently confused, and then said, 'Oh yeah.'

'Mine too,' I said, lifting it to illustrate. 'I had to get antibiotics in the end.'

'Awesome,' she said.

Celia extended her hand – all those childhood suppers with politicians, those charity dinners with captains of industry, came to the fore. 'I'm Celia,' she said, and the girl put out her own hand and said, 'Er, yeah, Amira.'

We began to walk in the direction of the house and Celia was saying how beautiful it all was and had she – Amira – been here long, and Amira said yes wasn't it and just a few days. 'Rey has been amazing.'

We walked across acres of polished stone past rows of sunbeds, a rolled-up navy towel on each. We were on a lower level to the entrance; there were steps up and to the right of them, a bar was carved into the wall and a woman in a white T-shirt was drying a glass behind it. She put the glass down and smiled expectantly at us; Amira asked what we wanted. 'You can have anything,' she said. 'Wine. Cocktails. Beer. Anything.'

Celia hunched her shoulders playfully as though trying to decide and then said, 'Actually, do you know what, just a glass of water would be great.'

The woman opened a fridge and brought out a bottle of mineral water, which she emptied into a glass on top of ice and lemon. She laid it down on a small paper coaster, pushed it towards Celia, and looked at me.

'Maybe I'll have a Coke,' I said.

Celia laughed and then said, 'This is very weird. Are you sure Rey won't mind?'

'No,' Amira said. 'He's really generous.'

I said, 'I didn't realise when we met that you were staying *here*.'

'Yeah. Rey's so nice. He took pity on me.'

'My husband actually knows him,' Celia said. 'They were at school together. Such a coincidence.'

Amira considered Celia for a moment. 'That's funny,' she said flatly.

'You scared him, the silly man.' Celia laughed. 'Ran off. Such a nincompoop. He'll be sorry when he hears what we've been up to.'

'I'd show you around the house itself, but you know he's having a party tomorrow? It's chaos up there. The DJ and the people from the restaurant are setting up. There's stuff and wires everywhere.'

'A party,' I said.

'Yeah. This one's for the whole village.'

'Oh!' Celia said. 'How generous.' Her smile was brittle. I

wondered if she was thinking that if anyone were to invite the whole village, it should be her. Her family had been here for generations, after all.

'Are you not coming?' Amira said. 'You should come.'

'Goodness, no. We couldn't do that.'

'Yes, you could. Rey would love it.'

'I don't think so,' I said supportively.

'Oh, you really should. Everyone's invited. He's ordered a goat.'

Celia said, in a high voice I hadn't heard her use for a while, 'What an incredibly kind and generous man, but no. We can't leave the girls.'

'Oh, bring them. Your husband too. Honestly, the more people Rey has around him, the happier he'll be. Come any time from nine.'

'We'll see.' Celia smiled.

I downed my drink so quickly the bubbles hurt at the back of my nose, and said, 'I think actually we should head home, don't you?'

Celia agreed and thanked the woman behind the bar. Amira followed us alongside the pool to the path as if she were reluctant to let us go. I wished I could think of a way to ask what her role here was exactly. She was too young – surely – to be sleeping with Rey. And yet she wasn't staff; not judging by the way she'd stood aside rather imperiously while the older woman had served us. I thought about how upset she'd been the night we'd encountered each other on the road. 'He took pity on me.' What did that mean?

We said goodbye and thanked her for the drink and set off back down the hill. As the angle shifted and the vegetation fell away, you could see Celia and Adam's house on the next headland – the cream walls between the trees, the terracotta roof, the curve of the balcony.

For all its size and grandeur, it looked flimsy from this distance, insubstantial, something inhabited by dolls.

7

If Adam had been waiting for us on Reynash's beach, perhaps it would have played out differently. We might have told him about the invitation and immediately disregarded it. We might not have gone to the party; the summer might have unravelled in its usual way; tragedy might have been averted. But he was already in the sea when we reached the end of the path, a hundred metres or so out. When he waved at us, it felt like a taunt.

It was much harder getting back across. The water felt colder now; the wind was roughing it into little tufts. Every time I lifted my head, I saw the surface had swollen. The distance stretched and the cove came in and out of focus above the tilting water. Celia was too far away to hear me even if I'd had the energy to talk.

Adam didn't look up from his phone as we dragged our

exhausted bodies ashore. I minded more for Celia than myself. He was cross, I could tell. Elbows on his knees, towel over his shoulders. Was it the wealth that rattled? The pool guy? The Saharan sand? Or was he annoyed we'd gone off without him? Or maybe he was simply embarrassed. It was his caper and he'd failed.

'Thanks a lot for abandoning us,' Celia called. 'Honestly. You are the limit.'

'You know where you are with Adam,' I said, 'when the chips are down.'

The girls were interested, though, and came over from their rock to listen. We hammed the story up – the huge swim, the pristine empty beach, the man with the gun, partly for their benefit, partly for Adam's.

'*Dad!*' Lydia protested, her mouth dropping in exaggerated horror. 'What if they'd been arrested?'

He looked up from his phone. 'They weren't going to be arrested.'

'And then this young woman appeared,' Celia said, 'out of nowhere, and she was someone Matt knew, so that was weird.'

'How?' Adam looked affronted.

'Just bumped into her in the village. I don't know how she fits in up there.'

'Probably his girlfriend?' Celia said.

'Too young, surely.'

'Why are you so interested?' Adam said. 'Do you fancy her?'

He was trying to rile me and I struck a pose to show I was above it. 'Far too young, but we do have a connection.' ('*You!*' she'd said when she saw me.)

Both girls laughed. Lydia said, '*Matt!*' just as she'd said, '*Dad!*' and I felt something inside me expand.

'I agree, though,' Celia said thoughtfully. 'It is baffling.'

'Why does it matter?' Adam said. 'She's nobody.'

The sun was behind the trees, the cove in nearly full shade, and I shivered. It was the second time he'd used the word. I wished Celia would pull him up on it, as she had about 'old women'. But she was leaning back, eyes closed, her mouth lifted at the corners in a small resting smile. It wouldn't have bothered her. People who were somebody, and people who weren't: it was her world, too.

I rubbed my shoulders with my fingertips – I hadn't brought a towel and no one had offered to share. I made the decision to mention the party then. I knew Celia didn't want to go, but the fact is, I liked the thought: there would be free food and limitless booze. Amira wasn't a nobody and nor was Reynash, and maybe it was time Adam and Celia acknowledged that.

Lydia and Jasmine were immediately on it, as I'd known they would be, firing off a barrage of questions – what, where, when, etc. – and, aware of the other two sitting quietly by me, I volleyed back with a series of enthusiastic answers.

'Who does he think he is, inviting everyone for miles around?' Celia interrupted at one point. 'It's quite weird, don't you think?'

I shrugged. I suppose you could say I manipulated the situation to my own advantage; I didn't realise I was sealing our fates.

'I'm not going,' Celia said. 'No way.' She picked up a pebble and threw it out over the water; it disappeared with a plop.

Adam shook his head more slowly, lower lip jutting. 'Me neither.'

He scratched the inside of his elbow.

I told the girls that, worse came to worst, I'd take them on my own.

'Cool,' Lydia said, nodding at me as if I'd grown in her estimation. 'You're the man.'

Celia went back up to the house to make some calls. An old lady she knew was having a hip op and she'd promised to check in. Lydia and Jasmine, needing showers, followed. Adam and I packed up the remains of the picnic. I said how lovely Lydia was – trying to coax him back to life: people like their children being complimented. He grunted in agreement. 'Costing me enough, though.' He often talked about money when he was low. 'You've no idea how much a seventeen-year-old can spend a month on Boohoo.'

'Boo hoo?' I said.

He laughed. 'Yeah. True.'

His phone beeped and he read a text, quickly typed a reply; then he stood, staring out at Arcadia. I shouldered the bag of rubbish and, trying to inject a bit of energy, clambered on to the first rock and shouted, 'Race you?'

'Fuck off.'

I heard him lumber behind, breathing heavily. He caught up

with me as I reached the proper path. Spiky plants scratched my calves.

'You all right, old man?' I don't know why I said it. The words just came into my head and then out of my mouth.

He took in a deep breath, and then released it on a hum. 'Yeah. Why?'

'You don't seem quite yourself.'

'Celia say something?'

I paused a millisecond too long. 'No, of course not.'

He bent to break off a piece of long grass and when it wouldn't snap, he yanked and twisted it until finally it detached, and then he used it to thrash at another clump.

'Is it Arcadia?' I asked. 'Do you and Reynash have a bit of history?'

He paused and for a moment I thought he was about to deny it but then he said, 'You could say that.'

'Bad?'

He let out a noisy horse breath from between his lips. 'I was a kid, Matt. I had problems of my own.'

I knew it was true – so I let it rest for a moment before I said, 'But still?'

He closed his eyes again, swaying his head as if he were moving it to music. 'He'd been at a private school but his dad had just died and money was tight so he'd had to leave. We thought that meant he thought he was better than us. And he cried a lot. He brought his lunch in a plastic Tupperware and we used to get it off him and throw his food around. We called him a few names.'

'Racist? Homophobic?'

'It was just a time when anything was ammunition. We were ignorant and mouthy. But you know what?' He wrinkled his nose. 'I think I was jealous of him. He was so sad about his dad. He loved his dad. And mine was a bastard.'

I thought about that time I'd picked Adam up and how, as he'd come down the stairs, he'd sidled around his father, his top half bending out to avoid him. The older man said, 'All right, son,' or something; it was all fine, but I had smelt violence and fear and, afterwards, on the step, Adam had punched my upper arm in greeting – overly hard as though proving something to himself.

'Maybe you were taking all the frustrations you felt at home, all your insecurities, out on him?' I said.

'Yeah maybe.'

He stopped at a cactus and peered at a bright yellow prickly pear. I had a flash of underarm hair in the loose sleeve of his T-shirt as he lifted his arm.

I started foolishly quoting that tongue-twister about pawpaws and prickly pears. The last time I was here, I'd recited the whole thing to Takara, showing off, I suppose, and it had led to a discussion of *The Jungle Book*'s outdated cultural depictions and whether or not it was OK still to appreciate the cleverness of the lyrics. She'd been right in her opinion, I'm sure. She was usually right.

'It's a long time ago,' I said, using the same untroubled tone that had failed with her. 'He might not remember.'

Adam sighed. 'He'll remember.'

Dead Heat

We were walking through the olive grove, the white walls of the cottage blinking through the trees. I said, 'You should go up immediately and tell him you're sorry. Show him you're a reformed character. Don't make excuses but be repentant; make it clear not a day has gone by when you haven't regretted your actions.'

He was still holding the piece of long grass and he raised it to his shoulder and hurled it. He was hoping, I think, for something soaring and dramatic, but it caught immediately on a branch of the fig and dangled there. He let out another horsey breath.

'I'm not sure,' he said. 'I'm not good at stuff like that. I'm not like you.' His tone was flat, defeated even. I could have helped him in that moment, I think, if I'd pushed it, if I'd let him be honest, but I felt a rare seductive flicker of power, and I gave in to that instead.

'I hope he's not carrying a grudge,' I said lightly. 'One man's already missing. You might be next.'

'Fuck's sake, Matt.'

'Don't worry.' I feebly flexed my biceps in a Superman parody. 'I'll protect you.' I threw an arm around his shoulder and said flippantly, 'I've got you.'

8

The night before their wedding – a big marquee in Norfolk – Adam sat on the edge of the bed in the B & B we were sharing and put his head in his hands.

'I'm going to fuck it up,' he said. 'I'm going to fuck it all up.'

I sat down next to him. He'd been tearful on the walk back from the house, and I assumed he was feeling overwhelmed: there'd been fish knives at the rehearsal dinner, and family priests, and a sea of people who'd known her since she was 'this high'. His own parents hadn't turned up, which he'd claimed to have been relieved about.

'Everyone thinks I'm marrying her for her money.'

'No, they don't.'

I wasn't going to tell him how months before at the

engagement party her parents had taken me aside. 'He's not what we'd hoped for, but he makes her happy,' her father had said, and her mother, who was so posh she spoke as if English wasn't her first language, had tapped my hand and said, 'We like *you*. You vouch for him, yes?'

'I'm not saying the money doesn't help,' Adam had said in the B & B. He'd looked up at me with vulnerability in his eyes. 'But I do love her. You know that, don't you, Matt?'

I nodded. 'Of course.'

'She doesn't have a bad bone in her body.'

I nodded again. 'I know.'

'I'm a shit, though. I've done terrible things.'

His face looked washed of emotion. He had a pale rim along the back of his neck from his fresh haircut and a couple of spots of blood on his shirt collar where he'd cut himself shaving.

'We've all done terrible things,' I said.

'Not like me, though, Matt. You know, when I was at school . . .'

'You were a bit of a bully.'

'No, worse than that. There was this girl. I keep thinking about it. She was just a kid really, two years below . . .' He started crying again and his voice was muffled as he told me that he and this girl had started talking on the bus, and that he'd coaxed her back to his house, and pushed her to do things he afterwards regretted.

I sat with the information, trying to get my head round it, and then I said, 'You had a bad role model in your dad.'

He lifted his tear-strewn face. 'I keep thinking: what if Celia knew what I'd done?'

'I don't know what to say, Adam. I mean, she knows you're no saint.'

'Should I have told Father O'Connor during private instruction?'

'Did he ask if there was anything you wanted to confess?'

'Not really. He mainly seemed to want to talk about marital intimacy.' He managed to smile. 'Cart after horse, or whatever the expression is.'

'I hope you didn't tell him that.'

'Of course not.' He rubbed his eyes 'But listen, now I'm with her, I'm going to be *better*.'

'Good.'

'All those Hail Marys of hers – some of them have got to rub off on me.'

I smiled. 'It's been a while since I was a practising Catholic but I'm not sure Celia can atone for your sins.'

'Can't she? I mean, Christ died on the cross for the whole of humanity.'

'Not quite the same thing. Christ was utterly without sin of his own.'

'And Celia isn't?'

I laughed, because his expression was so earnest, and suddenly he did too – cheered now he'd got it all off his chest.

He got into bed and slept like a baby whereas I lay awake, thinking about that girl, all night.

*

The night of the party, I went up to Villa Mimosa at 9.30 p.m., walking straight in through the open front door. In the kitchen, music was playing from a tiny pink speaker, and Lydia and Jasmine were mixing cocktails at the island. The room was in its usual state of chaos: open bottles everywhere, the pine table still covered in breakfast things; the picnic basket, undealt with, on top of the stove. A suitcase was open in the doorway, clothes, chargers, strewn. I was struck as I always was by the Murphy combination of extreme wealth and abject poverty: a painting above the Aga you'd die for a few feet away from a rusted open pedal bin.

Lydia danced towards me, all red lips and dark eyeliner. 'Mattski,' she said. 'It's party time! You ready to rock?'

I told her I liked her frock, was it a ra-ra skirt because that was something I'd remembered Celia once describing? And she said, 'It's cut on the bias, Matt,' and I said that was new to me, I was hopeless on the fashion front, and Jasmine said, 'We'll give you a makeover.' Huge silver hoops hung from her ears and her hair was pulled back in a tight bun. Her teeth were almost unnaturally straight and white.

I told her I looked forward to it and went across the hall to the lounge, a large, grand room, decorated like the house Celia had inherited in Norfolk: heavy floral curtains, delicate side tables and well-stuffed sofas. Adam was nursing a whisky in an armchair, freshly shaved in jeans and a crisp linen shirt. Celia was standing at the window in a long flowery dress she wheeled out every summer, bought from Jigsaw 'back in the day'. It had buttons up the front, though a couple seemed to be missing. I had the impression I'd interrupted something. Adam threw his glass down on the coffee table with what felt like relief when I said hello and Celia clicked her fingers to the music and sashayed towards me, hands pumping in circles as though pretending to be a train. Her eyelids were painted in various shades of mauve; her lashes were pale.

Adam got clumsily to his feet and tucked a loose edge of shirt into his jeans. 'Let's get this over with,' he said.

It didn't surprise me Celia had changed her mind; she loved a party: any excuse for her terrible dancing. I should have wondered more about Adam, but, after we'd gathered the girls and we were strolling along the dark track, with the fireflies and the bats and a distant owl, I let the companionship of the moment blunt my instincts. Celia had gone ahead, and was sandwiched between Lydia and Jasmine, one arm wrapped around each of them – every now and then she gave a little Morecambe and Wise skip. Adam and I were following, a few feet apart, both of us strong, dependable; like a pair of bouncers.

There were clues, now I think back. Adam changed his mind at one moment, stood still for a second and said, 'Actually, maybe I won't,' but then almost immediately said, 'Oh, all right,' though I hadn't said anything. He moved his lips a lot, moistening them, as if his mouth was dry.

He bent to say something in my ear. I smelt an apricot whiff of Metaxa and the vetiver of his cologne (Celia bought him Guerlain because it reminded her of her father). 'She's a wonderful woman. I don't deserve her.'

'You don't,' I said.

'You know she's the only thing that keeps me sane.'

'The whole world knows that,' I said – a reference to an interview he'd given in which he'd described her as 'my goddess'.

'You too, of course.' He dropped a heavy arm across my shoulder. 'I don't know what I'd do without you. My wingman.'

'We're all just here on earth,' I said, 'to pander to the great man.'

He grinned. 'I like to think so.' But he released my shoulder and for a minute or two we walked in silence, both lost in thought.

The road became busier as we drew close to Arcadia: cars parked on the verges and people hurrying up the drive on foot. As we hastened to catch up with Celia and the girls, I caught sight of a woman in a hoody standing off to one side of the entrance – Sara, the sister of the missing man. Her hair was pulled back in a clip, a few strands loose around her face. She was on her own, clearly out of place. When we got closer, I saw she was handing out flyers, though hardly anyone seemed to be taking one.

Adam swerved to one side, keeping himself out of reach, as if he were avoiding a chugger in a shopping mall. He kept a smile on his face, while being careful not to meet her eye.

I had a keen desire to do the same. And yet to keep walking – how heartless. She leant forwards to press a flyer on a man I recognised, one of the waiters from the village, and when she turned and saw me, standing there close to her, she reared back a little.

I said, 'I'm very sorry I didn't make it last week.'

She looked confused.

'The fingertip search?' I said and had begun to explain about my infected foot when she interrupted, 'It's OK. It was a waste of time anyway.'

'Why don't you come with me to the party?' I said. 'You could pass those around up there. I could help you.'

She lowered her eyes. 'I don't want to go up there. Not up to the house. I'm not ready for that. He's been great. He's done everything he can. And you know it wasn't his fault.' She shrugged.

'You mean Reynash?'

'Yes. He's been involved with . . .'

'Your brother's case?'

She flinched and I realised I shouldn't have said 'case'; it put her brother's disappearance in the category of closed, dusty things – files and coffins and courtrooms – while she was hoping for warmth and life: abscondment, lost memory, whatever stories her hope still spun.

'I don't expect people to put their lives on hold,' she said. 'I just don't want to go up to a party if that's all right with you.'

'Of course. Sorry.'

She turned away to hold out a leaflet towards a young couple who refused it.

'I'm here for the rest of July and August,' I told her, getting out the pen I keep in my shirt pocket. 'Can I give you my number just in case you think of anything I can do to help?'

I scribbled it on the edge of a flyer, using my hand as a

surface, and handed it back to her. She stared at me blankly, and then folded it into tiny squares and slotted it into the back pocket of her jeans.

The others were standing at the top of the drive waiting for me – they didn't say anything about Sara when I reached them – and we walked the last bit together, all rather skittish and nervous now, nothing yet to distinguish one from the other.

Fairy lights dangled from the trees and the way was lined with marble statues – naked men in loincloths and ivy-crowned nymphs. They must have been so hard to deliver, I said, so heavy. A lorry, Celia thought, with a fork-lift truck. Adam said, '*At least.*' At the front door, next to a bank of quad bikes, the music was louder, and the smell of roasting flesh stronger. Laughter and voices travelled. Adam threw his arm around Celia's waist. She craned her neck to look past him, and said, 'Oh God, Matt. What are we doing? It's way past our bedtime.'

Adam brought his mouth to her hair and whispered in her ear, his thumb reaching up to brush the underside of her far breast. I heard her quickly catch her breath, saw her lips part, her eyelids flutter.

The closer he diced with danger, I realise looking back, the more uxorious his behaviour.

A table piled with glasses and bottles of booze met us just inside the door. Lydia and Jasmine grabbed a can of beer each from a bucket of ice and set off into the house, walking very fast, but with tiny steps, casting a quick glance over their shoulders, as if they were trying to run away without it being obvious. Celia and I spent a long time choosing between bottles – they all had different labels and a woman in a red dress and dangly gold earrings said she'd recommend the Vidiano. 'He doesn't drink so he has no idea,' she said. 'But that one's good.'

'It's all very studenty,' Celia said after the woman had walked off. 'All that money; he might have shelled out for a few waiters.'

She looked up to find Adam – he'd enjoy her waspishness – but he had disappeared.

I said, 'I guess we should find our host and introduce ourselves.'

Celia wrinkled her nose. 'I hate it now I'm here, don't you?'

'I hate everything,' I said, and she laughed.

'And everyone,' she added.

'God, yes.'

Rooms, linked by huge open doors, stretched ahead, pockets of light and darkness, of noise and echoes. We walked through, affecting purpose, past small groups, elderly people on chairs. In a middle room a table of decks was set up; coloured lights running up the walls and across the ceiling; a woman with sunburnt upper arms dancing on her own; a man in headphones and a leather jacket twiddling knobs. I saw faces I recognised, including the woman who'd arrived in the harbour that first morning, the one with the tequila and the worm. A bald man in a floral shirt headed towards us, thought he knew me and gave me a high five, asking if I would be at the brunch tomorrow? The boat trip? The fireworks then? They were going to be awesome. 'One thing you can say about Rey, he knows how to birthday,' he said.

After he'd gone, Celia looked at me, and I looked at her. She said, with an upward tilt, 'To *birthday*?'

'How long have you and Adam been together now?' I said. 'It must be about time you anniversaried.'

'Yeah. Twenty-five years in September. We're planning to anniversary hard.'

I lifted my glass. 'It's just nice once in a while to have an excuse to wine.'

She clinked her glass against mine. 'I'm hungry. Shall we go and food?'

Outside on the terrace it was more crowded than in, or the darkness made it feel so. Braziers – artificial flames – lit people's faces from below, hollowed eyes and darkened cheekbones. Movement and sound eddied and flowed. However much money you spend, I thought, it's just a party, people deciding to have, or not have, a good time.

The food was on the left, beyond some steps. A dead animal was stretched on a spit next to a long trestle table where Dimitri was doling out portions of salad and meat on to plates. We joined the end of the queue. I said, 'Do you come here often?' and Celia said, 'What do you do?' and I said, 'Blah-blah-blah.'

She laughed, and then she took a deep breath and looked away and there was a long silence. I felt a current of tension. When she looked back, she said, 'I had lunch with Takara.'

I couldn't speak at first, weirdly. She put her hand on my arm and I flinched. 'I thought you had,' I said eventually.

'I have been meaning to tell you. I didn't want it to be a secret.'

'It's fine.'

'I've known her a long time.' Takara was the architect who'd drawn up the plans for Celia's first house; it was Celia who'd introduced us. 'I don't want to choose between you.'

It seemed unfair – Takara only ever bitched about her. 'Of course not,' I said and then, 'She seem happy?' I spoke so lightly the words seemed to dissolve on my lips.

'Yeah. I think so.'

I nodded.

'It's not all easy. I think she misses you.'

'Good for her.'

She considered me for a moment, and then did a strangely intimate thing, which was press the back of her hand against my cheek. I wanted suddenly to cry.

She kept it there, smiling sweetly at me, and I resisted the temptation to move my mouth to kiss it. I made a noise somewhere between my nose and the back of my throat instead, and she lifted her hand away.

'Do you think we should try and find our host?' she said.

I swallowed. 'Yes, maybe.'

'What do you think he looks like?'

I shrugged elaborately, to show I was OK now. 'Tall and thin. And very blond. Pale complexioned.'

'Really?'

'Yes. With a horn in the middle of his face.'

'Oh, I see, a unicorn.' She laughed more than was necessary.

'Yes, funny. I don't think he's blond, though, is he? Because he's not English, is he, not with a name like that?'

'I think he's British,' I said. Surely she knew; she and I had read the same article.

'Yes, maybe, but not originally.'

'I think originally,' I said, using the exact same intonation. She was staring at me blankly, so I said as a concession, 'I read his grandparents came from Pakistan, but . . .'

'Exactly, that's what I mean.'

I rolled my eyes, humorous but censorious. I'd had this kind of conversation with her before. It was like walking down a flight of stairs and missing the last step. It wasn't her fault, I told myself. It was her upbringing, the echo chamber in which she lived.

As if she sensed the distance between us, the tiny gap in my adoration, she stood on tiptoes suddenly. 'Oh, *there's* Adam,' she said, as if we'd done nothing but search for him since we'd arrived. She pointed over to a boisterous group beyond the spit under a row of orange trees lit by strips of neon lighting. Adam was in the middle of things, apparently holding another man in a headlock; the man, who was wearing pink trousers, was protesting loudly, and everyone around was laughing. They looked like school friends – the youthful spirits a bit forced, nostalgic; old mates performing old roles. I wondered if Reynash was among them.

We were getting to the head of the queue. I put my hand on her elbow to attract her attention and said, 'Shall we goat?' but she pulled away.

'Adam,' she called. He turned, grinning, as she danced towards him, kicking up her heels and twirling her arms above her head. I watched her reach him and put her arm around his waist. He introduced her to the man in the pink trousers, who made a stupid courtly bow and kissed her hand (it wasn't just me she had an effect on), and she smiled and flicked her pale hair. I saw how at ease with it all she was, despite her protestations and the tatty dress and plimsolls.

I waited. A few minutes passed. I let the people behind in the queue go ahead, and as I watched, I saw a women peel away from the group and head towards the house. She was wearing a tight black dress and heels, lots of make-up, her hair scraped back in a high ponytail. She looked different, but as she passed me, I realised it was Amira. 'Hey *you*!' I called, copying her cry from the day before. But if she heard, she didn't stop. She reached the top of the steps, leant against the glass wall, and, chin lifted, turned to look back the way she'd come.

Across the terrace, Adam was still chatting and laughing, his expression animated. I noticed him look in Amira's direction and Amira look back. Celia was in conversation now with two women. He whispered something in her ear, and then carefully laid his glass of wine down on the ground and started walking towards the house.

Amira slipped inside before he reached her, and he waited for a bit at the top of the steps, looking back the way he'd come, and then he lowered his head – not to duck; more to show an intent – and went through the doors after her.

I stood where I was, staring at the empty doorway. The

lights from the disco flickered. The music changed to something with a deeper bass.

I waited for Adam to reappear – clutching a fresh bottle, or doing up his zip, little tell-tale drop of pee in his crotch. For Amira to come back out, maybe with Jasmine and Lydia; she was, after all, closer to them in age.

I felt the bass in my chest, a dampness in my palms, a sickness at the back of my throat.

I walked up the steps and into the house, through the first couple of rooms. More people were dancing, more wildly now. Jasmine and Lydia were mucking about; scissoring their arms and kicking their legs as if they were running on the spot. They looked young and joyous and *innocent*. Past them, into the hall, with a wide staircase, going up and down. A toilet door opened and a man, who was on his own and wasn't Adam, came out, readjusting his belt.

I took the staircase up, and at the top started opening doors. If anyone asked, I'd say I had a migraine, was looking desperately for a paracetamol. The bedrooms were inhabited – clothes, toiletries, chargers obvious – but empty. No one was in any of the luxury ensuite bathrooms. One door led not to a room but a cupboard; it was full, and a bag of clothes fell down as I pulled the door open. The items spilled and I picked them all up – the black Lycra top, the joggers, the red cap, the pair of trainers – and stuffed them back in the bag. I had to squeeze the bag into a corner before being able to close the door.

I hurried back to the top of the stairs, and on a whim went to the window – big and arched – and looked down at the drive, with its statues and fairy lights. I say whim. Do I mean intuition? Or maybe I just knew him too well. 'Sex outdoors, Matt,' he once told me, 'when it's you and the elements, and you're bollock naked – that's when you know you're alive.'

I saw nothing at first. Dark and shadowy. The pale limbs of trees, ivy clinging. Reproduction bodies posed. When Celia was pregnant for the first time, she showed me the photo from the scan and I studied it for a long time before a human shape emerged from the umbra. Was that an arm? Was that a head? A tiny raised hand?

I wished I hadn't remembered that. It made it so much worse when the realisation came that, among the reproduction bodies, I could distinguish the squirm of two real ones – pressed so close together they looked like one.

9

I was back, standing numbly in the queue for food; I couldn't think what else to do. The man ahead of me was loading his plate up high and when he saw me looking, said, 'It's free.' Two women behind me were discussing how annoying it was not to be able to take fluids in your hand luggage – how the 100-ml rule was 'a joke' and I wanted to turn round and say, 'I'll tell you what's a joke. You and your silly little conversation – you're a joke.'

I didn't, of course.

As soon as I'd been served, I searched for a quiet spot and found, on the sea-side of the house, a pit arrangement under a loggia: a series of stone seats and tables, softened with cushions. Most of the booths were taken; a man busy on his phone in the third. I asked if he minded me sitting down, and he shook his head, eyes still on his screen.

I put my plate to one side – turned out I had no appetite.

Normally I'd have known. There'd have been phone calls, requests for cover: 'Say I was with you, old man.' This time, nothing. He was scared of me, that's why. For one thing he'd broken his promise – *never again*, he'd said, weeping, begging me not to tell Celia. But also maybe because, even for Adam, she was so *young*. Celia said he'd been distracted, and I threw my mind back over the last few months. Had there been clues? Actually, yes. He'd been less available. The last time we'd met up, he'd bought the first round and left after less than an hour, slapping the table as he got to his feet: 'Early start.' I'd just thought I'd bored him, gone on too much about Takara. Had he been seeing Amira all this time? Fuck. Had he arranged for her to meet him? No, that didn't make sense. She'd surprised him. He hadn't known she was here, not until today.

'*You!*' she'd called down.

It wasn't *me* she was addressing, but Adam. She'd given up hope – and then suddenly, out of the blue, there he was.

And Adam. He'd run away then, but he'd come tonight. He'd brought his wife with him, his own *daughter*. What was the matter with him? How could he have so much contempt for the people who loved him? Was he addicted to risk? Was life just a game?

I stared out to sea. Lights blinked where the sky hit the water. What was out there? We were too far east for Malta;

Crete would be over to the right. Egypt? No. *Libya.* Nothing but water between this house, this party, this flickering ball of gaiety, and Libya – civil rights violations, crime, uprisings, armed conflict. I thought about the guests piling their plates with free food; the couples killing dolphins on their jet skis. Takara having sex with Rick in our bedroom. All of them wanting *more*. More food. More status. More money. More sex. And there was Sara at the end of the drive, handing out leaflets, her heart-rending state of suspended grief. An outsider like me. The world seemed suddenly a horrible, dark place.

Celia was right. I hated everything and everybody.

'Not hungry?'

I dragged my eyes from the sea. The man across the table was looking at me over the top of his phone with an enquiring expression.

I said, 'I'm not mad about goat.'

'Or is it lamb?'

'I think it's goat.' I moved my plate towards me, looked down at it, and then pushed it away. 'Also I hate parties.'

He placed his phone face up on the table; he'd been in the middle of playing Candy Crush. He was about my age: a bland face behind a tidy beard, neat ears and buggy brown eyes. 'I know what you mean,' he said.

I told him about finding a list on my girlfriend's phone of ways I irritated her, and how my desire to leave a party five minutes after we'd arrived was number two.

'What was number one?'

'I think flossing in the bedroom,' I lied.

I looked across at the terrace. The music had ramped up; people were dancing erratically, arms waving.

I said, 'It's so tasteless, a party like this, when a man has gone missing.'

He considered me for a moment; then he said, 'The world is full of awful things. Wars. Famines. Floods. If we stopped and thought about it too hard we'd all sit at home in a dark cupboard.'

'But I think he actually *stayed* here.'

His expression was still impassive. 'I'm sure the police are doing everything they can.'

Beyond him, in the flickering light, I saw Amira come through the open doors, pause, and set off into the crowd. A few seconds later, possibly exactly ten if I'd counted, Adam appeared and looked around. There was an expression on his face I'd seen before: emerging from the stationery cupboard with Sonya the receptionist at the paper; coming out of a Portaloo at Hay with a buyer from WHSmith; exiting customs at Heathrow after the US press tour – sheepish, repentant, a tiny bit cocky.

His eyes fell on me then, sitting in the semi-dark on the edge of everything, and he saw that I'd seen. I kept my face still and emotionless. He put his head on one side and smiled – he couldn't keep it in – and I kept my own expression flat and unresponsive, and he came towards me, as I knew he would. He couldn't *not*. It was both the sweetest and most infuriating thing about him, the thing that made him vulnerable and human, his fatal flaw: the need to be liked.

In seconds his arm was looped around a stone pillar and he was swinging his body playfully in, Gene Kelly-style. Not that he'd have known who Gene Kelly was. Not in any real sense. He'd never have seen *Singin' in the Rain*, for example. Oh, he'd say he had. That very first TV appearance on the cultural panel – I may have briefed him about 'The Glory of Venice' but he still muddled Carlevarijs with Caravaggio.

'So helloooo,' he said, putting on a silly, high voice. 'You hiding over here?'

His face stalled as he realised I wasn't alone.

I said, 'Adam, this is . . . I'm sorry. I don't know your name.'

My companion had got to his feet, and Adam creased forwards, making a low gesture with his arms – sort of bowing his head. And the man made a similar gesture, only with his arms slightly raised. Adam dropped abruptly down on to the seat, so that for a few seconds the slighter man towered over him, and then Adam said, 'Long time no see.'

The other man nodded and, with a quick lick of his lips, said, 'Welcome.'

The truth – it should have been obvious all along – hit me then.

'Oh my God, you're Reynash,' I said. 'Of course.'

I started talking – and talking. I started on my plate as I did so. I wasn't aware of the taste. It was something to do, to pick up the plastic knife and fork and cut the lamb into tiny pieces and skewer a piece of tomato and to place it between my lips. I said how delicious it was. Of course it was lamb. Not that there was anything wrong with goat. I wished I could keep my mouth shut, but I kept talking, saying we were gate-crashers kind of, only we'd heard the whole village had been invited, and we couldn't resist, and Reynash eventually interrupted me, and with his eyes still on Adam said, 'Don't worry, Amira told me you were coming. It's fine.'

I brushed my fingers across the table; it was made out of tiny mosaic tiles, each one with a sharp edge.

'Such a coincidence,' I said, because I would do anything to put a firewall around Celia. 'Amira and I keep bumping into each other,' and I recounted our late-night meeting in detail. 'So, you could say I rescued her. I was her knight with a white hanky.'

He smiled at me. 'Yeah, well, that makes two of us – not that I had a hanky. I met her in a bar one night. She'd come out to meet a friend and misunderstood when they were arriving. I said she could doss here if she helped out with some of my guests. Poor girl.'

The air around me felt suddenly hot – so hot it was as if the heat were coming out of me. I expected to see the two men recoil from me in disgust. But they were just staring at each other, Adam, the untamed lion, and Reynash, the quieter, sleeker fox. Who was stronger in that moment? Looking back, I can't tell. All I can remember is how much I hoped Adam would use the opportunity to apologise for *one* thing at least: his history with Reynash. Own it, I willed him. Make amends. Start here. One step at a time. Be the better person. Be *a* better person. Say you're sorry.

But he didn't.

10

I woke the next morning, sweaty and hungover.

The BBC website was full of horror – floods and fires, bombings in the Ukraine. I flicked through story after story, but all I could think about was Celia and Adam.

They were lifeless by the pool when I walked into Villa Mimosa, and for a few seconds I stood at the kitchen door, watching them. The sun glittered on the surface of the pool; the plants and the trees trembled. I must have made a noise, or maybe he was on edge, because Adam lifted his head. 'Mattski! Fresh recruitments! Thank God.' He leapt to his feet. 'We're boring each other to death here.'

Celia put her novel down at her side, leaving her thumb in her place. (She was a slow but astute reader; though at book club, she'd told me, she pretended to love everything so as not to upset the person whose choice it had been.) She smiled as Adam leapt up the steps to greet me. In the kitchen, he headed straight for the fridge, took out two cans of Diet Coke and threw one at me. When I failed to catch it, he picked it up off the floor, and shook it up before opening it, spraying in my face. I told him to fuck right off – I was trying to stay serious, to let him know by my expression we needed to talk – but he came at me again and I began to laugh. The more we wrestled, the more the laughs came out of me in high-pitched gasps. It was a relief actually, a release of tension. Adam was a terrible, incorrigible person, a bundle of obnoxious cells.

'You're such a tosser,' I said. 'You're such a c—' I meant it – after last night. I could say anything. Words bounced off him. I got to the top of the steps, but he came after, wrenching his arm around my neck, trying to get my shirt off, his armpit brushed my chin. He had an animal smell of sweat, coffee, alcohol.

'Get a room,' Celia called. 'Honestly, you two.'

I managed to get away, down the steps to the garden. I was yelping and cowering now. 'I'm getting in the water. I'm swimming.'

I took off my shirt and trousers and leapt into the pool, still panting with laughter. He dive-bombed after me, surfaced, shook his head like a dog. He swam towards me, and, breathless now, letting out muffled squeals, I got away to the shallow end, hauled myself out and ran round the pool to lie down flat on the lounger next to Celia.

'Celia, help!' I whimpered as he lurched after me.

'You're such idiots,' Celia said amiably.

Adam rose out of the deep end, muscles flexed. He towered over me, dripping water, then pulled out the towel I'd been lying on. He perched on the end of the sunbed, grinning and triumphant.

'It's not funny,' I said, trying to signal with my expression that it really wasn't.

Celia started chatting away. She had no idea what any of this was about. She wanted to know about my evening – I'd left so suddenly there'd been no chance for a debrief. Had I seen round the house? Had I met Rey? He was surprising, wasn't he? Not at all how she'd imagined. Apparently, the two of them had met here in Greece the year before; they'd got talking in Dimitri's when she came out to close up the house. 'Clearly, I made more of an impression on him than he did on me.' She raised one coquettish shoulder.

'I'm sure you did,' I said.

'He can't swim, do you know that? Isn't that weird – to buy a house by the sea and not be able to swim?'

'Not sure about weird. But dangerous,' I said. 'A lot of water around to drown in.'

'Apparently, it's my fault he's here,' Adam said. 'He read that stupid interview I gave to the *Sunday Times*.'

'Fool,' I said, digging his thigh with my toe. 'Hoist by your own petard.'

'What did happen between the two of you at school?' Celia asked him. 'Did you behave very badly?'

He laughed awkwardly. 'I was no saint back then. You know that.'

'Oh Adam.' She sounded only mildly reproachful, as though he'd mislaid his phone. She bent her head to examine the nail on her big toe.

I rubbed my wrist. Adam had given me quite the Chinese burn. 'I think I know. Head-flushing? Food-throwing? Racist slurs?'

His eyes flicked back to mine and he gave me a quick smile. 'That sort of thing,' he said.

Celia was still looking at her toenail. 'I've gone and chipped it,' she murmured.

Adam pushed my legs to one side, trying to take more of the sunbed. 'I'm not sure it's worth being mates with a billionaire anyway,' he said. 'Steve said Rey asked him for some shit favour recently – using his account to clear some money or something. Sounded like money-laundering. Would you do something borderline illegal for a free holiday in Morzine? I don't know.'

I said camply, 'I'd do anything for a free holiday in Morzine.'

'I know *you* would,' he said, pushing my feet off the sunbed all together.

After a bit, I asked where Lydia and Jasmine were and Celia said they'd met a couple of local boys at the party, and had gone out with them for the day. It was good because Lydia had been worried Jasmine would be bored out here.

'She's quite the goer back home,' Adam added.

I looked at him. I didn't like his tone.

Celia leant forward. 'Now, what about you?' she said to me. 'Did you meet anyone interesting?'

I shook my head. 'Everyone was married. Or too young.'

Adam was breathing heavily. Moisture glistened on his upper lip.

Celia laughed. 'Don't worry. We'll find you someone lovely. I'll put on my thinking cap.'

I mentioned Sara then, asked if they remembered seeing her handing out leaflets on the main road. They both said 'kind of' in a way which made it obvious both that they did and that the memory embarrassed them.

'You know her brother's gone missing?' I said. 'I wish I could do something to help.'

'I'd stay out of it if I were you,' Celia said. 'You can be too nice. I don't want you being exploited.'

'Exploited? What do you mean: *exploited*?'

She wrinkled her nose. 'I'm sure the police are on it. She's bound to have plenty of people around her.'

She stood up and I watched as she found her goggles and earplugs and snapped on a pink swimming hat. 'We should sort the pool out,' Adam called. 'Convert it to salt water, like Rey's. It's much better for the environment.'

'*And* my highlights.'

'I thought you were a natural blonde,' I said.

'Matt! No woman of my age is ever a natural blonde.'

She walked to the deep end, climbed down the steps and pushed herself backwards. Once in, she began swimming lengths slowly: up, down, in, out. Beyond the olive trees, you could see the sea, a truer shade of gleaming aquamarine, hazy on the horizon, tufts of cloud squatting on the top of the far mountains.

Adam got up off the foot of my lounger and took over hers; he lay down, his eyes closed. I stretched out, too, now I had room for my legs. I kept my eyes open. I should leave – go back down to the cottage. Maybe even go back to London. Why did I feel in any way responsible for their happiness? Adam expected to carry on as if nothing had happened, and for me to do the same. Celia was all for doing good, but only within the prescribed boundaries of her own small world. It would have been different if Sara had been some lovely old dear with a flat round the corner from the Brompton Oratory. I felt exhausted by it. By them.

It was extraordinary how deeply blue the sky was; that such a colour could exist in nature. Small splishes and clinks came from the pool. Insects droned. From the kitchen, the fridge shuddered; ice dropped inside with a clunk. In this particular spot you could put Rey and Arcadia out of your mind. If you weren't careful, you could put everything out of your mind.

I forced myself to sit up. 'I'd better get back to work,' I said.

'Thanks for coming,' Adam said, lifting his hand sleepily. 'I'm glad you're here.'

I stood over him, blocking the sun from his face. 'Why don't you pop down with me. Pick up that book.'

His eyes were still closed, a small smile played on his lips. 'Which book?'

'The one you wanted to borrow.'

He opened his eyes then and finally realised I was serious.

I didn't say anything until the walls of the house were safely behind us. He was barefoot and walking comically, lifting his knees high and emitting little yelps as he stepped on stones and spiky plants, letting me know I was putting him out. He thought he could still make a joke of it, that he was already halfway to being forgiven.

I said, 'What the fuck, Adam.'

'What?'

'You know what.'

He raised his shoulders, wide-mouthed. '*What?*' He let out an embarrassed laugh.

'It's not funny.'

He let his mouth hang open, as if unable to find words – still camping it up.

'How long has it been going on? How do you even know her?'

'Oh God. Matt.' His arms fell to his side. 'You're like the fucking Gestapo.'

I stopped and glared at him. 'Don't put this on me.'

'Sorry. I . . .'

'What?'

'She's . . . she's . . .'

'Who?'

'I didn't *ask* her to come out.'

'Bloody hell, Adam.'

He let out a sigh and, as if forced against his better judgement, told a long, rambling, self-justifying story, full of anger and recrimination – directed everywhere but at himself. Amira was 'someone from the production company' who'd made 'a beeline' for him, staying after a meeting to ask him questions, and then turning up 'unannounced' at Hatchard's at a book-tie-in signing. 'We had a quick grubby grapple in one of those arcades off Piccadilly. I know. I know, I know, I'm terrible.' He put his hand up to stop me speaking. 'I was drunk. It was nothing. Supposed to be a one-off. Interns don't usually hang around for more than a week or two.'

'She's *an intern*? That's terrible, Adam. You could get into big trouble. It's an abuse of power.'

'She led *me* on. It wasn't me. She was *keen*, man. You know what I'm like. I can't say no. I got in over my head, but the summer was supposed to provide a natural break. I was coming here; she was Interrailing with friends.' He shuddered. 'Apparently, she got to Spetses, saw how close she was to the house, and thought it would be a laugh to surprise me.'

'But then you weren't here.'

'No. She broke into the cottage, decided to wait for me.'

'She broke into the cottage? *My* cottage.'

He laughed. 'Yes, Matt. *Your* cottage. Came back one night and you were there – proper little Goldilocks. Had to wait for you to go out the next day to retrieve her stuff.'

'I knew someone was hanging around. I thought it was Marc Ashley.'

'Marc Ashley?'

'The missing man.'

'No. Not him. Her.'

I brought my hand to the top of my head. 'You've outclassed yourself, Adam. I mean, last night – what were you *thinking*?'

'I was trying to talk to her, man. It's just *while* we were talking, she undid her dress. Unzipped it. Top to toe. All the way down.' He groaned. 'The sex – I mean – messy and frantic and dirty and up against the wall.' He made a clawing gesture with his hands. 'No one could have resisted.'

'I would have resisted. I'd have told her to put her dress back on.'

'Of course you would. We all know about you and sex. It's why Takara was forced to go elsewhere.' He put his hand up. 'Sorry, sorry. Below the belt.'

I stared at him unblinkingly, trying to think of the worst thing I could say back. I pulled at an olive branch, plucking off each leaf one by one, and then said: 'Did she tell Rey?'

He took a step away from me. 'Fuck. No, she's a good girl, Amira. She swore not, and I believe her.'

'If Celia finds out, it'll be the last straw – you know that, don't you?'

'Yes, I know. She'll kill me, literally kill me.'

'You have to end it. Once and for all. Completely. I'm not covering for you again. This is your last chance.'

He tucked his elbows close into his body, hunching his shoulders. It's what he did when he was cornered – that time at the paper when I'd told him he had to ring a contributor to apologise for errors he'd subbed into their copy. Or when

I'd caught him snorting coke at the Christmas party. But this wasn't like appeasing a classical music reviewer. Or keeping his recreational habits out of the workspace. This was his wife. His marriage. His career. He prised at a clod of red earth with his toe, unwilling to meet my eye. He hated taking responsibility. He wanted it to be my fault. He wanted to put the blame on me for forcing him into this position. But eventually he nodded, and I left him on the path as I walked back to the cottage.

11

What did he mean, 'We all know about you and sex'?

Of all Adam's deplorable revelations, this is what I thought about most. What had Takara said to him? When? I paced up and down the cottage, trying to think of an occasion when they'd been alone together. I thought back to that dreadful afternoon. I'd gone straight round to Islington and the Murphys had taken me in, plied me with tea and whisky and sympathy. I'd assumed they were on my side. 'Rick? Rick Vernon?' Adam had said, as if it were a personal affront. 'Adam's right: you're such a fusspot,' Takara had said during the breakup. Had she confided in him? In them? I'd assumed they were my closest friends. But was I the butt of a joke? And if so, what was I doing here?

I sat on the bed and scratched so hard at a mosquito bite on my ankle I drew blood. My thoughts turned nasty. Of course I loved Adam. We'd been friends so long – and I admired him. He'd emerged from the ashes of his childhood, done everything not to turn into his father, channelled all his anger into something different. But did he really deserve his success? Ever since his first break – the one I gave him – ever since that moment in the newspaper foyer, one opportunity after another had dropped into his lap. The worse he'd behaved, the better things had worked out. Just once, I would have liked for him to be caught out, for the consequences of his actions to come crashing down, for him to be forced to learn from his mistakes.

That night, Rey let off fireworks, sending the entire coastline into a state of wartime alert, and, while watching all that expensive glitter rain down over the Messenian Gulf, I worked my way through Celia's chocolates. After that, I rolled a joint with the dope and smoked it. I found the Durex – Amira's, I assumed, along with the bag of clothes she must have fetched while I was out – and put in my wallet. Of no immediate use, but you never knew.

In the morning, I felt calmer. It would be mad to pack up and go. Now I was here I should make the most of it. I'd forget the Murphys. I'd occupy myself with other things.

I resumed work on the screenplay that day, and I found myself for the first time in weeks properly absorbed. The words just seemed to come. The story was there, right in front of me, waiting for me to pick it up. I wrote page after page until it was dark, going to bed with a deep sense of satisfaction, resuming immediately the next day where I'd left off.

Dead Heat

Late afternoon, I lifted my eyes from the screen to see my cat Branwell edging out of the trees. He was a healthier specimen now, vertebrae less jagged, belly more rounded. But he was limping and, after enticing him with some tuna, I managed to get close enough to see his front paw was bleeding. I soaked it in warm salty water, just as I had with my own sore foot, and wondered about finding a vet. That would be ridiculous: I wouldn't be here for ever and I couldn't take him with me. (Could I?) His presence, I realised, was like most of my relationships: a comfort and a source of torment.

Over the next couple of days, I thought about Villa Mimosa, of the cool breeze that wafted through it, of all those air-conditioned bedrooms (of which they'd be using three at most). I wondered if Celia had noticed my absence. I missed talking to her – particularly when one morning, out of the blue, I received an email from Takara, asking if we could 'meet up'. I would have liked Celia's take on that. For the most part, though, I was content. They were, I think, the best few days of my summer.

On the third day, doing my washing, I came across Sara's latest flyer in the pocket of my best shirt. I felt bad for a moment because the whole fuss with Adam and Amira, and my worries about Takara, had put her completely out of my mind. The flyer began with the word 'PLEASE' in big capitals and asked for information, for any sightings of Marc Ashley, whose disappearance was so out of character, underlined. Among a new grid of photographs, one in particular caught my eye.

The missing man was wearing trainers – white with a silver pattern on the side and distinctive neon-yellow soles – which looked familiar to me. I'd seen a similar pair very recently. I racked my brain. Someone at the party had been wearing them, I was sure. I closed my eyes, tried to remember back: the dance floor, the terrace, down at the pool. Many trainers whirled across my vision; white with blue Ns and red ticks. It's 'the look'; I know that. I don't live under a stone. This pair, though. God, I could almost feel them in my hand.

I put the flyer on the table and carried on with the washing. I'd strung a line with a ball of string between two trees and I was hanging out my pants and socks when the answer came to me. I'd seen them in the cupboard at Arcadia when I'd been searching for Adam upstairs; in the bag that had fallen off the shelf when I opened the door.

I felt suddenly hot and clammy. Could those clothes have belonged to Marc? Wasn't there a red cap in there, too? And hadn't he been wearing a red cap in the very first poster I saw? In which case what was it all doing there? Shouldn't they have been given to Sara, who I already knew treasured anything belonging to her brother? Why had they been stuffed in a bag out of sight? Hidden, even.

It seemed wrong on all counts. I felt as if Marc *himself* had been hidden away, an inconvenience, while the parties went on around him. It led on to something that worried me from the beginning. I'd liked Rey when I'd met him and at the time I'd understood what he'd said about sitting in a dark cupboard if we thought about all the awful things in the world. But *really*?

Shouldn't he have cancelled the summer? I seemed to be the only person who thought this. Everyone else was putting their own self-interest above common decency. It was typical of a shift in the way we lived our lives, like the jet skis and the dead dolphin: people getting away with bad things, doing what the hell they wanted – and, after a bit, other people *not minding*.

I didn't stop to think any more. I picked up my phone and rang the number on the flyer.

Sara's voice, with its high reach, its glottal stops, was immediately recognisable. She seemed to remember who I was, but she sounded wary. 'Yeah?' she said. 'You said to get in touch, didn't you? I'm not sure if there's anything specific you can do. Just getting the word out, do you know what I mean?'

I told her I wasn't ringing with an offer to help, but that I had some information for her and perhaps we could meet so I could tell her in person. It was delicate, I explained, a bit sensitive.

The wariness was still there, in a long-drawn-out 'um' – for all she knew I was a weirdo – but hope won. She breathed in sharply and gave me some directions. I told her I'd be with her within the hour.

The address she gave led to a tower on the far side of the village. They're all over the Mani, these towers: feuding families of the past flicking the finger at each other across the landscape. On my last visit, I'd seen mainly ruins but, eight years on, many had been converted into chic holiday lets or boutique hotels. Sara's tower, just beyond a small stone church, was surrounded by lower buildings around a courtyard – sloping slabs of stone, a few sleeping cats. The walls were pinky cream, with fresh mortar in the cracks, and the windows were painted a fashionable pale grey. She'd told me to ring the bell at the main front door, which I did, even though it was open, and her voice echoed down the stairwell, telling me to come straight up.

It was much cooler on the stairs – those thick walls useful not just for defence. She was waiting for me at a door on the first floor, barefoot, in beige shorts and an outsized blue-and-white-striped shirt. I'd felt excited as I'd schlepped into the village, fired with crusading zeal as I sweated up the hill. But when I saw her standing there in her brother's shirt, I wished I hadn't come. My reasons were stupid, born out of loneliness. She looked flushed and sort of bruised, a muscle pulsing in her jaw, emotion jostling under her skin, pushing with little fists to get out. Her gaze went straight from me to the space over my shoulder; and her neck craned as if she thought someone might be coming up behind. I died a little then.

'It's not much,' I said quickly. 'I didn't mean to get your hopes up.'

Her eyes closed on a slow blink. For a second, I thought she wasn't going to open them again; when she did, she said, 'Come in anyway. Do you want a glass of water? Or' – she shook her head, as if irritated that she'd even thought to suggest it – 'a beer?'

'Actually, a glass of water would be lovely. It's been a bit of a walk. I'm quite parched.'

I mopped my forehead with the back of my hand and loosened my collar. I tried to smooth the front of the shirt with my hands. It had dried in time, but I hadn't managed to find an iron.

She walked away towards a sink at the other side of the room. The space was open-plan and simply decorated – mainly wickerwork furniture; there was a microwave on the counter next to the sink, and a small fridge. A duvet was folded on one end of the sofa, and an edge of sheet poked out from under the cushions. Underwear was drying on the windowsill. I wanted to say I'd just done my washing too, but I decided against it.

I said, 'This is nice.'

Handing me a glass of water – warm from the tap – she said, 'I had a room at the back of the village before, but it was very hot. It's better here.' She said it joylessly.

I nodded, and tried to look understanding. 'You'd rather not have to be here at all,' I said. 'It's horrible. I'm so sorry.'

'Yeah. I can't leave, you know? People say I should go back to Lewes, pick up my normal life, go to work, see my friends, but I can't bear to. I feel closer to him in the Mani. It's just the not knowing . . .' Her voice trailed away.

I asked her what she did in her normal life, and she said she worked for an optician. 'They've been very understanding, letting me have so much time off. I know it's probably futile – so many people have searched for him now and – nothing. But I have to keep at it, you know? It's like I'm letting Marc down otherwise.' She shook her head then, and did it again as if the movement soothed her. 'There's only me now. Lucia, his wife died in January. And both our parents are dead too.'

'I thought they probably were,' I said.

She looked at me for a second, her brows creasing in a little frown. 'Did you?'

'Yes, just because you're on your own.'

'Yes. I suppose I am.'

I wanted to reach out for her, but instead I said lightly, 'That makes two of us.'

She stared at me, looking doubtful – did she think I was coming on to her? – but then seemed to decide it was OK and gestured at me to sit by a small round table under one of the windows. I crossed the room and pulled out a chair, moving a laptop off it before I sat down. The table itself was messy – piled with leaflets and a writing pad, a pair of glasses with thick green frames.

'So this is the centre of operations,' I said.

'Yes,' she said curtly. 'So?' She leant forwards, elbows on her knees.

I felt foolish then, desperate to get it over with. I was overly apologetic in my explanation, said, 'It's probably absolutely nothing' several times, but explained that I had found a pair of trainers, a cap and some clothes, exercise gear, in an upstairs cupboard at Arcadia, and that I was almost sure they were Marc's. 'And I thought you should know about them, that you would probably want them back.'

'What do you mean they were Marc's clothes? They went through his room; the police gave me everything.'

'It's just the trainers. They're quite distinctive. The soles. You know.' I tapped one of the flyers on the table.

'If they were his, what would they be doing in a cupboard?'

'Exactly.'

Her face was red. 'Also, if it's exercise clothes, he'd have been wearing them. You know he was seen leaving for a run that morning? He'd only come for a long weekend, he wouldn't have had two lots of kit, two pairs of trainers with him. They can't have been his.'

I felt a prickle up my back. 'No,' I said. 'Of course.'

I didn't say anything for a moment and then, because I couldn't not, I said carefully, 'Unless they are his and he didn't actually go running that morning.'

'But people saw him,' she said. 'Two of his colleagues. They were coming downstairs for breakfast and they saw Marc leaving the house by the front door. It wasn't out of character. He'd done a half-marathon and he'd signed up for a full one. He finds it helpful for his mental health.'

The present tense. I picked up my glass and took a long swig of water, watching her over the rim.

I put my glass down. 'What do you think happened?' I said. 'Or what do you *hope* happened?'

She closed her eyes again briefly. 'That he set off for his run and thought fuck it and kept running. That he lost his mind, I guess, and is holed up somewhere, trying to make sense of it all. Lucia died really quite quickly after diagnosis. Pancreatic cancer. And, you know, it took it out of him. She'd been complaining of back ache for months and he blamed himself for not having suggested she see a doctor earlier. She first had symptoms around the time they were selling AdVent and he was very busy.'

'Oh I see – he was involved with that, was he?' I was surprised. I realised I'd assumed Marc had been some sort of underling at AdVent, a lowly employee, not at boardroom level.

'Yes.' She sounded distracted. 'As COO, he was central to the whole thing. He felt he should have picked up the signs, got her to the doctor sooner. He was in a state about it, but he wasn't suicidal. I know it's what everyone thinks. But I'm his sister. I'd know. He just wouldn't do it to me. He'll get in touch. He'll come back.'

She massaged the muscle in her neck. 'Listen, I appreciate you trying to help, but I doubt the shoes are Marc's. I've known Rey for years, ever since he and Marc met – on that coding course back in the day. And he's been amazing. You know, he tried to get me to stay at Arcadia and when I refused – I didn't want to be a burden – he insisted on paying for this.' She gestured at the room we were sitting in. 'And of course the reward money.'

'Oh, he came up with that, did he? The fifty thousand? I'm surprised it's not more then.'

'It's quite a lot. I assume that's why you're here.'

Horrified, I said, 'No, of course I'm not here for the reward. Gosh. No. That's not why I came at all.' I scratched my head. 'God. No.'

'OK.' She was looking at me again, quite coolly. 'Listen, Rey wasn't just Marc's boss; he was his friend. They built that company, and others before it, together. He and Rey knew each other inside out. Rey wouldn't keep anything from me. Nor would the others. It's just a pair of shoes. It doesn't change anything.'

I held her gaze. 'No. I can see that now. I'm sorry.'

Down in the courtyard, a dog barked. In the distance, a cockerel was crowing.

'Just out of interest,' Sara said. 'What were you doing upstairs in Rey's house, looking in cupboards, if it wasn't for the reward?'

I felt the heat come back into my face. 'Oh God, long story,' I said.

She was still looking at me, and because I was in a tight spot, I found myself telling her everything – about Adam's previous affairs and how awful it had been at the party when I'd seen the look pass between him and Amira and how I'd followed them into the house, and watched them from the top window.

'Like a peeping Tom?' she said.

'No. Not at all.' I felt my voice catch. 'Just to be certain, just to *know*.'

I cleared my throat and, to establish moral authority, told her I'd spoken to Adam and told him to finish with her and that I hoped that's what had happened.

She stood up. She wanted me out of her hair. It was all awful and I was awful. I should never have come. I'd made a series of mistakes. I stuffed my hands in my pockets. I felt a pain, a bit like longing, a bit like indigestion, in the centre of my chest.

I started walking to the door. She was behind me, and when

I turned to say goodbye, she was closer than I'd realised. I knew I couldn't hug her, though I wanted to. I had the urge to hold her, to bring the pieces of her back together. It would comfort me, of course, more than her. I thought we could at least shake hands, but she had already closed the door.

12

It only took him a day.

I was drinking coffee in Kardamos, sitting at a table closest to the water. The harbour was busier now schools were out, but not manic. A strolling couple in trainers and shorts stopped to inspect a rack of painted pottery. A young man was sweeping the pavement with a broom. From somewhere there was music – the ever cheerful bouzouki; a white cat stretched in the shade of an umbrella.

I had graduated to Greek coffee and, as I'd ordered it, without the prompt of my dictionary, in Greek, I enjoyed the thought of myself as practically a local.

I was watching a group of small boys – they were dropping bread over the wall and the water bubbled and frothed as tiny fish converged – when I felt a presence. The sun was in my eyes when I turned and I was dazzled for a second. I felt the air rearrange itself around me. The person stepped into the shade of a parasol and said, 'It's Matt, isn't it? Reynash. We met the other night.'

I got quickly to my feet, feeling a terrible self-conscious dread. I managed to say hello and stretch out a clammy hand.

He said, shaking it, 'I'm happy to bump into you actually.'

'You are?'

He nodded and asked if he could join me, and when I stammered, 'Of course,' he pulled out the chair opposite and sat down. He was wearing a blue baseball cap, white T-shirt, brown shorts. Nothing special. He was holding a carrier bag and he placed it on the ground. The white cat got up to investigate and he pushed it away roughly with his foot. The cat slunk off and sat a few feet away, still watching the bag.

I turned away to get the waiter's attention, and when I turned back, Rey was looking at me carefully. His eyelids were thin and wrinkled, as if he'd had eczema in the past, and he had a weak chin (one reason I suspected he had grown a beard). But there was something about his eyes. They were very acute, watchful. I know it's a stupid thing to say because it's true of all eyes, but they made you think of lenses – the pupils retracting mechanically in reaction to stimuli, tightly focusing when required.

'So you've been talking to Sara?' he said abruptly.

My mouth felt dry; I swallowed. 'I'm just trying to help.'

He nodded. 'I hear you went to see her at the Airbnb?'

I felt even hotter. 'It was probably a mistake,' I said at last.

'Was it the reward you were after?'

'No, of course not.'

'Yeah.' He shook his head. 'I told her it wouldn't have been the reward. It's not even that much, of course. You're right. We took advice from the police. Any more, they said, and you encourage crackpots.'

He looked at me for a bit, and then traced a circle with his finger on the table and, when he looked up again, he said I'd been kind, when not everyone had. 'I'm personally grateful that you're taking such an interest. It's been awful for all of us. The timing particularly. I feel terrible about the whole thing. Perhaps I should have cancelled all plans, but I had people coming to stay who'd bought flights, who were looking forward to it, and I couldn't let them all down. They've gone now. Poor Sara. I think she thought I'd forgotten about Marc, but I think about him all the time. I just want to do what I can to make her life a bit more comfortable – it's why I persuaded her to move out of the awful digs she was in at first, moved her up to the tower.' He smiled for the first time, but sadly. 'You know Marc disappearing is an absolute gutter, a terrible thing.'

'The two of you were close?'

'Yeah.' He sucked in sharply through his teeth. 'We went through a great deal together. Loads of ups and downs. He knew me when I was struggling. Helped me stay grounded when things got really . . .' He widened his eyes and shook his head. '. . . crazy.' He clasped his hands together and nodded. 'He was vital to the success of the company. I owe him a lot.'

He started to rub a small reddened area at the base of his right palm, saw me looking and said, 'Gaming callus. My one vice.'

The waiter came over with his coffee and I waited until he had gone to say, 'What do you think happened to Marc?'

Rey picked up his cup, but only nursed it in his hand. 'The police have obviously considered three scenarios. One, that he disappeared on purpose. Two, that he either fell or got lost in the mountains – both events, sadly, one has to assume at this stage, fatal. Or three, that he took his own life. Sara is obviously hoping for scenario one.' He took a sip from his cup, looking at me over the top of it.

I closed my eyes briefly. I could hear the small boys shouting to each other from the harbour wall, the scrape of the brush broom, the clink of Rey's cup as he replaced it on the saucer.

I opened my eyes. 'What about the fourth scenario?'

He frowned. 'What fourth scenario?'

'Foul play.'

'Foul play?' He looked appalled. 'You mean, murder? I don't the police ever considered murder.'

'I'm sure they must have done,' I said. 'I mean, you have to consider it, don't you? If someone goes missing?'

'I think it's unlikely.' His face, apart from his mouth, was very still. 'No one wanted to do Marc harm. We all loved him.'

'So . . . what then?'

He nodded. 'I think he was finding it hard to live with himself. Sara told you, I know, that he blamed both AdVent and himself for his wife's death. He was utterly convinced that if he hadn't been so busy with all the Google stuff – it was a manic time for us – he'd have saved her life. And he wasn't entirely happy with the deal itself – in the context, he thought the figures were obscene. He was that kind of person.' Rey stopped and rubbed his eyes. 'It doesn't have to be that way, you know. There are other options apart from guilt, other ways to make yourself feel better. One thing I'd love to do is look into earlier detection for pancreatic cancer. There's so much potential with AI. I'd love to have a chance to give back.' He laughed and sat back. 'I'm sounding like a tosser. Sorry.'

I cleared my throat. 'No, it's a good instinct.'

He downed his coffee in one, then looked at me again. I felt he was weighing something up. 'Sara mentioned you'd been snooping around my house, finding bags of my old clothes?'

I swallowed, aware of the colour draining from my face.

'I wish you'd come to me first.' He smiled lightly. 'You upset her.'

I felt the blood flow back into my cheeks. 'It was just the trainers,' I said. 'I thought they were Marc's.'

'Well, they weren't.'

I felt a shiver then. It was the flat way he said it, and the way those eyes drilled into me. I was being put in my place.

'Anyway.' He picked up his cup again, scooped any remaining froth out with his spoon, and ate it like ice cream. He smiled and said, like someone sharing a huge piece of gossip, 'So, your great friend Adam!'

'Yes, my great friend Adam,' I repeated, watching him carefully.

He stuck out his lower lip and nodded a few times. His eyes looked very knowing.

'She told you?' I said, and he nodded.

'Oh God,' I said. 'Please don't repeat any of it.'

'I'll try.'

'Honestly. *Please.* Not for my sake, but for Celia, his wife's. I adore her – literally adore her – and it would kill her. Adam is not a bad man. He's promised to reform and . . . oh, just please.'

'Of course,' he said then. 'It wouldn't be my place. Not that it wouldn't afford me some pleasure to blow up his life.' He laughed. 'Let's just say, I'd have hoped for a less comfortable existence for Adam Murphy than success, fame and a beautiful, *understanding* wife.' He raised his palms.

I said, 'I know he was awful to you when you were kids. I'm sorry.'

He shrugged. 'At the time, I didn't cope well. I had other stuff going on, and I ended up dropping out of school. But, hey, in the long run, being bullied probably taught me resilience, helped me get where I am today.'

'I know it's no excuse, but he was also having a hard time at home,' I said. 'His father hit him and his mother pretended it wasn't happening. He was fairly screwed up.'

He was watching me carefully. 'Well, whatever. Let's hope he's a bigger man now. I'm sure he is – to have someone like you for a friend. And the glorious Celia for a wife. Not that he deserves her.' He puffed out his cheeks. 'I'll just do my best to avoid him.'

Dead Heat

We both finished our coffees and I paid ('No, no,' I said, 'I insist'). Then he picked up his carrier bag – a little bit of fish for his supper, he told me – and walked off down the quay towards the speedboat that was waiting to take him home.

13

I felt tense the entire time now, beside myself with fear that Rey would tell Celia about Adam and Amira. I went over and over the conversation, trying to remember if he'd actually promised not to, and worried, even if he had, that he wasn't to be trusted. He made me uncomfortable – but maybe obscene wealth just did, the awareness that so much money allowed someone to do whatever they wanted, put them outside normal constraints. I wished I hadn't opened my mouth to Sara, and I hated myself for having done so, but I also felt renewed resentment at Adam for putting me in this position. There would have been nothing to keep quiet about if he hadn't had the affair in the first place.

When Adam rang the following day, I feared the worst – that my indiscretion had blown it all open. But he was his usual breezy self. 'Mate, where've you been?' he said. 'We haven't seen you for days. Get yourself up here. We're having a barbie.'

'No. I've got my head down. You know: work.'

'Don't be a wet blanket. James is over for a few days with his new girlfriend – bit of hot totty; you'll like her. And honestly . . .' He lowered his voice. 'Celia's beginning to wonder where you are. She's asking questions. Please. If you don't come, she'll think something's up.'

'Is something up?' I said.

He laughed. 'Ooh, missus, I don't know what you're referring to.'

'I meant, have you sorted what you needed to sort? Is it safe for me to come out?'

'Of the closet?' He laughed again. 'Matt. That's up to you.'

I tried again. 'Adam. Have you done what you said you'd do? Is it over with you know who?'

'Yes.'

'All done and dusted?'

'Yes.'

'Promise?'

'Cross my heart and hope to die.'

It was all bluster. He was hiding something. I knew it. I didn't yet know what.

I arrived just after one to find the kitchen empty. Wet towels and clothes were scattered on the floor. Fruit flies hovered above a bowl of peaches. Through the open doors, I could see a barbecue hissing unattended and various people lounging around the pool – no immediate sign of the hot-totty girlfriend Adam had so leeringly mentioned, but Jasmine and Lydia were sitting with their legs dangling in the water and Adam and Celia's son James, my godson, was lying on a sunbed. Celia, in her pink swim hat, was in the shallow end with her back to me. She seemed to be holding someone in her arms – a child? No, a man – using the buoyancy of the water to bounce him up and down. She was laughing hard, practically convulsed with it, and I felt a split second of joy – I'd missed hearing her laugh.

'Mattski!' A cold bottle of beer pressed against my neck, a heavy hot arm across my shoulder. Adam, wet-haired, bare-chested, smelling faintly of sweat, was standing behind me.

His elbow hit my ribs. 'Maud, meet Matt: our resident hermit.'

Standing beside him was an older woman, about my age, with a pretty, doll-like face and brown bobbed hair, elegantly dressed in a navy shift and tan sandals. She looked very small and neat next to Adam who, in his state of semi-nudity, was a great shameless hulk: his thrusting brown stomach, his flamboyant silver-chained hairs, his knotty biceps and knees.

'Adam's been showing me around the house,' she said. 'Isn't it gorgeous?'

'Isn't it?'

We shook hands and looked at each other. Adam told me Maud worked in the American school in Athens and was a newish friend of Celia's – connected by a couple he thought I might know but didn't. She was a big reader and a keen tennis player, he said, as if I needed to hear a list of her qualities.

'Do you play?' she asked.

'Only when I stay with the Murphys in Norfolk,' I told her, 'and am roped into a ladder.'

She laughed – though the wordplay was unintended – revealing an attractive overbite. I remembered Celia saying she was going to find me 'someone lovely' and, feeling immediately overwhelmed, walked away from her through the garden doors to stand at the top of the steps.

Celia was still in the pool laughing helplessly.

'Oh, oh,' she cried, spinning slowly round. 'I'm going to let you go. You'll be fine.' She threw her arms in the air and the person she was holding, the person whose skin, only moments before, had pressed against hers, was released from her grasp, flailed, went under and then broke to the surface, spluttering.

'Rey!' she cried. 'You OK? Rey?'

Rey?

He was laughing too. 'I'm a lost cause. What a lost cause I am.' His shoulders gleamed.

I felt dizzy.

Adam was behind me. I turned. 'What the fuck?' I mouthed.

'Celia's teaching Rey to swim.'

'*Rey?*'

'I know.' He was smiling flatly. 'You know what she's like when she sets her mind to something.'

'But *Rey*?' I could feel my face twist.

'Just leave it,' he said, his mouth hardly moving.

The barbecue was smoking more fiercely now and he ran down the steps to deal with it, calling out to James to come and help. I turned back into the kitchen. Rey? Here? He'd told me he was going to avoid Adam. Mechanically, I put on an apron to protect my best shirt and trousers and opened the fridge. When Maud came up behind me, I told her I was hurrying along lunch – 'They're not great at things like this' – and she laughed, though again I hadn't meant to be funny.

She gathered cutlery and plates, while I pulled together a salad and made a dressing, adding honey and mustard, which Maud tasted and approved. Adam shouted for sausages and Maud said companionably, 'Is he always this bossy?' She had gone out to lay the table and I was arranging some stale pittas in a basket when Celia wandered into the house, a sarong fanning damply down from her neck. The tips of her hair were curly and wet. Mascara was smeared under her eyes.

'Oh, marvellous,' she said. 'You've got ahead. Well done you.' Her fingers trailed across my back; I inhaled coconut and chlorine, a tang of sweat. She said, as if everything were absolutely normal, 'I've got ketchup? Will people want ketchup?'

The outside table was on a ledge, under a vine-covered loggia, overlooking the sea. It was high up and exposed; the cliff dropped away behind a low wooden fence; the view, breathtakingly, of unbroken blue. A hot breeze swept in and ruffled the paper napkins, and the olive trees to the side of us had a crippled form, as if rearing backwards.

We stood awkwardly together, Maud and I, while the Murphys milled. Celia was fussing around Rey, making sure he faced the view. He had dried off now and was wearing swim shorts, brown with a horizontal orange stripe, and a matching polo shirt in a soft towelling material. His eyes were hidden behind sunglasses – acetate tortoiseshell. He had shaken my hand without any reference to our coffee together, making it clear we were to pretend it hadn't happened.

'This is an amazing view,' he said, seated in the middle, the world at his feet. 'We're higher up than at mine, aren't we? I mean, you feel the sea is just *there*.'

'My view's bigger than your view,' Adam said facetiously. He had put on a T-shirt now – black with 'The Ramones' scrawled in red letters across the front. It was a bit short and tight. He yawned, releasing a noisy out-breath, and when he stretched, the T-shirt rode up; it had sweat marks under the arms.

Rey smiled and patted the chair next to him, and Celia perched there, legs pressed demurely together. She gave a self-conscious laugh. 'OK then!'

Maud walked round unprompted to take the seat on the other side of Rey, at which point Celia seemed to notice me for the first time: 'For God's sake, Matt, sit down!'

I slipped reluctantly on to the end, between Lydia and James. Adam sat down on the other side, next to Jasmine. He whispered in her ear, and I saw Rey notice, and Adam notice Rey. I felt as if the table were full of jagged spikes.

The platter of meat came to my end and I dug my fork into the smallest piece of chicken, burnt on the outside, uncooked within. Years before when I'd been staying with the Murphys in Norfolk, local friends came for supper and Celia had hissed 'FHB' to me across the table and, realising she meant Family

Hold Back, I'd felt such a warm glow of fellowship, I thought I might cry. I looked across at her now to see if she'd noticed my FHB today, but she hadn't.

Adam reached for the bottle of wine, poured some into his own glass and Jasmine's and then offered it round.

'Not for me,' Rey said.

Adam took a sip. 'It's really rather nice.' He laughed, as if surprised, and then picked up the bottle to look at the label. 'How do you choose, as a teetotaller?'

Rey let a beat pass and then said, smiling, 'Like most people, I just go on price.'

Adam laughed and noisily slapped the bottle back down.

'Have you never drunk?' Maud said and Rey turned to look at her.

'No, never.'

'Me neither,' she said with a small smile. 'I hate losing control.' It dawned on me, with a sinking sense of ... no, not disappointment, more like disgrace, that she hadn't after all been invited for me, but for *him*.

Was it for religious reasons? Celia asked and Rey said sort of, not really. He was explaining that it had begun with religion but had developed into a 'lifestyle choice', when Adam interrupted. 'How *do* you relax then?' he said.

Rey smiled at him. 'I find ways.'

'No, but really,' Adam said.

Rey laughed lightly. 'Gaming, I suppose. I have a weakness for World of Warcraft. For my sins. And Rollercoaster Typhoon.'

'And Candy Crush,' I said.

Rey looked across at me, surprised. 'Yeah. On my phone.'

He held my gaze for a moment.

I turned away, forcing myself to chat to my godson. He had Celia's soft features and hair, but Adam's squaddie way of sitting, knees wide apart. I said, 'How's life?' and James said, 'Not too bad.' He was tutoring, he added, fingers worrying at his fringe, hoped to do something 'in the media'. I nodded sagely. I was a hopeless godfather, I told him, I should have been a counsellor all these years, a guiding light. He laughed. 'No worry. No beef.'

A young woman in a vest top and tiny shorts emerged at the top of the steps, and draped herself, yawning, around James. She told Celia she was sorry to be late, but she had slept badly, the bed was very uncomfortable for her – 'I am used to a hard mattress, and this one was so soft.' She pulled her arms up on one side to stretch out the muscles in her back and squeezed on to the bench the other side of James. 'The bread please, Adam,' she said, 'I'm very hungry,' and he handed the basket across to her with a flamboyant servility, like someone doffing his cap.

When Celia got up to take the dirty plates into the house, I took my chance and followed with the salad bowl. I thought if there was any way Rey had told her about Adam and Amira, and she was putting on a front, she would drop it for me. But she hummed as she stacked the dishwasher. 'Bless you, Matt,' she said, putting the salad bowl in the sink, and then, 'Isn't he lovely?'

I pretended to think she meant my godson and said, 'Yes, adorable. I'm trying to think of people I can put him in touch with.' (How nice it would be to find him a job. How grateful she would be.)

'Oh, James, yes. He'll be *fine*,' she said.

When we came out again with pudding, a bowl of peaches, the table went quiet. Rey said, 'Adam here tells me you're writing a screenplay. Can you tell us about it or is it classified?'

Taking my chair, I gave the general gist, telling him about the sonar machine and how easy it was to use water as a murder weapon. Rey seemed to listen, properly listen, and when I mentioned how I'd got the idea from an article I'd written, said, 'By the way, I loved your Notebooks in the paper.'

'Really?'

'Yeah, and didn't you write a novel. Um . . .' He clicked his tongue.

I said, '*Paper Cuts*.'

'Yes. I'm not a big reader, but my mother loved it. They did it at their book club.'

'Oh really?' He hadn't mentioned any of this over coffee. Had he looked me up online since? Still, I couldn't resist making a face at Adam. (I'd sent him a proof, hoping for a quote, which he'd never given.) He stuck out his tongue.

I smiled wryly. 'That explains those six copies I sold.'

Rey smoothed his beard between his thumb and his forefinger. Finally, he said, 'Listen, I've got this friend who's peeled away from Sony. He's looking for interesting new projects, particularly thrillers. Your screenplay might be what he's looking for. Can't promise anything, but he's called Victor Cox. Sixth Sense Films. I'll put you in touch. You never know.'

'Really?' My face felt hot.

'Of course. No prob.' He smiled at me, nodding.

I felt a breeze cool the sweat on my neck. One of the napkins drifted to the floor. I felt uneasy, as if I was being played. Adam had never suggested helping me in this way, and he was even more connected. Was this Rey's way of keeping me onside, or was I over-thinking it? Maybe he genuinely meant it?

When I tuned back into the conversation, Lydia was saying, 'So how rich exactly are you? I mean, like insanely, obscenely rich?' She was leaning back, arms crossed behind her neck. The inside of her lips was stained with red.

Rey laughed. 'I don't actually know.'

'But rich enough to buy swim trunks from Gucci?'

Rey looked down to inspect. 'Are they from Gucci? I'm ashamed to say someone does my shopping for me. I hate shopping myself. But I like these. I've actually got two pairs.'

'*Two* pairs,' Lydia cried as if her heart were breaking. 'I'm stuck with the H&M dupe.'

'Are those the men's shorts you've been wearing?' Celia said.

'You should try them, Mum, update your look – it would be a good way to hide the old . . .' Lydia patted her own flat tummy.

Celia rolled her eyes. 'Thanks.'

'You look lovely as you are,' Rey said with a small smile. 'But if you wanted you could have a pair of mine?'

'I couldn't possibly accept,' Celia said. 'They're gorgeous. But obviously *horribly* expensive.'

Adam was beginning to look as uncomfortable with this love fest as I felt. 'Celia's church doesn't believe in wealth,' he said. 'It's better, darling, isn't it, to be rich in good deeds than rich in material goods?'

Lydia snorted.

Celia gave her daughter a reproving look and said melodramatically, 'Will none of my children take me to mass when I'm old?'

'I will,' I said.

A quick smile, and an outstretched hand that didn't quite reach. 'Bless you, Matt.'

'Though you're not *actually* one of her children,' Lydia said.

'More like a third person in our marriage,' Adam said.

I looked at the ground. A tiny ant was dragging the body of a dead cicada around a table leg. Adam's cruel laugh echoed in my ear. When I looked up, Celia had changed the subject and was telling Rey about the trips to Lourdes. Rey said he didn't even know Lourdes was a real place. He certainly didn't realise people still went.

'Oh, it's a real place all right,' Celia said. And she explained about the Grotto, the site of the Apparitions, how Our Lady had appeared to St Bernadette and how five million people a year took mass and bathed in the sacred waters and how there had been many miraculous cases of healing. And how, in her view, it was the trip itself that helped. Many of the pilgrims, she said, were lonely, and the friendship and companionship forged on the journey were in themselves transformative. 'Mock as much as you like,' she said. 'I wouldn't stop doing it for the world.'

Rey was watching her carefully. 'How much does one pilgrim cost?' he asked.

'About eight hundred pounds. More if they're wheelchair-bound.'

'And how many pilgrims do you take a year?'

'We hope to take eighty.'

'And the name of your organisation?'

Celia smiled. 'St Saviour's in South Ken.'

Rey shifted sideways to get his phone out of his back pocket. Celia pretended not to understand, to believe he was just looking up the church on his phone out of curiosity. But he typed and read and typed a bit more, seemed to make some mental calculations, pressed a few more buttons, placed his phone carefully face down on the table and said, 'There. Have next year on me.'

'What?' Celia looked flummoxed.

I was trying to do my own calculations – eighty times eight hundred; what was that? eight thousand times eight: sixty-four thousand.

I said, 'He's given a donation.'

'Rey, you haven't! Oh my God. No. *Rey!* That *wasn't* what you were just doing?' She looked at him and then at Adam, and then back to him, letting her mouth hang open to convey her shock. 'I don't believe it.'

'It's the least I can do. You're teaching me to swim after all.'

She leapt up then and wrapped her arms around him from behind, turning her head sideways and nestling her crown into the crook of his neck – a strangely childlike action. He reached behind to pat her, laughing. When she let go, I could see tears in her eyes.

14

Washing up, just the two of us, I asked Adam if he thought Rey had forgiven him his teenage misdemeanours and, up to his elbows in soapy water, he said, 'Yeah – my penance for stealing his food is watching him come on to my wife.' But he laughed because it was still funny then.

I looked over my shoulder across to the table at the far end of the terrace. I could see movement – arms rising, heads shifting position – but no human sounds, just the cicadas, the murmur of the sea. I wondered what was happening out there, what Rey's game was.

'Nice of him to pay for all those lonely pilgrims,' I said.

He gave a hollow laugh. 'He's buying her off, Matt. Just like he's buying you off with that producer friend of his. Can't you see it? Money and connections are all he's got. Friendship is transactional to him.'

I was aware of feeling resentful even though it was what I'd been thinking myself.

He handed me the salad bowl and I held it firmly in the grip of the tea towel.

'Really, Adam? Is it so inconceivable that he likes my idea for a film script, that he actually thinks it has a chance?'

He shook his head. 'Oh Matt,' he said sorrowfully.

I dried the bowl, put it in the cupboard and started carefully in on some cutlery.

Adam picked up the barbecue rack from the floor and plunged it into the water. Suds sprayed. His T-shirt rode up, revealing the soft cushion of brown flesh above the top of his shorts. I had a fork in my hand and I thought idly about plunging it in.

He started attacking the grill with the scourer. 'This is a nightmare,' he said.

'Maybe leave it to soak?'

'No. My life, I mean. It's a fucking nightmare.' He dropped the rack back into the water, wiped his hands on my tea towel, and crossed the kitchen to get a bottle of beer from the fridge. '*I'm* a fucking nightmare.'

A peal of laughter reached us from the loggia.

He used the counter-top as a bottle-opener, bashing the top with the palm of his hand, the lid skittering off on to the floor. 'I shouldn't have listened to you.' He took a swig. 'I should have trusted my own instincts.'

Dead Heat

I picked the bottle top off the floor and put it in the bin. 'Sorry – is this to do with Rey?'

'No – Amira. It was the wrong thing to do, finishing it like that. Out here.' He walked to the doors, checked the coast was clear, and then got out his phone and handed it to me. 'Take a look at these.'

His phone was open on a WhatsApp thread. I began to read and then, queasy at the intimacy of it, handed it back. 'Can you just summarise?' I sat down on a chair.

He gripped the counter behind him. 'She claims I told her I was going to leave Celia. That's why she came out here. I mean, she's insane, Matt. She says she was offered a proper job she didn't take because I'd told her to stay on as unpaid intern so we could be together – all lies – that she got into debt and now she's got nowhere to live and no job. It's not true, Matt. She's making it up.'

'So, it isn't all sorted. It hasn't gone away.'

'No. It hasn't gone away.' He was pacing now. 'She's threatening to go to the press.'

'The press? Oh shit.'

'I know.'

He stopped pacing and stared at me. His face looked naked, fearful even. 'That kind of exposure – it would be the end of my career. It's not my image, you know?'

'Middle-aged seducer of interns? No, I can see that's not your ideal image.'

He curled up his lip, not liking my tone. 'Well, none of

this would have happened if you hadn't ordered me to finish things. It would have just fizzled out.'

'It's my fault then?' I said mildly. 'All "this"?'

'Yes!' He glared at me but then smiled slightly, shaking his head in self-dismay, and began to laugh at his own gall.

I could have killed him, but I found myself laughing too.

He sat down next to me, tapping his phone on his knee. 'I've had to make certain assurances, just to get her off my back.'

'What kind of assurances?'

'I've promised to give her a bit of money to tide her over. Just to get her back on her feet.'

'So she's blackmailing you?'

'No.' His mouth twitched. 'More like extracting compensation.'

'OK. Fuck.'

'I know.' He threw his phone on the table. 'But I deserve it, don't I?'

'Oh Adam.'

'I've agreed to pay off her student debt.'

I nodded. 'And that's what? Thirty grand or so?'

'I think so. Shit. I hope it's just tuition and she's not stinging me for maintenance too. Fuck. No, I think it's just tuition.'

'At least you can afford it.'

'Maybe, but I don't know how to pay her off without Celia finding out. Everything's in the joint account.' He lowered his voice. 'Celia will wonder where it's gone.'

I craned my neck to look out of the doors. I said, 'It's OK.

They're all still just sitting out there, letting us wash up.' And then, turning back, 'Could you pay in instalments?'

'She wants a bulk sum.'

'Well, can you pretend it's for something else?'

He lifted his arms and let them drop. 'Yeah, but like what?'

I brushed crumbs on the table into a small pile. When I looked up, he was looking at me. He said, 'I mean . . .'

'What?'

'I mean, could I say I was lending it to *you*? She knows you're a bit strapped. Could you have run up a gambling debt?'

'Adam. Fuck off. No.'

'Or what about something to do with your sister? Some problem with her mortgage?'

'Adam. How could you even suggest it?'

'Please, Matt.' He was bending forwards now, watching me intently. 'There's no one else I can ask. You're the only person I trust. No one else knows.'

I put my head in my hands. It wasn't true. I wasn't the only person who knew and I wasn't to be trusted. I'd told Sara and she'd told Rey and any minute now Rey might tell Celia. He might even be out there doing it now. Fact is I'd betrayed Adam.

When I lifted my head, he had lurched backwards, so he was almost lying in his chair. His legs stretched out under the table and he was staring up at the ceiling, as if he were half dead with the stress of it. I'd told myself I wanted him to be caught out, but now he had been, I realised how ill-equipped he was for a world turned against him. I found myself saying we'd sort something out. 'Not gambling, though. We'll think of something else. Maybe we can say I owe Takara and you're giving me a bridging loan until the flat's sold?'

He leant forwards, rested his hands on my shoulders and kissed my cheeks, one after the other. 'Yes. *That* would work. You are the best friend a person could have. I love you, man. We both do.' He scratched his forehead. 'Celia probably won't even notice the money's gone until September: plenty of time to come up with a story. *Amazing.*' He handed me his beer and I took a swig. The bottle was warm from his hands; I tasted his spittle.

He rocked back again. 'You're going back to London, you said, in the next week or so?'

'Yes, just for a bit. I have actually got some things I should do, including seeing Takara as it happens.'

'So in terms of the whole . . . you know . . . administrative aspect, could I leave that in your hands?'

I genuinely didn't understand what he meant at first. 'What do you mean, "administrative aspect"? And what do you mean, my hands?'

'In terms of the delivery. It has to be cash. Could you deal with it?'

'You want *me* to deliver the money to Amira. In person? Me?'

'If you could just . . . fit it in while you're there?'

My mouth had dropped open. 'Adam.'

He gazed at me, shaking his head at first, and then nodding. 'It is too much. Of course it is.'

He lay back again, all the energy drained out of him. I thought about the lanky, shaggy-haired boy who'd arrived at the office, and how eager he'd been to prove himself. He'd won us all round – not just Sonya in reception and the cricket-loving op-ed editor and *me*, but Grumpy Sheila with the tea trolley, and Charlie the resentful chief sub, and that quiet mousy woman on Obits whose name I'd never bothered to learn whom he'd made a point of dancing with at the Christmas party. I remembered, too, how much I'd hated going to daily conference and how often he'd gone in my place, pretending he liked it. How the day of that TV panel appearance, I'd gone to the toilet and puked my guts out with nerves, and how I suspected Adam had been in the next cubicle and overheard.

I remembered then how at his wedding, in that marquee in the garden of that big house, I'd choked halfway through my best man speech. I'd lost my place, dropped the paper, felt tears at the back of my throat. If no one noticed it's because Adam had covered for me. He'd got to his feet with a 'Hang on, sorry, Matt', and pretended there was something he'd forgotten to say. Afterwards it wasn't my inadequacy but his irrepressibility guests joked about.

I now saw that all he'd ever wanted was to give love and be loved.

When I looked up, he was looking at me, still with that odd crooked smile, and I was aware I wasn't in control of my expression, that there was something mawkish and weak in the small movements of my mouth. I was still waiting for the right words to surface, when Adam gave a big sigh, a release of tension. 'Oh man: you're the best. I owe you.'

He stood up, kissed the top of my head, as if I were a child, and in two strides was out on the steps to the garden.

I got up to follow, but stood for a minute in the middle of the kitchen looking after him. Some of them had left the lunch table now. James was dragging his girlfriend's sunbed into the shade. Jasmine and Lydia were in the pool and Adam had ripped off his T-shirt and I could hear him taunting Jasmine, telling her she was ripe for a divebomb. And now Celia was coming towards me up the steps. I felt stricken at the sight of her, tormented by the job I'd been charged with. It seemed so disloyal, and yet it was her happiness I was protecting. I physically didn't know what to do with myself. She tried to get past me to get to the fridge and I stepped to the right as she stepped to the left, and she gave an irritated laugh and said, 'For God's sake, Matt, undo your top button. You look so hot.'

That evening, I tried to see Sara one more time.

A brown and white dog with a tufty neck leapt to its feet when I entered the courtyard, barked and then slunk back into the shade. A woman was cleaning the steps to the tower with a scrubbing brush, and she looked up as I approached. She didn't speak English and seemed unimpressed by my grasp of her native tongue. She shook her head when I pointed to the first-floor window.

I rang the bell anyway, careful to keep my feet off the wet tiles.

While I waited, the woman with the bucket stood up and went through an archway into the building opposite. She reappeared with a large man, bare-footed and bare-chested, a small towel over his shoulder, who had obviously been in the process of shaving. He asked me in English if I was looking for the guest upstairs?

I nodded. 'Yes. Is she out?'

'You've just missed her. She left five minutes ago.'

'Do you know when she'll be back?'

A big car had come, he said, and she'd got in it.

'Do you know where she went?'

'The airport, my friend. She's gone.'

He grinned, his mouth a pink hole in the white foam.

PART TWO

15

Less than a week later, I was back in London.

I'd always known I'd have to go for a bit, but I went sooner than I'd planned and I ended up staying longer. It was a mistake.

It was overcast when I stepped off the plane, warm and muggy, and the train up from Gatwick was packed, every seat taken, luggage in the gangways, the air throat-closingly tight. I'd been crashing, since Takara and I parted ways, in the basement of a friend from uni and I walked to the house from Clapham Junction, looking forward to seeing him and his wife, to looking at different faces, to having different kinds of conversations. I let myself in, though, to find a note from Angus explaining they had decamped to Cornwall for August and that they had a French au pair arriving in September who would need my room. In the meantime, I should feel free to spread myself around. (The note ended with an exclamation mark, as if to soften the blow, which I won't dignify by replicating here.)

I woke early the next morning and, unnerved by the silence above my head (the kids, surprisingly tiny in person, clomped across the ceiling like a herd of elephants), 'spread myself' immediately into their kitchen – a bright room smelling of garlic and Play-Doh. The garden looked inviting, but I couldn't get the back-door key to work so instead I sat at the pine farmhouse table to think through the practicalities of my mission.

Adam had already texted to ask how I was 'getting on' and I could see from my online app that 'Mr and Mrs Murphy' had transferred £30,000 into my account. I'd been tempted to put the task off – to keep him in his misery for as long as I could – but I also wanted badly to be done with the whole sorry business. Cash was the first priority, but I wasn't sure how one withdrew such a large amount – too much for a cashpoint. I tried to ring my branch – for historic reasons in Waterloo – to speak to someone, but the number didn't connect, so I abandoned my kitchen desk and trekked to the bank in person, only to discover the building was now a Wetherspoons. I returned to the house and, after an 'online chat' with presumably a bot, took myself and my passport into a random branch in Clapham Junction. As it was now Friday and they told me it would take three business days to clear, I wouldn't have the money until the following Wednesday.

I was annoyed at the delay, but at least had a distraction. Checking my inbox, I saw I had an email from Victor Cox,

Rey's producer friend, suggesting we put 'a face to face' in the diary and coming up with a few dates, the earliest of which was 13 August – just under two weeks' time. It would mean staying in London longer than I'd intended, but at least it focused my mind – particularly as the email asked if I could 'ping something over' before the meeting.

I replied, confirming the 13th and promising 'something' within a few days, and opened the document on my desktop containing my screenplay (ironic working title: 'Masterpiece'). There really wasn't that much left to do – just the structure to be tidied and the ending to be sorted (I hadn't decided yet whether to go happy or sad). If I worked hard enough, I told myself, I'd be finished by the end of the weekend.

That, at any rate, was my intention. Time passed. The kitchen table was scratched and I spent the first half an hour of creative endeavour picking at bits of engrained Weetabix. After another failed attempt to open the back door, I stared out through the glass at the garden. They'd replaced the lawn with plastic grass which the Murphys would abhor. Brightly coloured play equipment took the place of flowers.

I thought about my mother's small garden – behind the flats where, after our father's heart attack, she brought me and my sister up. Out there with her foam kneeler and her trowel, her constant battle with slugs – a devoured lupin the only time I ever heard her swear.

The house stretched emptily above me after that and I wandered from room to room – picking up vases and looking at photos, the faces of the children stretched in canvas above the stairs. Rails of clothes in the cupboards, bedside tables that looked like family antiques, the endless boxes of toys. Angus's office – he did something in tax – was full not just of boxed files and filing cabinets, but also computers and printers and serious stationery, including a shredder. It was all so substantial and grounded; I felt how little I'd achieved or accumulated in comparison. I started thinking about my upbringing, the scrimping and the God-saving. I thought about the high-rises where lots of my friends lived, and the boarded-up corner shop where I'd buy Tizer, later Strongbow. I thought about Adam and Celia, about how little they knew about my childhood, and how alien it would be to them if they did.

All in all I achieved very little but introspection that weekend, my head more in the past than the present, and was in a gloomy mood when on Sunday night I FaceTimed my sister Sally. She had just got in from her shift – still in her uniform, her feet killing her – and she made herself a cup of tea before she sat down 'so I can really concentrate on you'. She never made me feel guilty – even though it was ages since I'd been in touch.

We talked about this and that for a while – I told her I'd been away and she asked about the weather and the food and who I'd been with. 'Just friends,' I said.

At one point, her son Mikey came into view with his boyfriend Sam. About to 'go out out', they were dressed to the nines; Sam was wearing fake eyelashes. After they left, I told Sally how lovely they both were, how free their generation, and she said, 'One thing about Mum dying is the relief at not having to pretend.' It pulled me up short because we never said anything bad about our mother – such a pillar of the church, on the flower rota, organiser of coffee mornings and good works.

'Mum loved everyone,' I said. 'All of God's creatures – with the exception of slugs.'

Sally visibly shook her head. 'Don't forget the flat upstairs.'

There were two flats in our building – we were 28A on the ground floor and we shared an entrance with 28B. Two men lived up there throughout my childhood, but we never talked to them. Mum turned her face away if she passed them in the street. And then there was the gay nurse in the care home she was very rude to – she wouldn't let him touch her – but her brain was going then, or so I told myself.

'I suppose it wasn't really her fault,' I said. 'It was a sin to her.'

'She was homophobic, Matt. Let's not blame God.'

'She was a lovely mum, though, wasn't she?' I felt suddenly desperate for reassurance.

'Was she ever lovely?' Sally said. 'I mean, really? Didn't we all just say she was? It was the family myth – that phrase of hers, "If you can't say anything nice, don't say anything at all." You could never be angry or earthy or rude or wild. You had to repress all your emotions. You had to repress everything.' She looked at me. 'Didn't you?'

I looked back at the screen. Sally was smiling, a small, almost sad smile, and I felt I had to hold her gaze. It was all I could do not to burst into tears.

16

On Monday and Tuesday, I went to the dentist for a filling and saw the GP about a mole that turned out to be nothing. I exchanged emails with Takara. The sale of the flat was trundling on, but there were issues with the lease and whether or not the buyers could get planning permission for a roof terrace. I was copied into correspondence with the solicitor, and Takara and I messaged privately, arranging to meet for coffee for me to hand over my set of keys. Knowing I'd been in the Mani, her last email included a PS: 'Do you remember that night we skinny dipped – you, me and Adam?! I think I was happier that night than I've ever been.' I read and reread that sentence, feeling the green shoots of hope.

Before our coffee, though, I still had to deal with the money. On Wednesday morning I returned to the bank in Clapham

Dead Heat

Junction and collected a thick Jiffy envelope containing £30,000 in crisp new notes.

Adam had given me a number for Amira and I texted, saying I had 'something for her'. We messaged back and forth a bit and eventually, at her suggestion, arranged to meet on a park bench in Green Park the following afternoon. 'I'll be the one with the pink carnation,' I wrote to inject a note of levity.

She replied: 'kk'.

The sky was overcast and uniform white. No breeze, the heat trapped. I walked from Victoria, past the palace and through St James's Park, across the Mall and almost immediately right into Green Park and on to a path in the shade of the plane trees. It was busy. People milling, taking selfies. Tourists eating ice creams on striped deckchairs. Office workers grabbing fresh air on their lunch hour. In short it was cheerful and normal, and not at all sordid, which was good, because I felt horribly sordid.

The meeting point was a particular bench at the north end, on a path parallel with Piccadilly. As I drew close, I could see an elderly couple sitting there, tucking into a packet of sandwiches, and I was about to veer away and do another turn when I saw Amira sitting cross-legged on the grass opposite the bench, bent forwards, her arms wrapped tightly around herself. Pigeons were pecking at the ground and when one of them got a bit close she jerked her knee and it flapped off. I thought for a terrible moment she was sitting like that, so protectively, because she was pregnant, but when I said hello and she unravelled, I saw she was guarding not a bump but a

Daunt's book bag, the same dark green as her T-shirt. God. I hadn't thought about pregnancy; a whole chasm of horror gaped.

She got to her feet, tugging at the creases in her jeans, and shook my hand. I'd forgotten how pretty she was – a very smooth, open, symmetrical face, thick lashes. She said, 'I knew he wouldn't do it himself. He's just a jerk.'

'I'm sorry. You know, he's in Greece. He's got family commitments.' I wished I hadn't felt the need to defend him, but I did. I could see by her face that I'd made it worse. 'I'm sure he'd be here if he could,' I added.

At home, counting out the money, I'd imagined her hard-edged and avaricious, like a character in a film by Quentin Tarantino, but in person she seemed even younger than I remembered. She asked where my pink carnation was and seemed confused when I explained it was a joke, that it was what people said before a blind date. 'I guess my generation doesn't do totally blind dates,' she said kindly. 'We look at pictures – not that they're necessarily true to life.'

The elderly couple having moved off, we sat down on the bench. I asked if she had somewhere safe to put the money. I didn't want her to be robbed on the way home. She showed me a zip-up cross-body bag. It was a good one, from Uniqlo, quite roomy. Did she have far to go? I asked. Did she promise me she'd go straight there?

I drew the envelope out of the inner pocket of my jacket and held it out, but she just looked at it without taking it.

'He was all I thought about, you know,' she said. 'I stopped seeing my friends. I didn't go out. I got offered a job in Wales – at Dragon Studios – just a runner, but a proper paid job that might have led to something. He told me it was too far away, that it would break his heart to be so far apart. So I just hung around in that flat he got me waiting to see him.'

'He got you a flat?'

'It was only temporary – some friend of his was away – until he left Celia and then we were going to find somewhere together. I thought it was real. All those lines he spun me, how I was the best thing that had ever happened to him. But it was all lies. He mugged me off. I wasted two years. I should have been doing stuff with my life, *getting on*. Two years: the least he can do is pay for them.'

'Two years?' He'd led me to believe it was just a few months.

'Yeah. I was just a kid when I met him, just out of uni.' She looked down at the bench and traced a knot in the wood with her finger. Her lower lip had gone. When she started to cry, she shook her head and lifted her hand to ask for a second. I put my arm around her shoulder. She was still just a kid now.

We sat there for a while and after a bit, I said, 'You could invest the money, or save it. You don't have to pay off your student debt. I think I read somewhere it's more efficient to keep the loan if you have it, the terms aren't that unfavourable. Not comparatively.'

She shook her head. 'No, I want to put the whole thing behind me.'

'Well, yes. I can see that.'

'I might even give up working in telly. I don't want to be around people like him. Maybe a PGCE? Rey told me I should have asked for more. He said I should have ruined him.'

'Sorry?'

'Yeah.' She laughed wryly. 'He says Adam owes him, too, for emotional damage. You know he bullied him at school? Rey really hates Adam.'

I pulled my arm back and told her I ought to get going. I passed the Jiffy envelope across. She took it with a nod, and a little grimace, put it in her little bag, zipped the bag up and hoiked it across her chest. It looked very bulgy and obvious but she said she didn't have anything to cover it up with so I dug out my pakamac, used it to fashion a sort of parachute, and looped it around her shoulders so the bag was hidden.

I'd promised Adam I'd make her swear this was the last he'd hear of her ('You know what blackmailers are like') but, when it came down to it, I couldn't bring myself.

Instead, I said, 'So that's it then?' and she nodded.

I left her sitting on the bench. As I walked back up the path, I felt my heart tug – back towards the girl, or the money, maybe both. I expected to feel lighter once I'd completed the deed, but the relief didn't come. I wasn't sure if it was the references to Rey or something else. A figure was standing ahead, near a tree, and for a horrible moment, I thought it was Adam, come to watch me, but the person turned away as I got close and melted into the crowd by the gate.

At Green Park tube, at the top of the escalator, I texted

Dead Heat

Adam to say my mission was complete. I waited, watching the three dots, expecting him to ring – to ask how it had gone and whether she was OK (two years, and a flat!). Or maybe simply to thank me. But his reply, which didn't arrive until I was home, came in the form of emojis: a thumbs up and a celebration popper.

17

Takara and I had arranged to meet in a café on the South Bank where we often used to have brunch (or so we told ourselves). I felt excited and nervous as I walked there the following day. It wasn't just the PS. She'd told Celia she missed me, and she'd asked if we were 'doing the right thing'. I knew she might have been referring to selling the flat – there'd been other options, like her buying me out – but there was room for doubt and I took up residence there, made myself a bed and curled up on it. I felt trim – I'd been religious with my crunches – and as I got close, I rolled up my sleeves to show off my tanned forearms. The key to the flat was heavy in my pocket and I allowed myself a small fantasy that we would let ourselves in later, lie down next to each other on the bare floor, reset the clock.

Dead Heat

Our flat had been – or is, I guess; it didn't combust after our departure – in Waterloo, in a street behind the Cut, on the second floor, above a launderette. We'd bought it ten years before, when the area was on the turn, and we'd been happy there. Or I thought we'd been happy there. Takara had refigured the dark, poky rooms, knocking down walls and painting the ones that remained a gentle Farrow & Ball white called 'Slipper Satin', which she used in all her projects. It had been a lovely place to live. We felt in the centre of things: walking to work and enjoying the sense of ourselves as regular gallery- and theatre-goers, though reality didn't always match perception. We had also, like the new buyers, talked of putting in a roof terrace, although we'd never had the money or the energy.

When I reached the café, I stood outside for a moment, looking at her through the window. She had chosen to sit on one of the communal tables and she was wearing a navy shirt-waister that was part of her work wardrobe, even though it was her day off. She saw me, raised a hand in greeting, carried on reading an article as I walked in, only putting the paper down when I was in front of her. I'd been gearing up for one of those tight, fashionably long hugs, the sort Celia gave to convey special fondness, but Takara kissed my cheek, and I wondered if she'd had a static shock because she pulled back very quickly. She said it was lovely to see me, that I was looking well. 'Just decaf for me,' she said, which made me think she'd already had a caf – with someone else? – or was planning one later.

I sat down opposite, and she told me again I looked well,

and I told her she did too. She was growing her hair and it suited her – softer around the face. Her eyes looked huge. 'You always look so young,' I said, and she said, 'Thank you. I think.' We talked about my sister and nephew and her father and her work – she had a big commercial project in Limehouse and was 'in the office all hours God sends'. She didn't mention Rick Vernon and, as in therapy she'd described him as 'a symptom not a cause', I had no idea if he was still on the scene or not. She used 'we' several times, each 'we' a small paper cut to my heart – though they were mainly work-related. She asked after the Mani. Had it changed much since our visit? I told her about Arcadia – what a slap in the face it was for Adam, and she laughed as if the phrasing amused her. I told her Adam had been up to all his tricks and she rolled her eyes. 'Of course he has. And Celia – still the same combination of spoiled and needy?'

I laughed, but then I quickly made a face to say *come on*.

'All the fuss about the tennis court! Though I have to say the new surface is amazing to play on.'

'You've been to stay?' I said. 'Recently? The court's only just finished.'

She gave a funny laugh, looked at me and then quickly away, and said she'd dropped in when she was passing. 'But it seems like ages ago now.'

There were too many layers here. Norfolk? Passing from *where*? I felt the heat in my cheeks.

'Anyway,' she said with a note of finality. She tapped the table with the tips of her fingers.

Dead Heat

I saw the afternoon stretch before me, in all its emptiness, and I cleared my throat, pretended to have the last swig of coffee, although that had already happened.

She lifted a shoebox from the bench next to her and placed it on the table. 'I found a few things in the final clear-out which I didn't want to throw away,' she said. 'Not without checking with you first.' She pushed the box towards me, and I opened the lid. On top were a set of Allen keys, and an old bike lock, and beneath that a bucket hat, an envelope of ticket stubs from our first trip to Japan, several of my old spiral journalist notebooks, and an Amy Winehouse CD we used to play in the car. I lifted out a framed photo of the two of us, strangers now, at someone else's wedding. I looked stiff and awkward in my cheap suit, but she looked beautiful with her fringed bob and huge earrings, her silky orange dress, my hand on her tiny waist. It was baffling really what she ever saw in me. I laid the photo carefully back in the box, said thank you, genuinely, and we exchanged a meaningful look – full of sadness and wisdom and nostalgia and a little bit of dislike. And I thought how odd it is you can think you know someone so intimately and then not know them at all.

I handed over my key and we parted, promising to stay in touch. I waited until I was round the corner to look for a big enough bin. A huge wheelie at the back of the National Theatre was half empty, the lid already up. From the box of mementoes, I took out an empty notebook – still had some use in it – but the rest I stuffed down into the bin as deep as it would go.

18

I was desperate to get back to the Mani. If I hadn't been waiting to see Rey's producer friend, Victor Cox, I'd have left that day. I yearned for the sea, the cottage, my friends, my cat, panicked that the possibility of return was slipping from me.

There were still a few days until the meeting, and they dragged. I took my laptop to Battersea Park, a short bus ride away, and sat outside the café by the lake. I watched the world go by – children, cyclists, dogs, ducks – and tried to work on a new draft of my screenplay. I felt a sense of urgency but also lethargy. What was happening in my absence? How were they coping without me? I thought of myself, I think, as their protector. I worried a lot about Celia finding out about Adam and Amira – Rey telling her – but decided she would have contacted me if she had. When I phoned her a couple of times, and she didn't answer, I began to imagine Rey had taken my place, that he'd forgiven Adam and they were hanging out together: big meals, boat trips, private jokes. I imagined the phone ringing in an empty house; that they'd all decamped to Arcadia.

To my self-disgust, I didn't finish the draft in time, so I had nothing to send ahead of the meeting as I'd promised (which turned out to be fortunate – fewer copies out there in the world – though I wasn't to know that then). On 13 August, the day in question, I got up to Soho half an hour early, and wandered up and down Old Compton Street, propositioned, to my amusement, as I hovered outside the Admiral Duncan, by an older man in a leather jacket. 'Not your type?' he said cheerfully when I declined.

The offices were in a small courtyard behind Wardour Street, a converted industrial building of some kind – low-rise with a wrought-iron fire escape on the outside, lots of cool sliding glass and edgy artwork within. Sitting in reception – where a woman in her thirties in jeans and Converse typed frantically on an iPad – I felt a buzz of excitement. I was on the threshold of a different world. A bank of vertical plants snaked up one wall and a staircase whose open treads seemed to float, unsupported, led to a second floor where I could see young people milling. Ranks of framed posters celebrated films I'd heard of featuring Daniel Craig, Emma Thompson, Idris Elba.

Victor, pouchy-featured with soft blond hair and a slight stoop, met me in the foyer and took me up the suspended stairs and across an open-plan space full of desks to a small glass internal office, 'our conference room. Most people these days are on Zoom.' He apologised for the quietness of the place – 'it's Tuesday; hardly anyone comes in until tomorrow'. His assistant Albie – posh with shaved head and tongue-stud – brought us coffee on a tray.

Victor was dressed in a collarless shirt, shorts and fisherman's sandals. A pad of lined paper and a pen were splayed out in front of him and, as we chatted, he spun one or other of them round with his finger in a friendly, laid-back way. He asked how I knew Rey and I said, 'Mutual friends.' They'd met at Cambridge, he told me, and were in the same five-a-side football team every Thursday night; not that five of them always made it. I said I didn't know Rey was sporty, and he said, 'Oh yes, a natural athlete. He played water polo for the college. Good goalie.'

'Don't you need to swim for that?' I said. 'I thought he didn't swim.'

'Not really.' He laughed. 'Not properly. The thing about Rey is – well, you've met him. He's quiet, you know, unflashy. He's very intelligent, but he doesn't make demands. He tends to stand back, but if he's interested in something he's very focused. I guess that's why he's been so successful. And he's very empathetic. I think when you've lived through what he has – you know, the stuff with his sister – it gives you a different perspective on life.'

'What is the stuff with his sister?' I said. 'I'm not sure I entirely know.'

'Oh God. It was dreadful. Happened when he was at school. She took her own life.'

I blew air out through my lips. 'How old was she?'

'Only fourteen.'

'That's awful.'

He nodded a couple of times, clasping his hands together, and then said, 'What with one thing and another,' Rey had been 'extremely supportive' when Victor had cut himself loose from Sony. 'He invested in me,' he said, 'and as much as anything it was his confidence that I could go it alone that mattered more than the money.'

'That's good.'

'And the money, of course, opened our horizons, allowed us to be less risk averse, which in this business is the ambition, you know what I mean?'

I said I did.

'He speaks very highly of you.'

'Does he?' I tried to keep the surprise out of my voice.

'He's having a great time out there in Greece – really getting stuck in. He hasn't got many close friends – you know it's hard in his position. Relationships haven't come easily to him. It sounds like it's all happening.'

'What do you mean?'

He tapped his heart with his right hand. 'Making connections. I know it's complicated, but he deserves a bit of happiness. Bless him. Anyway.'

He swirled the pad of paper.

'He ran me through the rough outline of your project and I agree it's absolutely at the pinch point – the kind of unique and compelling drama we are keen to develop at Sixth Sense Films:

Fargo meets *Ripley* meets' – he sucked his teeth, made a rolling movement with his hands – '*Annika*. Is that right? You've got a sort of harbour-based, quirky investigator in mind?'

I hadn't seen *Annika*, but I nodded anyway. His enthusiasm was compelling.

'Did you send the script through? I told Albie to keep an eye out.'

I apologised and he raised his hand. 'Doesn't matter. Give me the elevator pitch. Go.'

He rested his chin on his hands and looked at me, listening, as I ran through the main points. I expected to feel self-conscious, but there was so much excitement in his gaze, I warmed to my theme – really gave him the whole hog.

'I like it,' he said when I'd finished. 'It's terrific! I'm even seeing a bit of *White Lotus* in there – let's face it, the Holy Grail.'

'God, yes,' I said. 'I love that you think that.'

'Good characters, intriguing setting – gosh, I'm suddenly thinking *Ozark* – and an unsolved murder. You might worry the market's saturated, but murder's perennial.'

'Hope so!'

He looked suddenly thoughtful. 'Do we need the whole sonic machine angle? Is it a bit of a distraction?'

'Oh, but . . .' I was about to say that maybe the machine was the *point*, but changed my mind. 'Maybe I could rethink that.'

'OK.' He sounded even more cheerful then. 'We can circle back.' He wrote a few notes, looked up. 'Casting? Any ideas?'

Bit early I'd have thought, I said, for that.

He laughed and rocked back in his seat. 'Yeah. It's just it's the first thing people – writers – normally want to talk about.' He folded his arm above his head. 'I was pre-empting the question, trying to keep you happy.'

'I'm happy.'

He looked serious again. 'We would of course definitely want you to be intrinsically involved as an executive producer.'

I said, 'I can't tell you how thrilling this is. All this on an elevator pitch. I thought you were just seeing me to appease Rey.'

He laughed quickly, stroked the skin beneath his chin with the back of his index finger and said, 'No, not at all.' His baggy eyes slipped away from mine.

He stood up then, and said, 'Let's touch base in a month or two. Pick up the conversation then.'

All in all, it was a very good meeting. He said it himself as he led me back down the open stairs. 'Very good meeting.' He nodded forcefully as he shook my hand at the door and wished me luck. 'Look forward to seeing where you take the whole project.'

I left with a real skip in my step – perky and rejuvenated, open to the world, to all its possibilities. If I'd bumped into my leather-jacketed suitor I'd have kissed him. The air was sticky and the streets were crowded but I decided to walk home – my body seemed to need it, just to keep the adrenalin at a rush, the endorphins pumping.

I took it at a pace, head bursting, humming under my breath. All the adjectives Victor had used, all the comparisons he'd deployed – I inhabited them all. It didn't matter that I'd had nothing concrete to show him. I'd written another *Ozark*; I was on a par with *Annika*. Fame and fortune were mine for the taking. Thank God I'd stayed in London. True, not much Victor had said tallied with what I'd actually written, but it was the kernel that mattered. I'd work at it. All night! He'd suggested a month or two. I'd have something for him by tomorrow.

As I crossed Vauxhall Bridge, I began to flag. The traffic was heavy, all four lanes of it, and the roundabout the other end – practically a gyratory system – was stressful to cross. A group of teenagers was playing football in a small green area to the left and as I walked past them, accosted by their noisy shouts, I felt bothered by something. I thought back to the conversation, prodded it until I felt the bruise. Rey had lost his sister – that was grim. But no, it wasn't that. It was the sports stuff. Football? Water polo? Even if you didn't need to actually swim – which seemed unlikely – it didn't tally with the impression of Rey I'd got from Adam: the 'dweeby' nerd. In my experience, the sporty kids tended to be the bullies not the bullied.

I turned right towards Stockwell.

Stop, I told myself, put *him* out of your mind. Concentrate on Victor. He's the one that counts now. *Own* this good fortune. And I was doing my best to own it, when I heard my name shouted and saw hailing me, across the road, a large man in a dishevelled navy suit.

Crossing, I realised it was a former colleague – Dave Baxter. He was a reporter on the City pages when I was arts editor on the paper – though he later moved to a desk job at the BBC. He was a lugubrious chap, always the first to let you know circulation was down, or redundancies were in the offing, or that they'd stopped doing Eccles cakes in the canteen. Two minutes in his company and you could feel any hope – engendered perhaps by a meeting with an energetic TV producer – drain out of you.

I should have said no to a quick drink, but he was persuasive, and I was thirsty, and five minutes later we were in the corner of an old-fashioned pub, hunched over a small table in the corner. After Dave had moaned about his job and sympathised about the loss of mine, with nothing else to talk about, we reminisced about old times. 'Funny about Adam Murphy,' he said, staring into his bitter. '*You* were the hot shot. We always thought it would be you who'd make it big.'

'That's nice of you,' I said.

'You were always so articulate about all that art stuff. Weren't you always being invited on that late-night show before he was?'

I told him it was amazing of him to remember, but that I hadn't actually ever made it to the studio, that articulacy was all very well, but confidence was what counted, actually getting off your arse, and that was where Adam had come up trumps.

'Of course, those books of his have had terrible reviews.'

'Yeah, but they sell,' I said.

He asked if I still saw him even and, for a moment, I thought about denial, but in the end said yes; in fact, I'd just been to stay with him and his wife Celia in the Mani where they had a villa. A village called Kardamos, I said: it was a beautiful spot.

'Of course – that rings a bell. Isn't it all becoming a bit glitzy? Like doesn't Reynash de Souza also have a place there?'

'A big one, yes.'

He said softly, 'And it was while staying there, wasn't it, that his COO went missing?'

'You know about that?'

He made a face. 'Yeah but you may have noticed it's not been very heavily reported, has it? These tech guys – they've got friends in high places.'

I felt a prickle down my back. 'What do you know?'

He leant across the table so his face was closer to mine. 'There were already rumours, that's all, that the sale hadn't exactly been entirely clean, you know?' He took a sip of his bitter and wiped his mouth of froth. 'And Ashley – that's his name isn't it? – was beginning to make trouble. It's worth looking at his social media, if you're interested.' He swung back across the table as if he'd said too much.

'I don't really know what you're getting at,' I said.

'Listen – AdVent wouldn't have been the first to manipulate their accounts before a sale. I mean, you'll have read about Mike Lynch and Autonomy.'

It rang a bell, but I asked him to remind me.

'Fellow Brit. He was imprisoned in the States, facing charges of fraud, on the grounds that he inflated the value of his company Autonomy – by five billion dollars – before selling it to Hewlett-Packard back in when? Two thousand and eleven? You know, there's a fine line between entrepreneurship and criminality. But anyway . . .' He raised his hands. 'He was released back in June, all charges dropped, so . . .' He shrugged again.

'Has anyone actually levelled similar accusations at Rey?'

'I had a friend, Jim Garcia, on the *Mail*, who looked into it for a while, convinced there were accounting improprieties – specifically that "free trials" were falsely included in the initial valuation, but you didn't hear that from me.'

'So your guy didn't find anything concrete?'

'Actually, no, because Jim ended up losing his job. A picture surfaced of him sniffing coke with a sex worker. He denied it all, claimed the pic was faked, but things went a bit pear-shaped for him soon after – job, wife, the lot. So, that was the end of that, on AdVent at least.'

I felt another prickle, more like a shiver this time. 'And Marc Ashley, AdVent's chief operating officer, is missing.'

'I guess the message is, unless you're very sure of what you're doing, don't mess with the big boys.' He took another swig of his beer. 'Anyway, what about you, Matt? What are you working on?'

'Not much,' I said.

19

I *knew* it. I knew there was something off about Marc's disappearance. I knew Rey wasn't to be trusted. All along I'd felt it my bones and yet I'd allowed myself to be lulled – flattered, distracted.

I raced home and opened my laptop at the kitchen table.

I started with Marc Ashley's social media. Nothing on Instagram, but he had a profile on X, which went back some years. I trawled through it, starting with the earlier posts, most of which referred to a video search service he and Rey had built, and then something called Prelink, which seemed to be some sort of car-hire tech. He began to post more frequently around the launch of AdVent, eight years ago. Announcements of targets hit: four million subscribers, six million, eight. A picture of the two of them celebrating the sale of the company, arms entwined. The caption: 'Tech Bros'. It was only this January that he'd started going off-message. Poetry ('Shame on you,/ You powerful people/Breaking rules and laws'), random phrases ('Honesty and goodness. Is it too much to ask?') and mish-mashed bits of the Bible ('Rich men are getting through the eye of the needle'). There were several links to the Mike Lynch extradition in May – all of them preceded by a list of hashtags: #tech #buyout #business #justsaying #readandweep #glasshouses #AdVent. His last tweet on 6 June, the day Lynch was cleared, read 'Look to your own. I won't be silenced'.

It was posted three days before he disappeared.

I closed X, snapped my laptop shut, and crossed to the other side of the kitchen. It was dark out now and, feeling exposed in the brightly lit room, I closed the plantation shutters, catching my fingers in my haste. Was it paranoid to think I was being tracked online?

I poured myself a glass of water, and then a glass of red wine to calm my nerves.

Why hadn't Marc Ashley's disappearance been widely reported? Why hadn't it been properly investigated? Christos had said he'd wandered off the path but was he being paid to say that? Where were the helicopters? Where were the dogs? Poor Sara, thinking how supportive Rey had been – paying for the Airbnb, the poxy reward when all the time . . . I was almost too scared to give shape to the thought, but . . . *had he silenced her brother*?

Steeled by a second glass of wine, I sat back down in front of my laptop.

Those white trainers I'd found in Rey's cupboard – with the silver pattern on the side and the neon-yellow soles – they were distinctive. Rey's explanation that they were 'old clothes' had never sat right with me. I went on various websites, including Nike's own, searching with no luck, until eventually I found them on a site for Rare and Collectables. They were a limited edition, eye-wateringly expensive, and out of stock in all sizes. Not exactly 'old clothes', even for someone as rich as Rey. He'd been wearing Gucci sneakers with twee little bees when I'd last seen him, not flashy street shoes. Rey's feet were small. The shoes I'd found in the cupboard belonged to Marc. *I knew it.*

I thought how quickly Rey had come to find me after I'd told Sara about finding them. He'd been sounding me out, trying to establish what kind of person I was. Was I dangerous? Could I be bought off? I'd acquitted myself well enough – been reasonable, apologetic; paid for the damn coffees. But I'd revealed a weak spot. I'd opened my heart about the Murphys, talked about them far too much. And there he was a day later up at Villa Mimosa, getting close to Celia, inveigling himself into their lives. I'd thought he was punishing Adam. But no. It was to *warn me*. Look what I can take away, he'd been saying. Look what I can destroy.

As for putting me in touch with Victor – painful as it was to admit it – it had been bribery, plain and simple. Carrot to the stick.

It was late but I rang Dave Baxter to ask him to put me in touch with Jim Garcia, his ex-*Mail* friend, and he said, 'No way, man. He wouldn't go anywhere near Reynash de Souza now and nor would I if I were you. Honestly, not if you know what's good for you.'

'But you're a journalist,' I said. 'Don't you care about the story?'

'Listen, Matt. Don't make me feel bad. Even if what you say is true, my boss was skiing with de Souza at Easter, probably been out to that house in the Mani. It's not worth it. Sometimes you can be a crusading warrior; sometimes you have to choose an easy life.'

Not having a boss can be an advantage. Not having a life, easy or otherwise, ditto.

I didn't think of myself as a crusading warrior – too little self-esteem – but I was a journalist and it was a long time since I'd had something meaty to chase. I burned to get back to the Mani, but before that I needed more information and the obvious person to talk to was Sara.

First thing the following morning, I called her on her mobile but the number, on repeated tries, cut off. Odd, but not disastrous. I had information to go on: she'd told me she lived in the town of Lewes in East Sussex and that she worked for an optician. I found the spiral notebook from Takara's box of mementoes and, with the help of the internet, set about compiling a list. I made myself a pot of hot coffee and rang each one in turn. Most were happy to tell me they had no employee named Sara Ashley, but two numbers rang out and the last person I spoke to was evasive: 'About what is this concerning?' It didn't matter. I'd whittled twelve opticians down to a manageable three (amazing to me a town could have so many; people, I suppose, always have eyes) and I was going to have to go to Lewes anyway – a matter of this delicacy should be dealt with in person. Three opticians: I was sure it wouldn't take me long to find her. (I was right, though it was to cost me.)

Afterwards, I would look back and realise I did the whole thing in too much of a hurry. I'd hardly eaten since the day before and I didn't stop to think. As Takara's therapist had rather painfully observed, I had a habit of hyper-focusing and easily lost perspective. I know it's probably true. Sometimes I find myself thinking about one thing, and one thing only, and I'm aware I get sucked in (though I'm not sure this makes me 'hard to live with').

At 11 a.m. I had my shortlist and ran to Clapham Junction station to discover the Lewes train was cancelled due to engineering works on the line, but that I was in time to catch the 11.20 a.m. Southern Rail service to Brighton. It was a very hot, full train – though the connection to Lewes was almost empty. On the last leg of the journey, which only lasted seventeen minutes, I felt increasingly nervous about seeing Sara. I thought hard about how to approach her. Maybe I'd ask how she was first, and bring the subject gradually round to her brother? Maybe I could even pretend our meeting was a coincidence? Or maybe that would lighten the seriousness of my mission? Wouldn't it be better if she knew I'd come on purpose?

Dead Heat

I didn't have it straight in my mind is what I'm saying – largely, I suppose, because I wasn't sure I would even find her.

As I've said, there were three possible opticians, and I started with Owl Vision, which was in a side street at the top of a steep hill. It was small and boutique, with racks of sunglasses and signs saying 'Prada' and 'Gucci'. No luck there, and I trekked back down the hill to Specsavers in the high street. I wasn't optimistic. She'd have said, 'I work at Specsavers' not 'at an optician', but I went in and pretended to browse just in case. The middle-aged woman, eating coleslaw behind the counter, was not her.

Thirkham & Breech, in a pedestrianised street across the bridge, was stylish and practical-looking; a sign said it was a family business. A cheerful man in a garish orange jumper looked up from the drawer of lenses he was tidying and asked in what capacity he could help. I recognised his method of phrasing from Mr Evasive on the phone. Taking a gamble, I asked for an eye test and, consulting a screen, he said nothing was immediately available, but I could, if my need was pressing, return in an hour.

I gave him my details and went down the road to Gail's for a very small and very over-priced salami and cornichon roll. It was the first thing I'd eaten since lunch the previous day. I still didn't have much appetite – maybe the nerves; maybe the hyperfocus – but I forced it down.

I was in the shop again an hour later and Mr Evasive led me through the shop, along a corridor and into a small room full of equipment. I knew immediately. Her back was to me – she was inputting data into a computer – but her boyish slightness, the delicacy of her shoulders, the softness of her hair were so familiar, I felt a jolt in the centre of my chest.

'Sara,' Mr Evasive said. 'Your next victim!' He left, closing the door behind him.

She turned and there it was – that sweet, sad face of hers. I hadn't realised until that moment how much I'd longed to see it again, how much all this had, maybe, been about that.

She had got to her feet with a pre-prepared smile. For a wonderful moment I imagined her crossing the room and falling into my arms.

'Er,' she said, frowning, and, 'Hang on. *What?*' And then she did cross the room – not to hug me but to reopen the door. She was all points and edges in her sharp navy suit. Her knuckles gripped the handle. She was taller, too, than I remembered.

'How did you find me?' she said. 'How did you know where I was?'

I said, 'Please, please. I tried to ring. I wanted to check you were OK. You told me where you worked.'

'Did I?'

'Well, OK, I did a bit of detective work. I needed an eye test and also I wanted to talk to you. I have some information.' Nothing I'd prepared to say seemed to be working.

She said, almost accusingly, 'What kind of information?' But she did let go of the handle. She was wearing heels; that's why she was taller.

I gestured to the desk and the two chairs next to it. 'Can we sit down?'

She left the door open but she did come back into the room and, though she didn't speak, she sat down and waited for me to do the same.

I perched on the edge of the other chair, keeping my knees to one side so as not to cramp her. I took the spiral notebook and pen out of my jacket pocket and rested it on my thigh. 'You left Greece so suddenly,' I said. 'I had no idea you were leaving.'

'I was offered a free ride home on a private jet.' She smiled, slightly bitterly. 'Who was I to refuse?'

I let that rest for a moment. *Rey's* private jet, obviously.

I opened my notebook. 'So you decided you would pick up your life?' I said.

It was supposed to be a gentle opener, but she abruptly moved her chair back towards the wall.

'Sorry,' I said. 'I didn't mean to offend you.'

Her eyes narrowed. 'I'm assuming this is about my brother and you should know the case is closed now. The police say accidental death, but I've accepted that he probably took his own life. So if that's why you're here—' She stood up.

I said quickly, 'Why? I don't understand. Did Rey pressurise you to accept your brother's death?'

'No,' she said. 'Rey didn't "pressurise" me, but he's explained a few things. The only way to heal is to stop fighting and accept it. I have to be practical. Marc's not going to be out there in those mountains alive. And it's better for me to come to terms with it. Otherwise, his assets are frozen and we can't bury him, by which I mean, of course, at least have a memorial service and . . .' She trailed off and sat down again as if suddenly tired.

'You're your brother's beneficiary, of course,' I said.

She gave me a hard stare. 'Can you leave?'

'I'm sorry. I know it's not about the money. I'm stupid and tactless. I messed this up.'

She nodded.

'I'm just trying to do the right thing. Just listen to me for one minute. Please.'

She rubbed her forehead and then kept her hand there, resting her head on her fingers.

Taking that as agreement, I opened my notebook. 'I know we talked before about Marc being unhappy about the sale of AdVent. You implied he was upset retrospectively that it had taken his attention away from his wife, but I'm wondering if he was also raising concerns about some of the facts surrounding the sale itself.'

She looked up. 'Go on.'

'Did Marc ever say anything to you about "free trials" inflating the pre-sale value of the company?'

'Maybe. Yes. He began to fixate about it, after his wife died. He did mention that he felt there had been an accountancy error. But it wasn't that important. It was only a small fraction of the overall amount.'

'A small fraction of an enormous amount is still a lot of money. Millions. And also, if true, it's fraud.' I explained about the journalist who'd been investigating Rey and how he'd subsequently lost his job. 'And Marc had been posting on X, stuff that I don't think Rey would have liked.'

She stared at me, her face pale. A few moments passed. 'Sorry. Are you implying Rey wanted to stop Marc from revealing company secrets? Are you suggesting that, in order to do that, Rey killed my brother?'

'It sounds awful to say it out loud, but yes.'

She released a gaspy laugh, and reached across the table for her phone. She started scrolling and eventually held it up to show me a series of photographs: Rey and Marc, much younger, on bicycles along a river; Rey and Marc arm in arm at a restaurant; Rey and Marc at a hospital bedside, with a beautiful, ill-looking woman lying between them.

'Rey loved Marc,' she said. 'I don't think you've quite grasped that. Maybe you don't understand because you haven't got a friend you're as close to. Their friendship was *everything*. Rey may not show his emotions to the likes of you, but he's *devastated*. Marc's obsession about this small accounting thing – Rey's explained it to me: it's one of the reasons why Marc might have taken his own life. And it's very hard for Rey even to think about it because I don't know if you know but his little sister died by suicide.'

'I did hear something about that. What happened?'

'She was raped at fourteen,' Sara said curtly. 'Discovered she was pregnant and was too scared to tell their mother. Their father had just died. It was a terrible time.'

I felt a chill come over me. 'I'm so sorry.'

'Thing is – sorry, I've forgotten your name.'

'Matt.'

'Thing is, Matt, Rey's a good and decent man. You're pally with that posh couple out there and I know they resent him. They think he's vulgar; that the house is vulgar; that having all that money is vulgar. It's an affront to their sense of how things should be. I expect you feel the same.'

'No,' I said, too quickly.

She considered me. 'I don't understand why you're so obsessed. Are you one of those conspiracy theorists? Is that what this is?'

I tried to gather my thoughts. It had seemed so clear back in the house and on the way down. The AdVent sale. The trainers. I'd come to warn her, maybe hoped the two of us might band together. I'd felt brave; I'd been fighting on her behalf. But now I was here, I felt foolish, petty even. A *conspiracy theorist*? Had I lost perspective?

I said weakly, 'It's the power he has. I'm a journalist. I don't think people should be allowed to get away with things.'

'You mean like being rich?' She stood up and walked to the door. She looked quite tall, standing there in her work heels. 'It sounds like jealousy to me.'

Due to 'trespassers on the line', there was an hour's wait at Brighton before the next London train. It was exasperating and, my head full of Sara, I decided to leave the station and fit in a quick tension-busting swim.

It was brisk and sunny on the seafront, waves clawing against the shingle, the air full of shrieks, the promenade patrolled by yawling gulls. I found a quietish spot and, leaving my clothes in a neat pile against the wall, entered the water in my underwear. It was rougher and a darn sight colder than Greece – the water a murky green, or muddy brown where the silt churned. Or I hoped it was silt. Another scandal of modern life: what the water companies were getting away with. I looked around at all the other bobbing bodies, the paddleboarders, the idlers on the beach and, with a flush of fury, thought: Why has no one stopped the bastards? *Why do we just accept it? Why aren't we all rising up*? A large wave came out of nowhere – the wake from a motorboat, I think – and knocked me off my feet. I waded back to shore then, suddenly scared I would be swept out to sea and no one would notice.

I texted Celia that night, and maybe because of what I wrote, she FaceTimed me immediately. It was the first time we'd spoken since I'd left.

It was late. We were both in bed. She was holding the phone close; I could see the cross-hatch of skin on her chest, the fleshy folds under her neck. When she turned on to her side, I caught a flicker of white nightie, the fuzz of underarm hair. She was alone, she said vaguely. Adam was downstairs playing poker with Lydia and Jasmine.

'What are you in a tizz about?' she said. 'What's the matter?'

I explained about visiting Sara in Lewes – I had to remind Celia who she was – and how I'd thought, mistakenly, that I had a lead on her brother's disappearance.

'Oh Matt. I told you to steer clear.' She gave a gravelly laugh. 'You fancy her.'

'I don't. It's not about that . . .'

Though maybe it was, I thought, maybe that's all it ever was.

As if she could read my mind, she said, 'What happened to that woman in New Malden? The one with the grumpy son. The *divorcée*.' She pronounced it the French way.

'Oh – Linda,' I said. 'She had enough of me.' It wasn't strictly true. She'd worn a T-shirt in bed that read 'It's always wine o'clock' and expected more from me than I was prepared to give. 'We weren't very compatible.'

'You mean in bed?' she said.

I laughed. 'I guess.'

'Do you think it's important? You know, with Adam, it's always been . . . well, it's always been one of the main things. Recently, I've been wondering whether it's a distraction, whether it blinds you to people's faults, that there might be other connections that are, I don't know, more rewarding?'

'Maybe,' I said carefully.

'I'm a bit off him at the moment, for various reasons.'

I said we all were from time to time, and she laughed.

Before she could confide any more – and looking back, maybe she was about to – I said, 'I saw Takara. That didn't go well either.'

'Oh dear, I'm sorry.'

'You didn't tell me you had her to stay in Norfolk.'

'We didn't have her to stay in Norfolk.'

'Oh.'

We were both quiet for a moment. I listened to her breathing, battling snakes in my head. Finally, I said, 'How are things at Villa Mimosa? How's my little cat?'

'Oh, you are sweet,' she said. 'Fine.'

It dawned on me, with horror, she must think I was referring to her. She said sleepily, 'You've got so much love inside you, Matt. You're full of it. It's such a waste that it just sits there. I wish we could find you an outlet.'

'Me too.' I felt a sudden powerful yearning for her then, for the kind of relationship where I could, without embarrassment, call her my little cat.

'What do you think you're looking for?' she said. 'When it comes to love?'

I swallowed. 'Someone like you.'

'Oh Matt.' I heard her breathe again. 'I'm married. I made a vow before God.'

I tried to sound upbeat, comically contemptuous. 'I know. I didn't *actually* mean *you*.'

'It's not the same here since you left,' she said.

Misreading the clues, I took that to mean she wanted me. I misread it to mean come back.

PART THREE

20

A day later, I caught an early-morning flight from Luton – packed with frazzled parents and screaming children – and then a bus going south from Kalamata. The views were incredible, fingers of land slipping into the sea like a line of giant sleeping creatures, and, despite my overriding sense of humiliation, it was re-energising to be back in this dry heat, this light.

I got off at the bus stop behind Kardamos and walked down to the harbour for a cold drink. Mid-August and it was in full flow, the streets thronging with tourists, the quayside packed with boats of all sizes. As I sat on a wall, I saw the loud clothing and sunburnt flesh through Adam and Celia's eyes, imagined how they'd wince at all those chips and kebabs eaten on the go. Sara was right: they found a lot of things vulgar. To me it was comfortingly familiar, the bank holiday buzz of childhood visits to Blackpool – the heady rush of other people enjoying summer.

Most of the missing person posters were gone from the main road; those that remained were torn, the writing faded. It was uncomfortable walking past them. I'd been overwrought. Maybe my screenplay had taken me too far into the dark side of human nature. Maybe I was just a sucker for a conspiracy. Best to put it all behind me, for things to go back to how they'd been before. As I drew close to Villa Mimosa, I felt a leap of excitement, an almost physical craving for the sanctuary of the pool and garden, for the company of my friends.

At the door, I shouted, 'Hello, hello.' No one came and, as I burst into the hall, I expected them to be arranged on their sunbeds as I'd left them; I imagined them leaping to life at the sight of me.

The kitchen smelt stale. My feet squeaked on the sticky tiles. I tripped on a loose trainer. The freezer door was open and water dripped, puddling on to the floor. Stepping into the glare, I could see down to the pool, the surface unruffled, the sunbeds beyond dry, uncreased, empty. The cicadas whirred, petals underfoot, and birds – sparrows, I think – fluttered in the bushes as I took the steps two at a time.

In the deep end, Adam was floating face down.

I had no time to think, though the image of his inert, motionless body has tortured me ever since, waking me with terror in the middle of the night: his arms outstretched, as on a crucifix, his hair streaming, his trunks – the ones with the pink flamingos – moving, filling with air, floating.

Dead Heat

It happens to me again and again. Sleeping and awake. I'm in, and under the water, my arms beneath his body, water in my eyes and up my nose, spluttering, splashing, and I'm down, under again, ears exploding, knees and elbows grating, bubbles and turmoil, and I can't breathe and when finally I flail to the side, my arms empty, dragged down by my clothes, shirt clinging, trousers half off, his face is already there in front of me.

'What the fucking fuck, Matt? You trying to kill me?'

I can't speak because my throat is raw, acid is rising at the back of my nose. He clambers out of the pool and dangles his hands to pull me out too, his big coarse freckled fingers bruising my biceps. I scrape my stomach, legs kick and I lie there on the side, unable to move, exhausted. My heart is pulsing and thudding. My head is ringing.

Eventually, I take a raggedy breath and say, 'Of course I'm not trying to kill you. I thought you were drowning.'

'I was fucking floating, Matt. Meditating. I didn't know you were even in the country. I thought I was being attacked.'

'Who by?'

'I don't know, Matt. A huge wet dog?'

Neither of us laughed.

I fumbled with my buttons; my fingers were shaking. My ribs hurt and he helped me pull the shirt over my head. I smelt alcohol on his breath then, saw that his eyes were unfocused. He said, 'Oh God,' with a deep groan, as if my dripping presence were the last straw.

I took off my trousers, rescuing my iPhone from the back

pocket. 'You're an idiot,' Adam said. 'You always have been. Haven't you?' He poked me, trying to get a rise, and I walked to a sunbed a bit away from him and sat down. My foot knocked something underneath it – it rolled out towards the pool. An empty bottle of Mythos.

'Well, I'm sorry for trying to save your life,' I said.

I fiddled with my phone, switching it off and on. 'It works,' I said crossly, and he said, 'Well done. Whatever.'

He lay on the bed next to me. A small dark shape floated at the bottom of the pool; a dead lizard, moving back and forth in the jet from the filter. At the far end, leaves were brushing against the side. Insects were floating; flies, still alive, flailed. I stood up and found the giant sieve leaning against a spiky tree and used it to try and flick out the insects and debris; only the harder I tried, the more they seemed to sink and disperse.

'So how was London?' Adam said. 'Get everything done?'

'Yes,' I said. 'You know I did.'

I expected him to ask more, and perhaps even express some gratitude, but 'I've been abandoned,' he said. 'There's no food – hasn't been for days – and I'm starving.'

'What are you? A child?'

He pouted. 'I am a child. You know I am.'

I went to look in the kitchen and he was right – no milk; the fridge nearly empty. None of the usual Tupperware pots with a bit of cold chicken or spare peas; no slices of desiccated tart on a saucer. I found two wrinkled peaches and made some coffee.

'So where is everyone?' I asked, coming back down.

He told me my godson and his girlfriend had gone back to

London; Lydia and Jasmine were at a market and Celia was looking at some churches with—

I interrupted. '*Some* churches?' I said. 'And you didn't fancy going?'

He stared at the peach, then rubbed it against his cheek. 'Not invited, mate.'

'And that's a problem because . . .?'

He hung his head, dropping the peach at his side, and looked up at me from under a lock of hair, and I felt a thud in the centre of my chest. 'Oh God, what now?' I said. 'Please tell me he didn't tell her about Amira?'

'What are you talking about? Not Amira. Who? No.' He frowned. 'Nothing like that. It's not even worth getting upset about.'

'So what is it?'

He forced a yawn. 'Honestly. Total overreaction. James's stupid girlfriend – she stormed into Celia's bedroom and said I'd propositioned her. But it was utter drivel. She walked in on me. You know – in the buff. My sin: not immediately covering myself up. I made a joke. I mean – it was nothing.'

'In the shower?'

'The kitchen.'

'And what was the joke?'

He looked down – towards his crotch, I suppose. 'I can't remember. No biggy.' He looked up, grinning. 'Or maybe it was a biggy.'

'Fuck's sake, Adam. Why can't you appreciate what you've got? Why is Celia not enough?'

'She is enough. It's just . . .'

'It's just what?'

He reached out and started pulling small pink petals off a nearby plant. 'You know once I told you I thought she'd make me a better person? Well, she hasn't. I'm on constant edge, like I can never be good enough. I will always fail. And now I've got the Primordial Emperor hovering—'

'That's just rubbish. She's not asking for much. Just basic decency. You have to try harder to behave yourself. Make it up to her.'

'I'm no good at it. I'm damaged. You know I am.' He put on a little boy voice. 'Help me.'

'Help you? What do you expect me—' I didn't finish because a drift of birds rose out of a shrub and there was Celia, standing at the top of the steps.

I sprang to my feet.

She stared for a second. 'Matt!' she said. 'You're back.'

'I couldn't keep away.'

'He's been trying to kill me,' Adam cried petulantly.

She came down to the terrace and walked slowly along the side of the pool. She didn't rush; I wasn't enveloped in one of her lovely hugs. She stopped and looked at me.

'I'm so sorry. I should have let you know I was coming. Is it OK?'

'Of course.' She smiled but there was none of the warmth of our recent FaceTime. Her mouth stayed tightly shut.

'I have to warn you,' she said, 'the kids have been using the cottage in your absence.'

'Gosh, that doesn't matter. I'm just very grateful to you both.'

'It's fine. I know you've been having a hard time.' She glanced at Adam. I felt something pass between them.

'I promise to keep out of your hair,' I said.

'It's fine,' she said again.

'So how were your churches?' Adam asked. 'Did the Primordial Emperor find enlightenment?'

'Who?'

Adam sniggered. 'His Supremely Mysterious and Primordial Emperor.'

I looked at him and then back at Celia.

'Reynash,' Celia said.

'*Reynash?*' I felt my stomach plummet. 'You've been looking at churches with *Reynash*?'

'It was fun,' she said. 'A few were derelict, but a couple were incredible. Do you know the difference between Western and Greek churches?'

I tried to respond, but only opened my mouth.

'Western churches are about looking upwards to the heavens. But Greek churches are about bringing heaven to earth; they're small and enclosing, they contain you in the space. That's what Rey says anyway. Rey's very interested in religion.'

'Is he?' I managed to say.

'I need a shower,' she said. 'You want anything, you two?'

We shook our heads.

'Reynash?' I mouthed as soon as she was out of sight.

'I've been trying to tell you. Fucking Reynash. Can't keep

him away. First it was the swimming. Then all that money to St Saviour's. Now it's Byzantine frescoes. Celia hangs on his every word. It's like he's taking over my life.'

A pressure in my temples, a sense of rising panic. *It's not the same here since you left.* It wasn't that Celia was missing me. It was just a statement of fact. Things had not been the same since I'd left.

I turned to look at Adam. He was lying back down now with his eyes shut. After a bit, his nostrils moved in and out and I realised he was asleep.

21

There was no sign of Branwell down at the cottage. I called for him, but he didn't come. The packet of food I'd left was untouched and the water bowl had been repurposed as an ashtray.

Up early the next morning, I walked through the olive grove, worried he might have got snared in one of the black nets. I was holding out an open tin of tuna and calling his name when Celia found me. She was wearing flip-flops and an aquamarine kaftan with pink tassels at the neck, a threadbare towel under her arm. She said, 'Oh Matt,' and then told me she'd been down 'religiously' to feed him the first few days, as I'd asked, but what with one thing and another, she'd been so busy . . .

'I'm sure the cat's fine,' she said when she'd followed me

into the kitchen. 'Cats are very resilient. And actually, to be honest, it probably wasn't a great idea to have encouraged it.'

'No, I know,' I said.

I was replacing the lid of the tuna, trying to make the metal stick without cutting myself.

'Matt!' She looked into my face. 'Aw. I'm sorry.'

I pushed her away. 'It's fine.'

'I'm a country girl. I'm unsentimental about pets.'

I put the tin of tuna in the fridge, being careful not to spill the juice. 'I know.'

'It was probably ridden with fleas.'

'Can we stop talking about the cat?' I said.

She felt bad, though; I could tell because she made a thing of persuading me to join her for a swim and slipped her arm through mine as we walked along the path.

'Adam tell you what happened with James's Anna? I'm livid. Flashing himself like some dirty old man. You can be arrested for things like that. Rey says I should cut him some slack, but honestly, I'm fed up.'

'I'm so sorry, Celia.'

'You're too nice to him,' she said.

'You too.'

'Well, I'm not sure if I am being nice this time. It feels like the last straw.'

'Oh Celia.' I was about to say something about Rey but she had dropped my arm to scramble down the last bit.

I turned my back to take off my trousers and T-shirt, folded them and lay them on top of my sandals and then undid my watch and placed that down carefully too. When I turned round, her kaftan was gone and she was standing there in a jewel-green bikini.

'How neat and controlled you are, Matt,' she said. 'Rey says you're wasted on the creative arts.'

'That's kind of him.' I kept my eyes on her face, away from her breasts and pale stomach, her freckled legs and arms.

'Do you like my new cossie?' she said, raising her arms in a self-conscious twirl.

'It's beautiful.'

'It was a thank-you present from Rey. I told him I was too old for a bikini, but he says age is just a concept.'

I was looking into her eyes and, her fingers fiddling with her crucifix, she looked into mine.

'How's the swimming?' I said casually. 'He must be Olympic standard by now.'

'Not really. But he can do a whole length!'

I tried to sound measured. 'And you're quite sure he's not been pretending not to be able to swim. You know, to get close to you?'

She sank down on the pebbles. 'Don't be silly.'

I sat too. The creases of her stomach made me feel tender towards her. I could smell coconut and a squeaky synthetic tang – her shampoo or face cream or lip-gloss.

'Celia,' I said, 'can I ask you a question? Do you trust him?'

'Of course. Why? He's really kind.'

'It's just the way he's inveigled his way in. It's all so sudden.'

'He's lonely out here. We're just across the bay. It's natural we should hang out.'

I wished I could tell her what Amira had said about Rey hating Adam, but obviously I couldn't. 'It feels a bit weird when he and Adam never got on.'

She pulled a face. 'That was at school. People change. And you know, he's been incredibly kind. He's helping you with your screenplay!'

'He put me in touch with someone,' I said stiffly. 'But I'm not sure that it was real.'

'Of course it was real. Why wouldn't it be real?'

I gave a small shrug.

'And you know he recommended James for a job?' she continued. 'A start-up off Piccadilly near the park. He went for an interview last week . . .' She trailed off.

'I'm very pleased for my godson.'

She picked up her towel and folded it over her knees and leant her chin on it. 'Oh Matt.'

'What?'

It was an old children's towel. I could see the faded blue and pink outline of Mickey Mouse.

She bit the side of her lip. 'Adam made me promise not to mention it.'

'Mention what?'

She sighed. 'Listen, James saw you in Green Park. With that girl. I know you swore Adam to secrecy, but I asked him about the missing thirty thousand and I got it out of him.' She bit the side of her lip. 'I'm worried about you.'

I felt the life drain from my face.

'I wish you'd talked to us earlier. I mean, I know you've been feeling terrible about Takara. But what were you thinking? Did you come on to her at Rey's party? Was it a moment of madness? She's so *young*.'

I bowed my head. If Adam had appeared then I think I might have killed him.

She was still talking.

'Can't you get that sort of thing on the internet these days? Pornhub, is it?' she said. 'And paying her off, Matt: was that wise? I really hope it's the end of it – are you sure she won't come after you for more? I hope you've erased all the pictures. I mean, I know you're not in the public eye and I don't really know how people like that operate, but you read things in the press.'

People like that.

I lifted my head. 'Adam shouldn't have said anything,' I said. 'I'm not really that person. Please try and forget it.'

'A moment of madness.'

'I suppose.' My voice broke.

She softened – she could never abide to see any creature, no matter how wretched, in pain – and she grabbed my face in her hands and said, 'Oh darling Matt, what a mess.'

We heard the crinkle of small stones and looked up. Adam was at the top of the largest rock looking down at us.

Celia sprang to her feet and waved her arms back and forth, as if she were signalling via semaphore to someone far off across a misty moor. 'We're dreadful,' she cried. 'Too busy gossiping,' and in that green bikini half ran, half flopped into the sea. I followed, turning when I was waist-deep, to see Adam still at the top of the rock, at the far edge where it overhung the water. 'I'm coming in from here,' he called, and he made the usual preparations – adjusting the position of his feet, looking over, checking the depths, arms up . . .

'Please don't,' Celia cried. 'Adam . . . Adam! ADAM!'

Too late. His body was in the air, and then disappearing from sight, hurtling towards the water. A smash; a triumphant shout. Seconds later, he appeared around the base of the rock. His arms circled, crashed towards us, his body churning, hair shaking. 'Yessss,' he hissed. 'That's how you do it.'

Celia was telling him he was an absolute idiot, that he would kill himself one day if he wasn't careful, but he was laughing, trying to kiss her. I sensed I was about to be dunked and I tried pathetically to swim away, but he was on to me, and water was up my nose and my knees were scraping the rocks and the weeds. Celia was a few metres away when I surfaced.

'What's wrong?' Adam said. 'You look like your dog's just died.'

'Celia knows everything,' I said in his ear and enjoyed the flicker of panic on his face.

'Everything?' he said.

'She knows Amira was blackmailing me.'

'Oh yes, for getting her to send you photos.' The corners of his mouth twitched. 'Yikes. Sorry, mate. Game was up.'

I stared at him dully. Tiny fish and weed swirled at my feet.

'We should set up a repayment plan,' he said.

I lowered my shoulders, felt the water spill over them. 'Two years and a flat,' I said.

'We'll do mates rates on the interest,' he said.

I flicked my hand, splashing him, and began to swim away. I hated the way he turned everything into a joke, that nothing was allowed to matter. Maybe once I'd loved that about him, the way he infused the world with air, lifted a heaviness in my own soul. Not today. He'd *used* me. I *was* a joke.

'How about an outing to cheer you up?' Celia called over. 'The caves at Diros. The mouth of Hell. You haven't been, have you?'

I said I hadn't, though the last few minutes had felt close.

'We could go tomorrow,' Adam said. 'A change of scene always does one good.'

'Fab idea,' Celia agreed. 'Boys' trip. I could have a day's peace and quiet.'

In the past, which is to say a few days ago, I would have liked nothing more. Not now. Celia was unashamed in wanting rid of us.

But it was irrelevant. It was never going to happen. I knew that the moment I heard the enthusiasm drain from Adam's voice. 'Yeah, whatever.'

Because that was the thing. That had *always* been the thing. He didn't want me. He wanted her.

22

The next couple of days were awful. It was very hot, the temperatures scaling the mid-forties. Wildfires raged in other parts of Greece; pictures on the BBC website showed holidaymakers running along roads in their bikinis, black clouds of smoke billowing behind. An old woman stood with her hand pressed to her chest, her face devastated, as her house burned. Over a period of hours, flames engulfed whole villages, homes were destroyed, livelihoods lost. Hundreds were injured. Eight people died.

Here in the Mani, was it my state of mind that gave me the impression things were rotting? Black sticky stuff appeared on the beach, streaked across the pebbles: tar from somewhere, which got on your clothes and stuck to the bottom of your shoes. Dead fish floated in the harbour, white and bloated. The streets smelt of drains. One morning, on a walk, I came across a dead cat. (Not black and white: a tabby.) At Villa Mimosa, heat caused a problem with chemicals in the pool. I found Adam crouched at the edge, dipping in pH strips and checking them against a colour chart.

'Does a bit of slime really matter?' I said. The night before, a firefighter plane had crashed on the island of Evia, killing both crew members, so I was testier than I might have been.

'Standards, Matt.' He'd put on a posh headmasterly voice. 'Standards.'

I'd been into town and had brought him a printout of my script, which I had jostled into some sort of shape. I placed it neatly on a sun lounger next to his phone. 'My masterpiece, as you keep calling it,' I told him. 'I thought you might like to read it.'

'Beautiful,' he said, getting to his feet. 'I'll read it tonight.'

He ambled into the kitchen and I followed. Celia was out, he told me. She'd found a yoga class in a nearby hotel.

'I wanted to go too.' He flexed his biceps and struck a pose, half he-man, half-Bruce Forsyth. 'But she says I'd cramp her style, that she wants something "of her own". I mean, fuck off. Why does she suddenly need something of her own?'

'Maybe she's still pissed off about Anna,' I said.

'She say anything to you?'

I shrugged.

A noise in the doorway and he turned his head.

Jasmine was standing there, in a T-shirt and a pair of very short pyjama bottoms. Adam made a noise, an almost imperceptible moan.

She smiled. 'Is there anything to eat?'

'What is this, a hotel?' He chucked her a peach which she caught. Her teeth were very white and small as she bit into it. Juice dripped down her chin, and she looked at Adam over the top of it.

'It's not going to keep the wolf from the door,' he said. 'We'll have to get something more substantial into you.'

I considered his tone, trying to flatten an unwelcome thought, as he opened the fridge and took out a carton of eggs. He fried them bare-chested, leaping to one side as the fat spat. She sat at the table.

I waited for Lydia to emerge before I left.

The next day, I was in Kardamos drinking coffee as Rey's speedboat purred up to the jetty and I saw Celia leap on. She was wearing a bikini with men's shorts that clung to her curves. As the boat accelerated away, she let out a girlish squeal and I was convinced I saw Rey put his arm around her waist to steady her. A church trip or another *swimming lesson*? I brought the cup to my lips but I wanted to smash it against the wall.

In the evening, Adam announced 'a gala supper' in the village. His treat, celebrating a certain number of books sold or something. *Horta* and horse mackerel were back on the menu and Adam was in full mine host mode. Lydia and Jasmine were brimming with high spirits, coaxed by Adam to recount the details of a full moon party they'd attended: the antics of some hilarious boys from Salford. 'I hope they didn't have their wicked way,' he said, 'because I'm not having that.'

Lydia squirmed; Jasmine giggled. I felt so stiff and awkward, I thought my face would crack. Celia, sitting opposite me, was playing the role of good wife; her arm along the back of Adam's chair; now and again she absent-mindedly stroked his neck. He teased her about something – a mispronunciation – and she pushed him, rolling her eyes in a way I'd seen her do a million times. They talked about September – a trip they had planned to Vienna; the logistics of various Norfolk weekend visitors. She caught me watching and the new post-Matt-as-nude-photo-procurer pity came into her eyes.

'What's up, Matt? You're very quiet.'

I bowed my head, befitting my role as Disgraced Person. I felt something inside me flare – a reckless urge to do damage. 'Just thinking about Takara,' I said. 'Her being in Norfolk without me.'

Celia folded her napkin and stood up. 'Don't worry. She won't be invited,' she said firmly before heading for the loo.

'But she already has,' I called after her.

Adam was looking at me, eyes narrowed. I smiled at him.

He said, 'What did she tell you?'

'Who?'

'Takara. She's OK, is she? She hasn't said anything to . . .' He made a swirling motion with his hands, biceps knotting. '. . . upset the apple cart?'

I felt suddenly sick. I reached for a fresh napkin from the dispenser and held it for a second against my mouth.

'I think the apple cart was pretty well upset already,' I said, after I'd taken it away. 'Most of the apples were already in the gutter. There were none left to bruise. Anyway, even if there were, I'm over it. Fuck it.'

His eyes shifted sideways. 'Good man.'

That night, I decided I'd had enough. It was stupid of me to hang around. Adam had said nothing about the screenplay and I felt both bored and tense while I waited. Needing something to do, I spoke to my sister. Work was 'same old, same old'; she'd been off the tills and on shelf-restocking this week: more tiring, less boring. Her tone was valiant, determined to stay up, and I felt a wave of admiration and love. I was a loser. Why was I even here? Why was I so protective of the Murphys? They weren't *my* people. And yet, even as I thought all this, I could feel my heart cleave to them, a kind of longing. I lay awake for hours, hot and restless with it, but when I went outside the air pressed into my throat. In the deathly quiet, I felt a terrible middle-of-the-night terror, a sense of impending apocalypse like the moment when the sea is sucked back before a tsunami.

23

At dawn the following morning, a group of Italians hiking on Mount Taygetus, alerted by circling ravens, spotted the skeletal remains of a body.

I went straight up to Arcadia to tell them. I was breathless, my heart pounding. I ran most of the way, wanting to explode with the enormity of it. I'd seen the entrance to the trail blocked off with tape, the police cars and ambulances parked up on the road. Standing on the outskirts of a gaggle of locals and officials, I'd picked up that the body was in a ravine only about fifty metres from the main path, close to some wheel tracks. Deterioration had taken place – heat, insect activity, scavengers – and most of the clothes had been picked away: *only sandals remained.*

The Murphys, who were sprawled around their green-tinged

pool, hardly lifted their lizard heads when I told them. The girls, busy with some hair treatment, were 'grossed out' by the thought of a body rotting so close to the house. Adam made a coarse joke about 'the sister', how I should be the first to offer a shoulder and a sympathy fuck. 'Surely she'd be particularly receptive.'

'Honestly, Adam,' Celia said, but she was smiling. She must have noticed my face, because she added quickly, 'I wonder what happened? Do you think he fell while out running?'

'No. He was wearing sandals. He wasn't running – someone lied about that – and those trainers I saw in Rey's upstairs cupboard *were* his. This is serious. This means I was right all along.'

'Oh Matt,' Celia said mildly.

'Do you lot not see what I'm getting at?' I said.

Adam, brushing a fly away from his face, laughed.

'God's sake, Adam,' I said. 'Why is everything a game to you?'

Celia patted her sunbed. 'I want you to sit down here in the shade and I'm going to get you a glass of water. It's a terrible thing, assuming it is that poor woman's brother. Or even if it isn't, of course, it's a terrible thing full stop. I know it's a shock, and you have been following the whole thing more closely than we have. It's understandable that you're upset. But I'm not sure it's anything to do with us.'

'Don't you get it?' I said, sitting down next to her. 'Rey's involved.'

Her face clouded a little. 'It's been dreadful for him, having it drag on,' she agreed. 'All those people trampling through the house, all the questions. And now it'll be raked up again. It's just not what he needs.'

'I can't believe you're thinking that way,' I said. 'A man's dead.'

'Matt.' She looked shocked that I'd raised my voice at her.

'Sorry.' I lowered it almost to a whisper. 'You're not thinking straight. You've got too close to him.'

It was overcast as I walked down the track to the cottage – there were storms, I would later discover, all over the Mediterranean and the Adriatic – but still so hot I could hardly think straight.

Would the police reopen the case now they had a body? Would they search Arcadia? Should I contact Sara, pass on my condolences, or had she not yet been informed? It seemed indecent that I might know, along with all those other people gathered up on the road, and she didn't. What would I say anyway? I was pacing outside the hut, trying to compose a message in my head, when Celia approached down the track.

Her hair trailed from an untidy bun and the buttons of her dress were half undone. Everything about her was loose and untethered. 'Matt. I realised you might need this. We borrowed it when you were in London. But now it's so humid, without even a breath of air.'

She was holding out a fan. I put my hand out to take it but she held on to it a second too long. She was very red in the face; flickers of mascara were smudged under her eyes. 'Um.' She bit the corner of her lip. 'Have you got a minute? It's about . . . Rey. Shall we go to the beach?'

I thought: She has her own suspicions about him after all. Maybe even *information*. But she didn't say anything at all as we walked down the path – she stayed slightly ahead of me the whole way. She tugged at a long piece of grass and pulled it apart, scattering bits of seed head.

In the cove, she sank on to the pebbles, wrapped the dress across her knees and let out a shuddering sigh. She looked at me sideways with an embarrassed, little-girl expression on her face. All she said was, 'Oh Matt,' almost despairingly, but it was enough.

I'm outta here, I said in my head. I'm over you all. I'm outta here.

She folded one arm over her head and started rocking slightly. 'Matt, Matt, Matt,' she repeated like a lullaby, like a love song.

I noticed the red marks where her straps had rubbed and the pallor of her neck where her hair normally protected it from the sun.

Less than a mile away, the remains of a body were being lifted on to a stretcher. Wildfires were raging. People were dying. In a room, somewhere in Lewes, maybe Sara was crying. Didn't one have a responsibility to bear witness to all that, to rise above one's own needs and desires?

A few seconds passed. I looked out at the headland, at the house, and the yacht at anchor. Next to the grey sky it looked flat and uninteresting.

'Have I got myself in a bit of a pickle?' she said.

'I don't know,' I said. 'Have you?'

She looked up at me and, for a moment, it was like it had been before. Our special closeness. With my thick, clumsy thumb, I wiped the tears from under her eyes.

'What's happened?'

'Nothing. Nothing at all, I promise. It's all in here.' She pressed her hand to her heart.

'Rey?' I said.

'I knew you'd guessed. It's why I had to come. It's insane. He's not like Adam. He's not alpha. He's not *handsome*. But he has something, you know?'

Yes, I thought, money.

'I'm not used to the attention – the gentle, solicitous, wonderful kindness.'

'Aren't you?' I said lightly.

'And Adam. I've just been so angry, so hurt. Our own son's girlfriend. I let a crack show, just a tiny sliver, but it was enough.'

'So you and Rey . . .?'

'No. No. Matt. No. Nothing has happened.'

'Nothing at all?'

'No. Well. Not really.' A secret smile. 'We've talked about it.'

Their bodies touching in the pool. In church, gazing at an icon. Hands brushing. The agony of their restraint. Her open mouth. The small sound she makes. Through the open door, the boyish pallor of her legs, those little cries. Her utter loveliness, her utter goodness.

'I've always felt my place in the marriage was to be loyal, that if one of us behaved themselves it was OK. Now, this?'

She lifted her shoulders. 'I don't know any more. Can I leave Adam? No, I don't think I can. I made my vows in front of God. Divorce is out of the question.'

'As bad as murder,' I said.

She laughed. 'Did I say that? It's just we get on so well – we talk about everything. You know his sister died, don't you?'

'Yes, I do.'

'Rey says we could run away and join a religious retreat – there's a brilliant "stillness" one in Andalusia apparently. Nothing matters, he says, as long as we're together.'

'Does he know about your tooth?' It was cruel, but I couldn't bear the way she was arguing herself into it, arguing herself out, inhabiting both realities, trying to have it both ways.

'God no!' she said. 'Matt, honestly. I shouldn't have told you. Anyway, I'll have my implant by the end of September.'

'There you go then.'

She moved her hands to her shoulders, ran them around her upper arms and over her elbows, enjoying the feel of her own skin. 'I mean, there is always annulment.'

'*Annulment?*'

'Don't look at me like that. If someone is having an affair when they *actually* get married, it proves they never had any intention of sticking to their vows, and the sacrament therefore can be disallowed. I knew about Adam and Teresa, my maid of honour. I just chose not to make a fuss.

'But anyway,' she went on, 'I'm not going to leave Adam. There are the children. Of course I won't. It's just Rey says . . .'

'I don't trust him,' I said. 'I think he's got an ulterior motive in getting close to you. I thought it was to warn me or damage Adam; now I'm beginning to think it might be both.'

She flushed. 'Matt, will you listen to yourself?' She patted her chest. 'It's *me*. He wants *me*. You should have heard him. He fell in love with me last summer when he saw me in Dimitri's. He's never felt like this before. And he's a good man. He gives lots of money to charity and . . .'

I stopped listening. I realised how blank her mind actually was; how, for all the theories and analysis, everything she said was uncoupled from rationality, the shiny excitement of her sentiment too engrossing. She didn't want to be challenged; she didn't want anyone to take it away, she just wanted to talk about it, live in it, be gloriously tormented by it.

Eventually, I interrupted. 'I adore you. You know that. So I say this with love: you're on a dangerous path, Celia. You'll take these tiny steps, thinking each one doesn't matter, but if you want to protect your marriage, you should understand that each step takes you a little closer to the edge and before you know you've gone over it.' I felt wise saying this. It was all stuff the counsellor had said during couples therapy.

'I *know*.' She wasn't listening; nothing was going in. She didn't care what I knew or thought.

'It'd kill Adam if he found out,' I said. 'Or he'd kill Rey.'

'I don't know what to do,' she cried. 'Darling Matt, will you help me?'

I loved her. I had no choice, so I said of course.

*

The night before Adam and Celia's wedding, after Adam's meltdown, I lay there, listening to him snore, and somehow in the early hours I coaxed myself into believing it was a wonderful thing that was happening. Adam and Celia, separately so important to me, would be even more so together. In the church, as I handed over the rings, I told myself I was part of it. All these years, when I'd lied for him and been at his beck and call, it was to protect their union, this beautiful, precious thing. And it was beautiful; it was precious: it had to be to have caused me so much pain.

After Celia left me that evening, I took a pill and must have fallen asleep because I dreamt I was out on the yacht with Rey and he dived in – a perfect swallow dive – and he called for the ladder to be dropped, but the staff were busy, and I leant over the side and pushed him under with the net thing I'd used to clean the Arcadia pool. He fought back but finally stilled and I watched as his mouth turned into an 'O', his limbs dissolved and he melted into the depths.

The clouds had cleared by the time I woke. I gazed up at the light flickering through the fig leaves. My heart was beating as it had when I saw Adam floating and thought he was dead. I remembered something Patrick Leigh Fermor had written about Greek superstition, about dreams under a fig tree coming true. I hope it was a sign of my bleak distress rather than anything more sinister that I squeezed my fists tightly and hoped mine would.

24

Dave Baxter texted me the following morning to ask if I'd seen the 'Mike Lynch bombshell'? I'd been too much in my own bubble to look at the news, but I went on the BBC website right away.

Lynch's yacht, the *Bayesian*, had gone down the previous day in a freak storm off Sicily – most of the crew, apart from the cook, survived. Lynch and his daughter were among the seven dead.

Had I also seen – Baxter texted – about Lynch's financial VP? He'd been knocked down by a car and died of his head injuries in Suffolk over the same weekend. 'Weird coincidence, no?' he wrote. 'Turns out no one's untouchable. Hard not to see a conspiracy.'

'Divine retribution?' I wrote.

'Or . . . human intervention?' he replied.

I didn't act at first. I waited, learning what I could about the investigation from Andrea in the shop. The track marks near the body belonged to a quad bike, but no quad bike had been found. The decaying sandals turned out to be Birkenstocks. The body was in such an advanced state of decomposition, they needed dental records for formal identification.

Life went on. The blue and white police tape they'd erected over the entrance to the trail where Marc Ashley had died tore. Bits of plastic littered the bushes on either side; someone had stuck a polystyrene cup on the head of a cactus.

I walked a lot over this period of limbo. I found it calming. I discovered new paths, including one that led up to the main road just before the drive to Arcadia. Much of the land was overgrown with banks of thistles and ivy, but it was peaceful, with only twittering birds flitting out of the undergrowth ahead of me, and the occasional jangling goat.

I looked out for Rey and Celia – though it's wrong to say that I spied. I picked up bits of her: a pair of green bikini bottoms dropped on the rocks; a crumpled towel. Once, I saw flickers of movement, red and blue and brown, through the trees and crept after them. The path wound through the olive groves, then dipped down to the ruins of an old stone house. I heard voices, and saw the two of them – dressed like twins. I watched, the light flickering like broken chips off the white stones, as their bodies pressed together. Cicadas screamed as they kissed.

I took a photo on my phone.

When a week later the body was formally identified as belonging to Marc Ashley, I was more upset than perhaps I should have been. It led to the decision to confront Rey – which was spur of the moment, though I realise that sounds implausible now.

It was late afternoon the day I heard and I was sitting in the cove below the cottage when I heard buzzing and saw Rey's tender heading out from his jetty. He wasn't alone – he had one of his men with him – and as the boat churned in a wide semi-circle towards me, I saw Rey was looking my way, scanning the shore, and I realised he might have thought I was Celia. I stood up quickly; his arm lifted in a salute, and the tender abruptly swung to the left and puttered off, carving a more direct path now towards the yacht.

I sat down again, feeling winded. Perhaps I shouldn't have stood up, but waited until he was close, realising his mistake too late to back off. I hadn't seen him since I'd been in London – surely by design, not accident. He'd been avoiding me.

It felt suddenly urgent that we squared up to each other. I took off my shoes and my trousers and top and stood there in my trunks. I didn't have my neoprene slippers, and it was painful underfoot, but I felt confident. The yacht was dauntingly far out, but the sea was flat, the water warm. 'You can do this,' I muttered to myself. 'You got this.' I kept my strokes and my breathing regular, my eyes tightly closed (pausing every ten strokes to adjust the direction) and I tried very hard to ignore the dark depths of water beneath. A couple of hundred metres out, in a sudden panic, swallowing water, I almost turned back, but I regathered my strength and kept going. The difficulty of the task gave it an urgency; the more effort I had to put into it, the more important I convinced myself it was. When, finally, the straight white sides of the yacht towered above me, I gaspingly feared my dream was coming true, only I was the one who would drown – my hands sliding, legs slithering hullwards, my pitiful call lost in the slapping of the waves. I summoned my last atoms of energy to reach the anchor chain and was clinging on when a head appeared and a man, shouting, guided me back around the side to where a solid ladder slowly, electronically, descended.

Sharp pains in my chest, salt in my throat. My eyes stung; everything wobbled. My arms felt too weak to lift my body. At the top, I doubled up, drenched, gasping with exhaustion. The man handed me a thick grey towel and I threw it over my head, sucked in and out a few enormous breaths. He told me to follow him. He was in his mid-twenties, muscles bulging in tight beige shorts and a beige polo top. The towel, I noticed, as I wrapped it around my waist, was initialled RdS.

Rey was sitting at the stern of the boat, in a sunken area of polished chrome and white leather seating, a pair of binoculars slung around his neck. He looked cool and dry in his usual brown top and Gucci swim shorts, the ones that were so incomprehensibly admired by Lydia and Celia, hands crossed behind his head, his legs open and apart. I had time to think it was the stance of someone who owned a luxury yacht, that he was learning to inhabit the role, when he closed his legs and, touching the binoculars, told me he'd watched me swimming over, that I'd looked to be struggling a bit.

He raised an eyebrow. 'Could you have made it back to shore?'

'I think it's highly unlikely.'

He nodded and stared at me for a moment longer than necessary. 'Good thing I decided to let you up then.'

I thought: He's a threat. I hadn't known for sure until that moment.

We talked about nothing for a bit – he said, 'Long time no see' and hoped I'd been well, blah blah, and then he started telling me about the boat – 'she' was just a bit of fun really; he'd seen her in Athens and bought her on a whim. Of course, he'd had to spend a fortune kitting her out and the price of diesel was off the charts, so he was an idiot really. He shrugged. 'A fool and his money.'

Another young man appeared at his shoulder and Rey asked him to bring me a drink – anything I wanted – and I asked for a Coke. Full fat, I added, I needed the sugar. All three of us laughed; my feebleness had somehow, unfairly, become a joke. It arrived on a tray with a small bowl of crisps and another of olives. Rey told me he often came here for sundowners, there was nothing so romantic as being out here on the water as the sun slipped behind the horizon, and I realised – because he'd said 'romantic' – he meant with Celia.

I took a few gulps and put my glass down on a miniature paper doily.

Rey was looking at me expectantly.

I said, 'Yes. So, I wondered if you'd heard today's news: it's definitely Marc Ashley they found.'

'Yes. I know. Christos called me. Not a surprise, of course, but devastating. Absolutely devastating. Poor Sara. I've got a call out to her later. Dreadful business. Poor Marc.'

'So he didn't go out for a run,' I said. 'Despite what your colleagues said.'

He nodded slowly.

I tried to keep my gaze on him steady. 'I keep thinking about the trainers and the running kit in your cupboard.'

He laughed and let the laugh die away. 'Dog with a bone,' he said.

This time I shrugged.

'OK.' He leant forwards, pressing his elbows into his knees. 'I'm going to tell you something. I don't need to, but I will. Those trainers, the running stuff: they did belong to Marc. You're right. But it's nothing sinister. I held them back. I realise it was probably wrong now. Silly really. But when we handed over Marc's things, I thought it would be better if Sara didn't see them. Marc had told us he was going for a run, but he was just wearing ordinary clothes when he left. I do feel guilty, but that's because I should have realised what he intended to do. That's all it was. I was protecting her.'

'So you admit it: you held back evidence?'

'It wasn't evidence as such.' He flicked some invisible dust off the leg of his shorts.

Flames from the setting sun licked the back of his head and I was adjusting to his confession when he said, 'I know why you're really here. Celia's told me you've been snooping around us.'

'What?'

My face felt wooden. I pressed the pads of my fingers together. The skin was white and wrinkled, slightly numb. One of my cuticles was bleeding.

'It's OK. She told me you can be trusted. You're "on our side".'

'I'm on *her* side.'

'Look, Adam's your friend. I get that. But let's not beat about the bush: he's been a terrible husband. She should have left him years ago.'

A swallow of Coke. I said, 'You've known her a handful of weeks. I've known them for years; years looking out for her and knowing what's good for her and what isn't.'

He said, carelessly, 'Yeah, yeah,' as if time wasn't important, dedication wasn't important, putting in the hours, slow, hard work, hope – none of it was important. 'Listen, I'm sure this is difficult for you, and goodness knows what's going to happen. I've been alone a while, and I'm not going to do anything rash, but you know how you just know when something feels right?'

He was doing that upward-speaking thing – going up at the

end of sentences – which has always annoyed me. I said, 'I know you've got reasons to harbour resentment against Adam. Fuck it, at some time or another, we've all harboured resentment against Adam.' I forced out a jovial laugh. 'I had this idea and now I can't get rid of it – that this whole thing is a plot. Coming here to the Mani, buying the big house, stealing his wife, taking away everything he loves – some elaborate revenge.'

He laughed as if I'd made a good joke, though afterwards I realised he didn't deny it.

'*Can* you swim?' I said.

He held my gaze. 'Better than I could.'

'It's just I thought you might need to be able to swim to play water polo.'

He breathed out slowly. 'You don't need to swim very *well*. You're mainly in your depth. And I was a stand-in; I only played a couple of times. I have to ask myself why it matters so much to you. Because it seems you're more invested than you should be.' This time, his mouth, as well as his tone, curved upwards.

'It's only because—' A sharp pain at the back of my eyes, an obstruction in my throat. What was I going to say? That I had a place in the world when I was with the Murphys. I swallowed, and tried again. 'It's only . . .' Eventually, I said, 'Don't underestimate Celia's faith. She takes her vows seriously and all this with you may be exciting now, but . . .' I shrugged and waved my hand to suggest the 'all this' I mentioned was transitory. '. . . her Catholicism goes very deep. It may be that you're not aware of how traumatic this could end up being.'

'When she comes to her senses, you mean?'

'Yes. I suppose I do mean that.'

He gave me a slow, gracious nod. 'Duly alerted.' He was telling me I was a prig. I shouldn't have talked about 'vows' and 'faith'.

I said, 'Plus their marriage is, despite everything, very strong. They adore each other.' And then I added, 'I don't know what he would do if he found out about you.'

'Oooh.' He pretended to shiver. 'Should I be careful?'

I thought about Adam's strength, even in horseplay, the way his emotions were always given physical expression. How he so often acted without thinking about consequences. And I noticed again how slight Rey was, how narrow his torso, how delicate his hands.

'Yes. I think you should be careful.'

He seemed to note the change in my tone. 'Yeah, yeah,' he said. 'I remember. God.'

'Rey, honestly. You think you know but you don't. She'll never sleep with you.'

He laughed then, like someone relieved of a worry. 'Oh Matt, I think you'll find that horse has bolted.'

My face felt suddenly flooded with blood. It throbbed in my ears, and in my neck. I could feel it pushing to get out of my chest.

Rey scanned the deck of the boat. The man who'd lowered the ladder was standing, arms crossed, to the right of a door to the cabin; the other was out of sight. They were dressed as stewards but they doubled as bodyguards. The gardener at the house *had* been packing a gun. Too much money made you scared. I felt empowered, thinking that. There was something so sad and sterile about the white leather and the beige uniforms, the monogrammed towels. Sara had said I was jealous, but I wasn't.

Rey rubbed the bridge of his nose. 'I hear what you're saying. You hope people change, but you're right: we've been a bit reckless, got a bit carried away. I'm used to keeping my emotions to myself. I'm self-contained; work's really my thing. I'm not used to opening up to someone like this.' He pressed his left hand to his heart. 'We should tread carefully, work it all out. We need to get her back to London. It'll be easier then.'

He'd used 'she' and 'her' in relation to the boat earlier, and for a second I hoped that's what he was referring to. But no, he meant Celia.

'I wouldn't rush anything,' I said reasonably. 'But maybe back off for now.'

'Yes, OK.' He nodded. 'I appreciate you having her best interests at heart.'

I looked out towards land; the lights were on at Villa Mimosa. When I turned back, he was watching me.

He smiled slightly, crooking his head. 'On a happier note, did the meeting go well? With Victor? He sounded pretty psyched when I spoke to him. He loves your idea, says he's waiting for some material? I'd love to read it myself if you felt comfortable with the thought.'

'At some point, yes. And I should have thanked you for putting us in touch. So thank you.'

Dead Heat

'It's my pleasure.'

I drank the rest of my Coke. The ice had melted. The sun still hadn't quite set. It was suspended, an elongated red disc, in vertical streaks of cloud. He asked if I'd like a lift across in the tender, but I said I felt better now and wanted to swim back, that it would do me good. I needed the toilet first, and one of the men took me downstairs and showed me 'the head', as he called it. He'd gone when I came out, and I *did* have a little snoop – opening a door on to a huge bed, with a mirror on the ceiling. I closed the door quickly and went back up the stairs where the same man was waiting for me, the electronic ladder already deployed.

It was quicker going back; maybe the current was with me. I felt as if I were escaping prison. I imagined my pale body encircled by the lens of the binoculars; searchlights scanning the sea around Alcatraz, and I tried to make my strokes strong and confident. It was dusk when I reached the shore, and my muscles had turned to jelly – I was to sleep better that night than I had for weeks – but it didn't matter. I'd made a decision. I felt virile, invigorated, alive.

25

Celia was back on my doorstep, as I'd expected, the following morning.

I heard stones crunching and the rustle of undergrowth as I was brushing my teeth – she was waiting when I came out, a dressing gown open over her old swimsuit. She was red in the face; flickers of mascara smudged beneath her lower lashes.

'We don't have long,' she said, speaking quickly. 'Tell me everything. He's lovely, isn't he, when you talk to him? So intelligent and so interested. Did you adore the yacht? Am I mad? Am I going insane? But do you get it?' She clutched both my hands and stared frantically up at me. 'Darling Matt. Do you forgive me?'

I put my arms around her and kissed the top of her head.

I'd do everything, I said into her hair, everything in my power to make things right. 'You love him, do you?' I said. 'And he loves you?'

She pulled away, laughing through her tears. 'It's ridiculous, but yes. Yes.'

None of it mattered to her, I thought as she disappeared up the path. She just wanted a witness to it, to make it real within the context of the two of us, which in itself wasn't properly real because I didn't really count. I was too malleable, no threat to anything or anyone.

The police station at Aetolia was a low white building, with curved windows, approached by sweeping steps and widely spaced palms. A blue and white Greek flag fluttered against the gleaming brickwork.

I'd tried to argue myself out of coming. There's a thing when a person pushes themselves into the centre of an investigation and becomes the suspect. Was this about to happen to me? I thrashed it back and forth until late afternoon when I concluded it was worth the risk.

The heavy-set man at the desk spoke some English – used, I suppose, to dealing with tourists – so I kept the bits of Greek I'd prepared to myself. I sat on a red bucket chair, shivering in the air con, next to a woman and a teenage boy, until eventually a different officer came, younger and slimmer, and took me into a room. He wrote down my name and address – currently, I told him, a little uncertain – and asked if I wanted a lawyer. I realised maybe the first one had misunderstood and thought I'd come to confess. I tried to laugh it off, but it put me on the back foot.

As I started talking, I tried to keep my eye on the stars on his shoulder, on his twin patches of receding hair, on the tiny stain on the lapel, anywhere but the gun slung around his hips. I explained immediately that I believed the death of Marc Ashley to have been murder and that Reynash de Souza was involved.

1) In terms of motive: they were, I was sure, aware that Reynash de Souza's company had recently been sold to Google. Marc's last tweet was about the apparent financial irregularities – suspected fraud – surrounding Mike Lynch's sale of Autonomy. He must have been drawing parallels because he'd hashtagged AdVent. Marc's sister had said the death of his wife had refocused Marc's mind on things that mattered. It was my contention he was about to blow the whistle. He had become a liability both to AdVent and to Reynash de Souza.
2) Sara Ashley, Marc's sister, had initially been adamant that her brother would never take his own life. She'd been otherwise persuaded – I put heavy emphasis on the word – by de Souza himself. But she and Marc had been very close. I believed her initial instinct should not have been dismissed.
3) Marc's body was found wearing Birkenstocks. Obviously, if Ashley had intended to take his own

life, he wouldn't have cared what he wore on his feet, but witnesses at Arcadia – the house belonging to de Souza where Ashley had been staying – claimed he had left for a run. Trainers belonging to Ashley– I showed a screenshot from the shopping website – had been concealed in a cupboard in Reynash de Souza's house. I'd seen them with my own eyes and de Souza had admitted to me personally that he had hidden them there. Getting friends to lie and then concealing the trainers, along with other running gear, looked like a cover-up to me.

4) The vehicle tracks that had been found near the gully where the body had been found. Had anyone checked them against any of the quad bikes that were kept at Arcadia?

The officer looked at me throughout. Occasionally, he wrote something down, but mainly he compulsively rubbed to one side of his mouth where he'd missed a bit shaving. When I ran out of steam, he waited for a few moments, still looking at me, before thanking me for my contribution.

When he stood up and scratched the back of his neck, I saw dark sweat marks under his arm.

'So what are you going to do now?' I said, still seated. 'Surely you're going to follow some of this up?'

'We are waiting for an autopsy on the body, so I shouldn't comment,' he said. 'If he was in sandals, however, then it makes it more likely that he fell.'

'Did you listen to what I said? He didn't fall; it's foul play.'

He smiled as if he found my phrasing quaint. 'All this sounds a little personal. Mr de Souza was with friends the day Mr Ashley went missing; he has an alibi.'

'Yes, but they owe him,' I said. 'Those friends are in his pocket. Everyone is. You probably are.'

I shouldn't have said that last bit – I was frustrated – because he looked annoyed and asked if there was anything else, and when I said no, that was it, he unlocked the door and walked ahead of me back into the main foyer. It was empty now. I followed him to the circular doors and out the other side.

He was shaking my hand when a woman came up the steps towards us. I recognised her; she'd been one of the officers standing at the bottom of the trail close to the ravine. She nodded at me and, as she passed, asked him, in Greek, what was happening. He replied quickly. His head was turned away, but he said one phrase twice, and she repeated it, underlining his point, and then, laughing, she walked back into the building.

I hadn't understood, just as they knew I wouldn't, but those sessions on Duolingo weren't a complete waste of time. At the bottom of the steps, I wrote it phonetically into Google Translate, and the answer flashed up: 'man who masturbates'.

I'd hitched a lift to Aetolia with an English couple on their way to a boutique hotel in Gerolimenas. It was harder getting a lift the other way. I stood by the side of the road for fifteen minutes; and then decided to have a beer at the taverna opposite. It was more of a local than a tourist bar – flies and football on the TV and old men playing backgammon. The sun had dropped. I drank quickly – throat suddenly raw with thirst – and asked for another. Time passed. The match went to penalties. It was dusk when I checked my phone and saw a missed call from Adam.

'Mate, mate,' he said, the moment he answered, 'I've got to talk to you. We've got to meet.'

I paid for my drink as soon as I'd hung up and it was maybe an indication of my obvious fluster that the first vehicle on the horizon – a mini-van with a sliding door – stopped for me. It was driven by a sweet Belgian couple with young children and, squeezed in the back between two toddler seats, I spent most of the twenty-minute journey dodging sticky hands and breadsticks. I tried to be friendly, but I was roiling with tension. I think they were relieved when I got out.

He was waiting for me, not in Dimitri's, but in a small bar/gelateria we sometimes went to afterwards. It was in a narrow claustrophobic lane behind the harbour, near the supermarket – an odd choice on a hot, airless night, not even a slight breeze lifting off the sea to cool the sweat on your skin.

He was outside on a white plastic chair, eating ice cream from a pastel-pink pot. He hollered 'Matt' when I was still some distance away and, even though I raised my hand in greeting, whistled as if I were a dog coming to heel. 'Mint choc chip,' he said when I reached him. 'I challenge anyone to find an ice cream as delicious.'

'Salted caramel?' I said.

'You can shove your salted caramel up your arse. What even is salted caramel?'

A woman passing with lots of piled-up blonde hair said, 'It's what we used to call caramel!'

'Or toffee,' he countered roundly. 'Nothing's toffee any more. Toffee's been cancelled.'

She laughed, adjusting her hairclips, and I think she might have taken the empty seat if I hadn't slipped in first.

He used the plastic spoon to scoop out the last smears of ice cream; his tongue flicked. The tiny pot and the tiny spoon were both doll-like in his huge hands.

He'd showered and shaved and, in my dishevelled state, I felt immediately at a disadvantage. His demeanour was sober and businesslike – he had ordered a bottle of wine, with two glasses, but it was untouched on the table in front of him, like a prop.

I went inside and ordered myself an ouzo. I needed the hit. And the short delay. It was all white and brightly lit in there, ice cream as autopsy. I knocked back my glass with a wince, keeping my eye on him through the open doorway.

The woman with the piled-up hair had circled back and I watched Adam respond to her, eyes engaged, head at an apologetic tilt. Any other time, his body said. He turned his head to look for me and lifted a hand for her benefit. A regretful shrug. He didn't want to disappoint her. Any other time . . . I felt a huge surge of emotion. I felt I knew him, in that moment, as well as I knew myself. I thought maybe I loved him.

The woman was swaying away up the road when I came out. Adam rolled his eyes.

'It's your pheromones,' I said. 'Must be. Certainly not your looks.'

'Flies on shit,' he said. His moments of self-deprecation, often surprising, were one of his saving graces.

He scrunched the ice-cream pot in his hand and threw it into the bin. 'Wine?'

'Sure.'

I asked if he'd eaten as he poured and he said he had. I looked at my watch; it was later than I'd realised, past ten. Celia had gone for dinner with a school friend, he told me – some ghastly woman who was staying up the coast. He and the girls had had 'a bite' but they'd dumped him for some Greek lads; cheeky minxes, he was going to have to put a stop to that. Where'd I been all day? When I told him, he screwed up his forehead, half laughed, and shook his head, as if he thought I was mad. 'The police station,' he repeated. 'What the fuck, Matt?'

It seemed pointless to explain. I'd already gone over it too many times. But I told him, as briefly as I could, my concerns about Marc Ashley's death. 'No one else cares,' I said. 'Rey seems to have this power over people. Including you guys.' I watched him closely because of course, by 'guys', I meant Celia.

He shrugged. 'No power over me, mate.'

I felt pity for him, then.

I kept drinking, looking at him over the top of my glass. I put it down and wiped my mouth with my fingers.

'So?' I said. 'You wanted to talk?'

He was chewing the inside of his lip. A long moment passed. He swayed his head. Finally, on an exasperated puff of breath, he said, 'I think you've worked it out.'

Celia and Rey? Is that what he meant? He was being so calm.

I nodded carefully.

'The last few days, knowing you know and neither of us saying anything . . . it's been hell, man.'

'I'm sorry.'

'Let's have it out, lance the boil. Whatever.' He scratched his head. 'I mean. Fuck. Matt. Sorry, man.'

He stared at me, and I stared back at him. A group of rowdy lads passed, half shouting, half singing.

'I'm a fucking arsehole,' he said eventually. 'I should have told you before. I suppose I hoped you'd never find out.'

I moved my head from side to side, acting non-committal, playing for time. Not Celia and Rey then.

He half rose from his seat and sat down again, resting his elbows on his knees. 'Fuck, Matt. It meant nothing.'

'I'm sure it didn't.'

'We bumped into each other in Lamb's Conduit Street; Celia was away, and I was on my way up to Norfolk, and she ended up coming with me, and it just sort of happened. One thing led to another.'

He was still contorting his limbs. 'You hate me. And you should. But she shouldn't have told you. Why would she hurt you like that? What a bitch. You're better off without her.'

'Please don't say anything else,' I said. 'I want you to shut up.'

'I don't know what came over me. I mean, she was up for it, but—'

'Shut up,' I said.

'Yeah, fair. It's all in the past now. Just one thing – you haven't told Celia, have you? I mean, you wouldn't, would you? I'm on a yellow card here, man.'

'No. I haven't told Celia.'

He threw his head back. 'I'm such an arsehole,' he said, this time with relief.

'You are and you always have been.'

'It's like you said, pheromones.'

'And arse-omones.'

'You're right. I'm an *arse*. I always have been. Even as a kid. Even as a teenager.'

Of course I'd known about him and Takara. I'd closed my mind to the details. But here he was, rubbing my face in it. I'd felt sorry for him, because of Celia and Rey; I'd gone to the police partly on his behalf; I'd put my neck on the line for him. But he wanted me to ask: *How long did it go on? What did you do with her?* It was an illness with him.

I poured myself another glass of wine. 'Tell me about that girl you abused at school,' I said.

'Which girl?'

'That girl you raped,' I said. 'It started then, right? Your behaviour with women?'

'Which girl?' he said again, and then guiltily, 'I didn't actually *rape* her.'

'That's not what you said the night before your wedding when you told me about it. You cried.'

He shifted uncomfortably. 'Don't say *rape*.' He poured himself a glass and me another one, which I knocked back. 'Look, she's fine. I saw her the other day on Facebook. Married. Loads of kids. Husband in insurance.'

'That's a relief,' I said, feeling bleak with fury.

'Yeah.' He shook his head.

We talked about something else then – I can't remember what now. And after a bit he asked if we were good and I said we were. Anger had ruined me. My brain and my mouth had disconnected. I was very hot. I could feel the heat inside me, coming off me, spilling from my pores. The narrow street we were on was busy: a queue was building for ice creams; the table kept being knocked; pop music blared from the bar. I remember Adam saying it might be time to get me home. When I stood up, the world slipped sideways, pavement and sky and window – I put my hand out to steady myself. 'Easy.' Adam was next to me, holding me up, and we navigated the street together. I had lost my sense of direction a bit, but he seemed to remember what to do and soon I registered we were walking along the main road towards Villa Mimosa. It was dark. Lights came towards us. 'Whoa,' Adam kept saying, pulling on my arm. I fell into the bushes. Tripped. Or he pushed me. 'OK, OK, man,' he kept saying. 'All right, fella.' Once, I pushed him back. 'Whoa,' he said again. 'Mate, mate, mate.'

'I'm not your mate,' I told him. 'Don't mate me.'

He was in my head. His big hands and his big body. Takara's

smooth skin, her slim boyishness. Celia's little cries. Adam thrusting. His breath on Celia's neck. His tongue in Takara's mouth. I hadn't wanted to think about it. I hadn't wanted to know. I'd done everything I could to stop myself.

I shoved him harder, palms open, and this time he shoved me back; my fingers caught the collar of his shirt, and I yanked him to me. He was ducking, trying to hold me away, as I thumped him, and then his face sort of snarled and I felt a blow to the stomach and, winded, I went down, pulling him with me, into something that gave way under us, soft and sharp, scratching and suffocating, a bed of thorns, and, as I sank into it, he didn't move away, he was still there, his body inert, heavy, and I lifted my head and found his mouth. Felt the scrape of his skin. The touch of his lips. Tasted his spit. There was a moment of softness and surrender. My tongue probed. We opened to each other as I sank deeper into the thorns. I heard his breath and then his elbow met my eye, my head was knocked sideways, my cheek in the earth, and he was towering above me. 'Mate, mate. Fuck.' He stood like Hercules. 'Fuck. Man. Mate.'

I lay there, motionless, imagining my own death.

26

A glass of water splintered in the light. I hauled my head from the pillow and drank it down. A saucepan was on the floor next to me, and I was sick into it. Bitter acid. My brain rolled in my skull. I lay back down.

When I came to properly, the sun was burning on my eyelids. I dragged myself up and drank more water and was sick again, in the toilet this time. I poured bleach into the bowl, then retched – flecks of spittle – and poured in more bleach. I hauled my body around the cottage, trying to erase my presence: clothes in my case, leftover food in a binbag. I emptied and washed out the saucepan. I wanted not to exist, never to have existed. I swept and cleaned, keeping my head upright – dipping my head turned hot magma around my skull. I straightened the furniture and ran a cloth over the hob and the interior of the fridge and then I crashed back on to the bed before I brought up the rest of the water sloshing in my stomach.

I went through the mental process of finding my laptop and booking a flight and walking to the bus stop and waiting and travelling and changing and checking in and getting through security and queueing at the gate – the endless queueing at the gate.

Chargers. Adapters. I could see one from here. Unplug it from the wall, coil it up, place in the case with everything else.

I should get up and do it now. Unplug the charger. Coil. Case. Laptop.

When I woke again, the light had changed. A thin blade of afternoon light under the crack of the blind. The sun had moved. Or the earth had moved. I was the thing that hadn't. I didn't want to think, to go over anything. Of course I knew Adam had fucked Takara. He'd taken her, just as he'd taken Celia. Just as he'd taken the broadcasting career I might have had. He'd taken everything. What hurt was him wanting to *tell* me, the way he'd forced me to confront it, to imagine it. He had to be the centre of my thoughts. It was all about Adam. It always had been. I groaned, remembering my tongue in his mouth. I buried my face in the pillow; the cotton sticky, salty, as if there were blood.

I thought of Adam's father and his limp wrist; 'Gaynash', Adam and his mates had called Rey. I thought about the men upstairs when I was growing up. I thought about an elderly gent Celia had talked about after one of her trips – how he'd told her 'the love of his life' had died of Aids. She'd lowered her voice. 'So he must be a homosexual,' she'd said, her lips pursing as if it was a word she didn't want in her mouth. Abhorrence was in her upbringing and in her church and her faith. My faith.

I tried to work out the time. Midday? Early afternoon maybe? Too late to think about buses. I was damp with sweat and my body throbbed. I'd find a taxi. My face had been squashed into the pillow by heat and weight. My legs had been bitten to pieces. All that mattered was that I got out without being seen. I could kip at the airport if I missed the plane.

The headache raged in a lower key – more of a dull ache than a convulsion. I closed my eyes again.

The sound in my head was high and distant, a chirrup, or a gurgle. A moan: Celia building to orgasm, her limbs pale beneath the mosquito net; Adam's body, thick, muscular. And me behind the crack of their door, holding my breath. The plastic font of holy water above my mother's bed. Her fingers on the rosary. The darkness of the confessional, cedar-wood, the musky sharpness of the priest's robe.

Retching, I got myself upright. Too quickly, the world spun in black and white. I got out of the bedroom and through the main room and reached the front door.

In the garden, flickers of movement, a clash of textures.

A creature under a tree separated from the shadows. Something sinuous, alive. It took a minute for my brain to process, to believe it.

Branwell, plus two kittens, two small leggy bundles of fur,

one playing with his – no, *her* tail, one stalking a leaf, back arched in a ridiculous display of machismo.

I found some food and put it down under the tree and stood back to watch as they ate. It was such a small thing. And Celia was right. Two more stray cats, two more mouths to feed. After a while, I realised I was crying.

I didn't hear him approach. The first I knew of his presence was the cats skittering into the bushes; I got up too quickly; my stomach lurched, the world spun. For one suspended, reeling moment, I thought it was Adam, but the steps were lighter, the breathing quieter. It was Rey, coming up the path from the beach. He must have motored across on the boat.

'What's happened?' He crossed the grass towards me, light-footed. 'What have you done?'

He was up close now, frowning. His fingers grazed my face, and he said, 'Your eye. Your cheek. Looks like you've been in a fight!'

'I have.' I brought my hand to my face. It felt odd, bumpy and swollen.

He laughed, and then abruptly stopped. 'What you mean, you have been in a fight? You're not joking?'

'Celia hasn't told you?'

He shook his head.

When I brought them away, my fingers had blood on them.

'Christ,' he said. 'Well, I think we should get you cleaned up.'

He took me into the bathroom at the back of the house. I caught sight of my face in the mirror above the basin – my cheek was purple and swollen, my right eye half closed. He sat me on the toilet and used paper and cold water to clean it up, his eyes narrowed in concern. I smelt coffee on his breath.

It was hot in the bathroom. A mosquito whined. I could see hairs clogging the shower drain. His hands were small and he stuck his bottom lip out as he concentrated.

I thought about Adam helping me home, thinking to leave a jug of water by the side of my bed, a saucepan on the floor. Had he not told Celia what happened?

Rey asked me if I was hurt anywhere else. I was aware of feeling a sharp pain when I breathed in. I said no, I was fine.

'Who was it?' he said at last. 'Someone in the village? Some drunk holidaymaker you got on the wrong side of?'

'Kind of,' I said.

He let me go then, moving out of the way as I stood up and left the bathroom and walked back round to the front of the building. The light was pinking, glimmering low between the trees. No sign of the cats. They'd licked the plate clean, and pushed it right up to the trunk of the tree.

I sat down because my legs didn't feel as if they'd hold me much longer.

Rey perched on the edge of a chair, leaning forwards. 'You OK?'

'Yes. Thanks.' He was in a flash of sunlight; the colours around him seemed very bright and clear. 'Good thing you were passing.'

'Actually.' He paused. 'I wasn't passing. I came to find you.'

'Oh yes?'

He looked away from me, tapping his hand against the side

of his leg. 'I heard you were at the police station yesterday. I just thought it might be worth clearing the air.'

'OK.'

'Christos tells me you've still got concerns.' And then added, with ironic exasperation, 'Still going on about the trainers!

'As for the wheel tracks near the gully – I mean, lots of people ride quad bikes up there.' He was smiling gently now. 'I understand it. You don't make a lot of money without making enemies. You're suspicious of me; you think I persuaded my friends to provide me with an alibi – that I was with Marc, and I pushed him to prevent him from . . .' He moistened his lips. '. . . what? Blowing the whistle on some nefarious business?'

'Something like that.'

'Meaningless death is upsetting. Celia says your dad died young of a sudden heart attack. It's personal for you. It's much easier to find a narrative in which someone can be a hero. Fact is, shit happens. Horrible things happen. It makes us all feel helpless, no matter how rich or connected we are. But I would really advise you to stop poking your nose in. Certainly, steer clear of the official investigation. Christos said they're beginning to be suspicious of you.'

The blood rushed to my head and I leant forwards into the bushes and retched. When I sat back up, he was looking at me with his head on one side. 'Are you sure you don't want me to take you to a doctor?'

'I'm fine,' I said. 'I'm sorry for everything . . .'

'It's OK. You're a decent bloke. I can see that, even if Celia didn't keep telling me.'

I probed something dark and nasty inside me. It rose in my chest and I opened my mouth and it came out. 'I thought Adam was going to kill me.'

I heard a creak and a snake-like hiss of breath. 'He did this, did he?'

I brought my hand to my cheek and left it there. I closed my eyes and wasn't sure I'd be able to open them again.

'He's a thug,' he said. 'Can I ask why?'

I looked at Rey, levelly now. I could taste vomit and blood at the back of my throat. 'You know his father was violent? He used to knock Adam about and his mother pretended it wasn't happening. He's got a lot of anger inside. He gets jealous. If he's triggered, if he thinks he's being betrayed, he lashes out.'

'Why did he think he was being betrayed?'

'He decided I was sleeping with Celia. He's guessed something's up and he's got it into his head it's me.'

I held my dropping lid open to watch his reaction, but his face didn't change. 'You and her?' he said, and his eyes grazed me. 'You and Celia?' His mouth moved up at the corners.

'It didn't feel very funny last night,' I said.

His face darkened then. He realised I was serious. 'Is she safe?' he said.

'I don't know. But please don't tell her about this. It could be dangerous for her.'

'The sooner I get her away from him the better.'

I was going to write that something died in me, but I think it was more that it grew in me. My face suddenly flooded with blood. It throbbed in my ears, and in my neck. I could feel it pushing to get out of my chest.

I said, 'There's something else I should tell you. I think it might have been Adam who raped your sister.'

I felt him recoil. His face darkened and his breath seemed to stop in his throat. I reached out to put a hand on his shoulder and he flinched. He bowed his head. I heard him swallow. His eyes were closed.

I got him a glass of water and he drank it down and then wiped his mouth with the back of his hand. He asked more questions – what year, what had Adam told me, when? – and I just kept shaking my head and saying I didn't know, and maybe it hadn't been Adam after all, I didn't have the details, it was just something he once mentioned, and I'd carried the information all this time and didn't know what to do with it.

We walked into the kitchen for more water and he sat down at the table.

He said, 'He's a worthless human being. He brings nothing but unhappiness to everyone. He deserves *nothing*. His success. Kudos. Celia. None of it.'

'I know.'

'Would you tell the police what you've just told me? You're worth ten of him.'

I hung my head.

'No, seriously. You're the one with the talent. You should get out from under him.'

'That's nice of you to say.'

A printout of my screenplay, the one I'd kept for myself,

was sitting on the table and he tapped his fingers on it. 'This it? Your script?'

I nodded and he said, 'Would you let me read it? If I think it's any good maybe I could hurry things along with Victor, come up with some early finance. If it worked out, it might make me some money. And if it didn't, well, you never know, maybe you can do me a favour in return.'

I think I shook my head again because he frowned slightly, and said, surprised, 'Or not?'

'No. Yes. Whatever you want.'

I was in a dream for what was left of the day – a fugue state. I was starving and, after Rey left, I found my way down to Kardamos, anxious every minute of the walk that Adam or Celia would walk towards me or drive past. I ate on a back street inside the dingiest of bars – ordering a spanakopita with fries – and afterwards bought some fresh food in the shop, enough to last a few days. Not too much; I didn't know how long I'd be here. I slunk home, laden down, keeping to the shadows.

According to the Maniots, a man's blood is supposed to cry out the day before he dies. If I'd heard it, I hope I'd have behaved differently.

27

I was lying on my bed the following morning, the sun sending flickering patterns on the ceiling, when my phone pinged. I sat up when I saw who it was. Celia. An ordinary message. 'Cuppa?'

It seemed unthinkable that anything could carry on unchanged. I didn't understand. Had Adam still not told her about our fight? *Our kiss?* Or was it good manners? Had she – they – discussed the most civilised approach to the problem of me? Had they agreed to pretend nothing had happened? If so it was death. Death to honesty and openness and friendship itself because what is friendship without honesty?

I let a few minutes pass. A Hail Mary came into my head. I recited it through and then repeated it four times over. When the last 'Pray for us sinners now and at the hour of our death' had left my lips, I typed: 'On my way.'

The pool was still green and the teenage girls were peering down at it. Adam had a bucket of chemicals in his hand and was adding a spoonful to the filter. He was wearing trunks and a pale grey T-shirt with 'Tom Petty & the Heartbreakers' across the front in swirly black writing. Celia was lying on a sunbed in the shade, reading a book.

She saw me first, rested her book on the ground and got to her feet, coming to meet me with her hands outstretched. She was wearing her green bikini top but not the bottoms, because I had them, and those swim shorts. Lydia was right; they suited her. She frowned. 'What have you *done*? What's happened to your face?'

Adam straightened. He held his hand above his eyes, though the sun was behind him. I was the one almost blinded. I did the same, mimicking him; it was like a salute. He dropped his hand, half smiling.

'Oh,' I said. 'Silly thing really.'

Across the pool, Adam shrugged. Both hands were clasped in front of his body. What did he think I was going to do? Lunge at him?

I turned my gaze back to her. 'I . . . um . . . I got into an altercation in the village.'

'An *altercation*?'

I remembered Rey's assumption and repeated it. 'A drunken

tourist took exception to my presence. He thought I was eyeing up his missus.'

'Oh my giddy aunt,' Celia said, appalled. 'Are you OK?' She peered at my injury, frowning in a way that balanced concern with slight revulsion. 'Oh, for goodness' sake. These numbskulls shouldn't be allowed on holiday. Have you seen a doctor?'

I told her again that I was fine, and she said 'poor old you' several times, and tutted again about the 'utter toerag' who'd behave like that. She asked a few questions about where and when it had happened, and I answered vaguely, occasionally glancing at Adam. Had I contacted the police? Got the chap's name? If he was one of those yobs from the big all-inclusive up the coast, I should let them know, warn them their guests were running amok, ruining everything for everyone else.

I used to find it comforting, her view of life as a rowdy children's party. Now it just seemed naïve, tenaciously so. How much easier it was to live in a world of numbskulls and nincompoops and giddy aunts, to ignore real evil, real nastiness, all the dirty secrets that make up the dark side of human nature. How entitled her existence, tucked up with God against 'yobs', how cowardly.

'I looked for you yesterday,' Adam said, addressing me for the first time. He was speaking flatly – signalling clearly that he had no personal response to anything that concerned me, but that motions, for the sake of others, were being gone through.

'When?' I asked.

'Ten-ish – on my way for my morning swim. You were out cold.'

I thought about him finding me unconscious. Had he checked I hadn't choked on my vomit? How long did he stare down at me? Had I moaned? Had I drooled? I imagined his revulsion.

Celia led me into the kitchen and put the kettle on for tea, unless I fancied something stronger – she wouldn't blame me if I did. 'No, tea is fine,' I said.

'No biccies, I'm afraid.'

Out of earshot of Adam and the girls, she lost interest in my injuries. She bustled around the kitchen – opening cupboards and clattering mugs. 'I hear you went to the police about Rey,' she said. 'Honestly, Matt. Why?'

'I don't think he's been entirely honest,' I said.

'Look, what happened to Marc Ashley *was* an accident. He's promised me and I believe him.'

'Are you entirely objective, though, Celia?'

She began to answer, but then her shoulders sagged. 'Oh God.'

I put my arm around her, and for a moment her head fitted into my neck. I smelt sweat and suntan lotion, the slight sourness of her breath. She let out a heavy sigh. 'Oh Matt.'

'I know.'

'What am I doing?'

'It must be very hard.'

'It is. I look at myself and I don't understand who I am. I should stop before it all goes too far.'

I thought it had already gone far enough.

'Tell me to stop,' she murmured.

'Stop.'

'Oh God.' She sighed again. A strand of her hair brushed against my mouth. 'What would I do without you?'

She detached herself, though, laughing as she made a little twirl to untangle herself from under my arm.

I had an urge to hurt her then and I told her I had decided to leave, to head back to London. She said, 'Oh gracious, when?' and I said I wasn't sure, but in the next few days.

'You're abandoning us! I can't believe it.'

She carried the tea tray out to the steps and called down to Adam, 'Matt says he's leaving us for good! We have to stop him.'

'You're leaving?' Adam was sitting at a small round table under a tree, his legs outstretched. Lydia and Jasmine were lying on sunbeds a few feet away. He dipped his fingers in his glass of water and flicked it at them. 'Fuck off, Dad,' Lydia said sleepily. Jasmine's shoulder blades sprang together. She looked up at him, her mouth quivering. He laughed quietly at the back of his throat. And then, returning his eyes to me, said, 'Why are you leaving?'

I sat down. 'Work, meetings, bits and bobs.'

'Ooh, get you.'

'Did you have a chance to read my screenplay yet?' I said. 'I'm longing for your thoughts.'

'Yeah, yeah. I'm going to get to it.'

Celia laid the tray on the table and pulled up a third chair. 'I'm sure there's no rush,' she said reassuringly. 'You're not going *now*. This *minute*.' She poured tea out of the big brown teapot and handed me a cup. I took a sip.

'We're escaping for a day tomorrow, me and the girls. I met up the other night with an old school friend who's staying up the coast and, as we can't use the pool, she's invited us to spend the day with her at her hotel. Adam's refusing to accompany us.'

Adam rolled his eyes. 'Her husband's so pompous.'

'It's just a bite of lunch. I'm not asking you to move in with them.'

'It's still a no.' He caught my eye then and his expression was so lugubrious I couldn't help but laugh. After a moment, he laughed too. When he stopped, he kept looking at me, his head on one side, his mouth in a lopsided smile. There was appeal in his eyes, embarrassment, even guilt. I felt my heart and my stomach lurch. Maybe it would be OK – all of it. I'd sort things out with Rey. Adam and I would muddle on. This was just a blip. Marriages had blips. The good ones were like heartbeats, sometimes things went a little awry – arrhythmia, palpitations. But then they settled. Adam and Celia's marriage would survive. *Our* friendship would survive. We'd all go back to London and things would return to normal.

Celia was still chatting away about Karen, how once at school the two of them had climbed out of the bathroom window to meet some boys and been caught running across the quad by 'the head of Geog', who'd said, 'Oy, oy, oy, young ladies, no way, José,' and how all these years later it's how they always greet each other. 'Oy, oy, oy, Karen/Oy, oy, oy, Celia.'

'Anyway,' she went on, 'it'll be fun. Please come, Adam? They do a set menu for lunch and a great cocktail, apparently.'

'No way, José,' he said. 'My morning swim, maybe a walk. I want to sort the pool out one way or another.'

'When will the water be a normal colour?' Lydia asked. 'It's so annoying.'

'Not long. I can't rush it – the chemicals are basically poisonous.'

'It's good to have a break from the pool,' Celia said. 'You feel freer in the sea, don't you? Do you think it takes us back to the womb?'

'I'm not sure the womb is somewhere I want to go back to,' I said.

Celia said, 'Anyway, Matt, you can keep an eye on Adam. I don't trust him on his own. He's so reckless – all that hurling himself off rocks. Join him for his morning coffee and swim, won't you?'

Adam looked at me again and I looked at him and he gave a small shrug.

A creak as Jasmine turned on to her back. Dropping my gaze, Adam dipped two fingers in his tea and repeated the flicking thing, aiming for her bare brown stomach. She yelped and slowly moved on her side to face him, flopping her arm protectively over her breasts. She looked at him from under her eyelashes and he looked at her, and I felt the heavy, dark weight of premonition.

It's hard to remember now quite how it felt: the sense that Rey had a godly presence, was all-seeing, all-knowing. I've erased the email, so I can't read it back, but when I opened my laptop on returning from Villa Mimosa and saw his name at the top of my inbox, I felt he was inside my brain, listening to my thoughts, and that this email was in direct response to them. A call and answer, like at mass.

Rey had loved the script; had read it in one sitting, 'gulped it down'; it had problems, sure, and he'd jotted down some suggestions – file attached – but he couldn't wait to discuss it further with me and with Victor. 'Exciting!' the message ended. I should call him, 'to chat'.

He answered after the first ring. Had I looked at his notes? I said I hadn't yet. They were reasonably straightforward, he said, nothing to frighten the horses. He said his main concern was timings, pacing. I agreed that timings could be problematic. I was new to this. 'Me too.' He laughed. 'Me too.'

Rey said other things, too, detailed points about motivation which surprised me. I hadn't thought of him being that thoughtful, but it made me feel he really *got* what I had been trying to do. 'Let's meet soon while it's all fresh!' he said. 'How are you fixed tomorrow morning?'

I said I was supposed to be joining Adam for an early swim.

'Is it important? Can you blow him out? I mean, what do you owe him?'

'Nothing,' I agreed. 'Nothing at all.'

'Because it would be good to put in a proper stretch of time, and the morning is always so much more creative, don't you think? If you came here at ten-ish? And then if anything I have to say inspires you, you could stay here at Arcadia to work. The peace and the view are very energising.'

Dead Heat

I lightly tapped my cheek, still so painful to the touch.

Arcadia, I thought. Until now I'd been scared of the place, repelled by it.

For the first time I was genuinely looking forward to being there.

28

Early the following morning, not wanting to arrive empty handed, I made a quick trip to the shop in Kardamos for baklava.

In the end, it wasn't as quick as I'd intended. Andrea's father had just come out of hospital and I felt I needed to listen to her chat. She had some heavy boxes that needed lifting and I helped her with that too. Before I left she took my hand and, patting it, said, 'You're a good man. You ever need a favour, you come to me.'

Cutting it fine, I was hot and breathless as I hiked the drive up to Arcadia. The gate was open and so was the front door, but I rang the bell anyway. My hairline was wet with sweat; I could feel it collecting in my armpits. I stood back to try and catch a breeze, fill my lungs with air. My heart pounded in my chest. I realised I was trembling. It was a big moment. I wasn't a conduit for other people. I possessed something worthwhile of my own. Today could change my life.

I heard the soft shuffle of Rey's footsteps on the marble floor and he opened the door, wearing brown espadrilles and his trademark tight brown shorts. He beckoned to me to come in and clapped me on the back. 'Good man,' he said, when I handed him the baklava. 'You shouldn't have.'

He checked out my eye, said it looked worse if anything – 'Quite a shiner' – then, seeing the emotion in my face, gave me a proper hug. I got a whiff of aftershave – it smelt of expensive leather, or the inside of a confessional. I thought about Celia in his arms, felt once more overwhelmed, and had to swallow to stop myself from retching.

Once he'd released me, he led me through the house to what he called our 'workstation': a sleek elm table in the room where the disco had been. The wide glass doors were open, and air from outside lifted the edges of a lined paper notebook. A jug of water, ice and lemon slices floating, sat next to two glasses. The printout of my screenplay was sitting there piled neatly next to a Sony laptop. The air smelt of fig and cedar. A young woman in tan shorts and a white polo was dispatched to make me a cappuccino, and when she brought it back, the baklava had been plated up next to it, on a little round tray.

I drank down a glass of water; then I took a sip of cappuccino; the sweetness of the milk made me feel sick. I thought about Adam's penchant for strong coffee, the thermos he'd have taken down to the beach. I laid the cup back clumsily and some of the foam spilt. 'I'm sorry,' I said. 'I'm all over the place.'

Rey smiled.

'It's just your enthusiasm. Your support. It's a long time since anyone . . .' My voice caught at the back of my throat. I shook my head. 'Sorry.'

He smiled again and I bent my head to bring my laptop out of my bag. I had to pull myself together. What would he be thinking of me? My laptop creaked as I fumbled to open it. He put his phone face down on the table in front of him. Once again, I noticed how delicate his fingers were. He didn't open his laptop and I wondered if he was having second thoughts. I think I must have wondered out loud because he said he was 'super psyched' and he'd spoken to Victor, who couldn't wait to get me in the writers' room. He felt his notes were self-explanatory and what he'd recommend was that now I went through them and had a proper think, see if I agreed. I'd be perfectly happy working here, wouldn't I? Wasn't he right, it was just the best place to let one's creative juices fly?

For all this, the engagement he'd displayed on the phone wasn't quite there, and I fished a bit – 'But you do think it's good?' and 'Are you sure we're not just wasting our time?' – hungry for the high, the positive affirmation that I'd felt the day before. 'Yes, yes,' he said, and, 'Of course.'

And then he tapped the printout with the tips of his fingers. 'You know, it's *your* support I'm grateful for. You've been such a good friend to both Celia and me. It would have been impossible without you. And you were so understanding about the whole Marc Ashley business. I'm grateful for that.'

The 'Marc Ashley' *business*? And what did he mean: *understanding*?

I looked at his fingers on the printout and I looked at his face and the last part of me that had been soft and hopeful hardened. It was no use pretending. This wasn't about my value as a writer. I thought back to his interest – first putting me in touch with Victor; and then offering to put up some money – both times I'd been asking too many questions, and both times he'd thrown me off track. It was a negotiation, a transaction. It always had been.

Leaning back in his chair, he said, 'So I hear Celia's out for the whole day?'

He can't have noticed the stiffness in my jaw. 'Yes. Visiting a friend up the coast.'

'And Adam refused to go with her?' He shook his head, tutting slightly. 'If she were mine, I wouldn't let her out of my sight.'

I didn't plan what I said next. 'She's never going to be *yours*.'

I meant because she wasn't a possession; she could never belong to anyone; only herself.

Misunderstanding, his eyes darted to mine, his lips tight. I saw the saliva stretch white in the corners. 'Why? What's she said?'

'It's over,' I said. The lie filled up my mouth.

'What do you mean "It's over"?'

'Adam knows.'

I felt the power in the room shift. I could say anything.

'What do you mean, he *knows*?' He was frowning now.

'She loves *him*,' I said. 'He'll forgive her like she's always forgiven him, and they'll carry on as if nothing has happened.' It felt as real as if I believed it myself. 'You should steer clear for a while.'

'Steer *clear*?' He rocked back in his chair, like someone bracing for impact.

'Yeah. Stay away from them both. For your own safety.'

He bit his lip. 'Is he coming for me?' he said. 'Will he hurt me?'

I lifted my hand to the bruise on my cheek. 'I wouldn't put it past him.'

'Is she safe, do you think? Would he hurt *her*?' He was scratching the back of his neck, his cheek, one side of his scalp.

'I don't know.' I spoke very slowly, as if each word were painful.

'Fucking hell.'

He stood up abruptly then and, leaving his phone on the table, walked out through the open doors to the terrace. I watched as he disappeared down the steps.

I sat there motionless for quite a few minutes, in shock at my own capabilities. Why had I said what I had? I'd be caught out. I stood up and looked down the steps, but I couldn't see him. I paced the room for a bit, trying to breathe, and then I sat down. He'd left his phone on the table; he wouldn't be long. I opened his email and reread his notes. He felt the main character needed a trigger event before the blood bath of the penultimate scene. I got it; he was right. I heard myself laugh. I could still get what I wanted from him. He'd been playing me, but I could play him back. Fuck it. I could be as bad as the rest of them.

I forced down my coffee and managed a piece of baklava and had another glass of water. Then I stood up and walked over to the doors and again looked across the upper terrace and over the lip of it, down to the pool. No sign of Rey.

I went back into the room, picked up both his phone and mine, and then walked down on to the terrace. Unsure which direction he'd taken, I took the path around to the front of the house – the quad bikes were all there – and then retraced my steps and climbed the spiral staircase to the lower terrace and walked along the edge of the pool to the path that wound down to the jetty.

I felt exposed – the sea so huge and empty, the glaring sun and sky, the empty mansion behind me with all its doors and windows open. I took the path to the first bend where Villa Mimosa came into view – it would be empty now: Celia, Lydia and Jasmine on their trip up the coast; Adam down at the cove. Nothing here but the lonely cries of birds. I kept going until I could see through the trees to the private beach. The sunbeds were empty, the tender bobbing at the end of the jetty, the sand newly raked, the breeze ruffling the loose ties on the parasols.

At the edge of the water was a small bundle of clothes.

I ran the rest of the way. When my feet sank into sand, I

could see the whole bay, and out there, halfway across now, a figure churned.

Disbelief first, panic, and then terror. What was he doing? Where had he gone? And then fear shifted sideways, replaced by a sort of admiration as I watched him plough through the water. He was doing crawl, arm over arm, face down. He was a dart, a missile. Straight line. A strong, confident swimmer, as you'd expect from a 'natural athlete' – five-a-side football, *water* polo. I took my phone out of my pocket and filmed him – I'd show Celia the evidence – keeping my eye on the surface of the sea until I could no longer distinguish a head from a buoy. I raised the lens to the muddle of rocks, imagining I could see Adam. But what with the sun, the shadows, the crags, it was impossible to tell the difference between a tree and a person.

The time on Rey's phone said 10.45 a.m. when I walked back into Arcadia. I'd been alone for about half an hour. The house was quiet and seemed deserted, so I carried the tray with my coffee cup and the plate of baklava through various rooms until I found the kitchen tucked away in the basement. The woman in the white shirt and tan shorts was tidying up the fridge; she looked appalled at the sight of me. 'No, no, no,' she said, taking the tray from me, but I said it was no trouble. I went all the way upstairs then to the top floor, and checked the cupboard where I'd found the trainers and the other clothes. They'd gone.

Back at the 'workstation', I stuffed my laptop and Rey's

copy of my screenplay into my bag, and left the house, walking quickly down the drive, and reaching the main road a couple of minutes later.

There was a split second here when I almost turned right and headed towards Villa Mimosa. I wanted to put distance between myself and whatever was happening between those two men. I wanted to play for time, to be around people. *Normal* people. It was more than a premonition, as I marched towards Kardamos, it was dread – for Rey, for Adam, for Celia, for myself. Something horrible was about to happen, or already had. Ghosts roam the Mani in the hottest hour of the day in summer. If their mortal predecessors have been killed by an enemy, the ghosts wail for revenge.

The sweat poured off me; the sun blazed overhead. All I could think was to keep moving. Cars passed me, including one laden with kids, waving through the back window. I held up my thumb – I thought they might stop – and their faces creased; the joke was on me. It usually was.

In the village, I went back to the shop, hoping to see Andrea but she wasn't there. I had a quick distracted chat with Georgios, her son, and then headed to the harbour where I gave directions to a honeymooning couple who had mislaid their hotel. Too sick to eat, I found myself possessed of an overwhelming need for something I hadn't felt since my father died, and my feet led me through the back streets of the village past the tower where Sara had stayed, to the stone chapel. I turned the handle in the door, expecting it to be locked, but it opened. Inside was a small altar, a chequerboard floor, and rows of ladder-back chairs. I lit a candle and knelt, my head bowed, for what felt like a long time. I thought about Rey going to find Adam, the iterations of that, of what might be happening. There was no going back now, no *carrying on*. It was over, my relationship with the Murphys and indeed with him.

I became aware, after a while, of a human smell and the sound of breathing. When I raised my eyes, a man was standing above me. He said something to me in Greek and then, in English, asked if I was OK. He had a short beard, almond-shaped eyes and large knobbly hands. He was wearing a thick black robe, but it was his manner more than his clothes, or the heavy scent of them, that told me he was a priest.

I told him I'd made a mistake, done something I should never have done, and he asked if I wanted to pray with him. I shook my head, remembering the priest behind the wooden grille in the confessional at the church when I was growing up, the tap of his beads, the terrifying murmur that would emanate from the back of his throat, how you'd think that murmuring would never end.

He sat on the chair next to me then and asked if I had come far and if there was anything I would like from him. I told him I'd been thinking about my father, who was long dead but whose shadow lay over me, and the man whose body was found in the gully up to the mountain. He nodded, cupping his hands together, and said both of them were at rest, and spoke about how, for forty days after a death, the soul of the departed wanders the earth, visiting people and places they have loved.

'Why would they do that?' I said.

Dead Heat

He smiled, as if the question had surprised him. 'We are all restless,' he said. 'We are all searching. It takes faith to bring us peace.'

I got up to go. Behind me, as I pushed open the door, I could the mumble of his voice as he blessed me.

29

It was 4.30 p.m. when I walked past the entrance to Arcadia; I turned my head away to avoid looking up the drive, at the long stretch of black tarmac, and a few metres beyond took the back way down to the cottage. At one point I went wrong and had to scramble over piles of stones and push back the limbs of thorny trees to rejoin the trail. I checked my phone repeatedly, as I had all afternoon. No messages. No missed calls.

    Branwell was waiting for me at the door, both her kittens asleep in a mat of dried leaves under the fig. She had a small scabby area above her eye and I coaxed her inside with the tuna. She was thinner than she'd been, her nipples distended. I poured her a saucer of milk and she lapped at it. I thought about what Celia had said about my untapped reserve of love and I felt emotional, thinking about her and especially, I suppose, Adam. I felt lonelier than I'd felt for a long time. The cat sat and washed herself in the doorway, and I sat on the stone floor, with my back against the oven, and watched her.

I walked down to the bay at one point, stood with my hands in my pockets, staring across at Arcadia, thinking back to the party we had all gone to. It looked deserted now. Our little bay was peaceful, too. Nothing on the ground – no blood, no scuffle marks. Should I have looked more closely, peered here and there, looked under rocks, gone to investigate that pile of seaweed? Maybe I should have done. But I didn't. I've learnt there's no point going over and over these things. You can torture yourself with regrets.

I had a shower and, when I came out, I'd missed a call from Celia. I stared at it for a long time.

I decided not to ring, but to go up to the house to see her in person, which I'm glad about now.

She was in the kitchen, on a high stool at the island, drinking tea from a mug that read 'Coffee Tea Biscuits' and doing Wordle on her phone. Around her the house was silent.

She looked up when she heard me in the doorway. I didn't know what I was expecting, but she just looked puzzled. 'Are you on your own? I thought you were with Adam.'

I told her I hadn't seen him all day, that I'd been with Rey.

'*Rey*? He's not answering my calls either. Both my men have abandoned me.'

I told her Rey was interested in financing my TV series.

'Your *TV series*?' She smiled before she could stop herself. 'That's nice.'

I kept my gaze steady. 'We were supposed to meet up again this afternoon, but you're right, he's gone AWOL.'

'Oh God.' She pressed her hand to her mouth. 'I hope they're not off somewhere together. Can you imagine?'

She fired off a text and then smiled at me brightly. 'Can I get you anything, Matt?' I could tell then she wanted rid. Always over the years I'd felt we had something special, that I was as important to her as she was to me. The moments when I felt her friendship was consciously given, like a gift or an act of charity, were, to her credit, relatively rare.

I kept her talking – asked about her day, whether the girls had enjoyed themselves – she'd dropped them in the village, she said, to meet those Salford boys. As the time ticked by, I watched the doubt begin to flicker in her eyes. She picked up her phone and dialled a number, held it to her ear. 'Nope. Still straight to voicemail. Oh Matt.' She laughed, and then shook her head. 'Did Adam say anything about going for a walk?' She looked once more at her phone. 'And Rey's probably working. Anyway . . .' Her smile faded.

It was another hint for me to leave – she was hoping Rey was about to ring her back and they'd have time to meet up, make the most of Adam's absence. Or maybe she just wanted a few minutes to finish Wordle, eat chocolate, *pray*, whatever it was she did when she was alone.

I told her about my conversation with the priest.

'You've been to church,' she said. 'Good for you.'

I said, 'If there has been some personal conflagration between the two of them, I'd back Adam in a heartbeat.'

'Don't.'

'Any day.'

Her phone chirruped, and she picked it up quickly. 'Lydia,' she said. 'She and Jas are staying out for supper.'

I checked my phone too. Still nothing.

We talked about calling the police – at what point in the distant future it wouldn't be stupid to ring.

She went quiet for a bit and then she said, 'You did meet for coffee this morning, though, didn't you? You did swim?'

I was rocking very slightly back and forth and it must have looked as though I was nodding because when I told her we hadn't actually swum, she looked as if I'd played a trick, as if all this time I'd purposefully hidden the truth from her.

She stood up. 'I'm going down to the cove to check. You'll think I'm being stupid, but I just . . . I hate those rocks. I mean, I am being stupid, aren't I?'

I was reassuring. I'd been to the beach that afternoon and—

'Did you look all over? Did you check where he dives in by the rocks?'

She was being paranoid, I told her, though we could wander back down there together to be on the safe side, take a couple of cold beers with us, watch the sun set while we were at it. It would be romantic.

'I don't want to watch the sun set, Matt.'

'No. Of course.' I stood up. 'Let's go.'

*

I want to write about the walk down to the beach. I want to describe the surface of the path, and the light flickering in the olive grove. I want to dwell on the temperature, the way the air held all the concentrated heat of the summer, and yet also a hint of its decline. I want to go back to the kitchen, to recount more of our conversation: the fanciness of her friend's hotel, and the smallness of the portions at lunch, and how she'd forgotten how smug Karen could be, how *brilliantly* her kids were always doing and how, of course, Celia was pleased for her, but did their achievements have to be thrust down her throat? (I'm not sure that conversation even happened. It might have been a different hotel, a different friend.) I want us to have stopped at the door to the hut, to have played with the kittens and pulled out chairs and drunk wine and for Adam and Rey to have strolled up the track, towels slung across their shoulders, all wide grins, and for them to have joined us.

I want to delay our arrival at the rocks. I can't bear it, now I've got this far.

We walked in silence. She was twisting her lips, biting one corner; when she saw me looking, she shook her head. 'I'm being stupid,' she said again. 'He's gone for a walk. He's lost his phone. He's in a bar.' The path to the cove ended and the rocks rose ahead; to our right was the short scramble down, but Adam's diving-off point was a few metres ahead. The rock rose smoothly and then became more jagged, ending in a series of pock-marked crags.

'Beach first?' I said.

She shook her head. 'Please, Matt. Humour me.'

She turned her back, closing her eyes, waiting for me to go and look. She laughed, lightly. It was still almost a joke, as if I were checking under the bed for a monster.

I took the first few steps and then turned. She hadn't moved. She was standing with her head bowed, not daring to look.

I turned back to face the sea; the water below me was a very dark blue; but glittering on the horizon. The sun was low, in my eyes. My feet slipped; my brogues had leather soles: stupid. My legs were shaking. I checked to see she wasn't looking and got down on my hands and knees and crawled the last few feet until I was close to the edge and then I lay flat on my front and wriggled forwards until I could go no further.

I peered down.

Cones of blackness, shafts of light, shoals of fish, pools of the purest turquoise. The cliff to the left changed colour as it entered the water; you could see the whole shape of it, the formation of land, a skirt of rock with a circle of debris. Waves broke against a single rock, which stuck from the surface of the sea, but here, straight down beneath me, the water moved gently, stirred back and forth, as if it were breathing. In places the water was so still you could see all the way to the bottom, each pebble magnified. Nothing. Just the quick movement of fish; twirls of weed; the light shifting. Nothing. Nothing.

The air left my lungs. Something sharp cut into my chin. I closed my eyes. One push of my feet and I'd be propelled over, head first. It wasn't even that high. I imagined the shock of the water, the silence as the surface closed above me.

'Matt!' Her voice was shrill, closer than it had been. 'Is it OK?'

I made to turn, to call yes, there's nothing, and then, pressing my palms down, I wriggled to the left, to where a crevasse in the rock gaped, and pushing my chest forward I hung my head right over. With the shift of perspective, the water suddenly seemed very close.

'What, Matt? What?'

I felt the noise leave my throat. I could hear it break the air. The sea curled back on itself; the sun withdrew. I managed to articulate the word 'Don't' and I could hear her calling my name and then his with increasing urgency.

He was on his back, his hands moving in and out, towards his body and away, to keep himself afloat, and his eyes were staring up at me. He was looking into my soul. His mouth curled in that lopsided smile. He'd waited for me. He knew me. He knew what I was. What I'd done, what I *hadn't* done, my sin of omission.

I was shouting and sobbing and urgently – so he would respond and close his mouth because it was open and water was getting in – screaming his name now.

Celia was still saying my name, his name, over and over. Her voice was further away.

He was alive, shaking his head, his hair, his body vibrating. A seabird fluttered on the surface, and there was a dart of movement; all the tiny fish in his hair and his mouth scattered.

I forced myself to look behind me. Celia was curled in a ball, rocking back and forwards, saying no over and over again. She staggered to her feet. 'I can't look. I'm going to look. I've got to see him.'

I crawled towards her and we collided halfway; I grabbed her wrists and tried to stop her from getting closer, but she wailed and pushed at me, fought back. My feet slipped, and I fell to my knees. She came with me; her head sank on to my shoulder, her hands braced against my chest, and she sobbed that it was my fault, I'd told her I'd keep him safe, I'd promised.

She said, teeth gritted, 'Bring him to me. Go down there. Get him out.'

But now I was the one sobbing, rocking. I shook my head. 'I can't. I can't.'

Time passed. I was aware of Celia talking and crying and then on her phone, talking and crying into it. I could hear her body shaking in her breath, and ages later the high-pitched drone of a boat leapfrogging across the bay and then shouts. I heard Celia take His name in vain: 'Oh God, oh God, oh God,' and other voices, too, the dark shapes through my fingers of men in wetsuits, and though I didn't move from my spot, from the direction of the noises and voices, the buzz of the engine and the slopping of water against rock, I knew they were doing what I hadn't, what I couldn't, which was get around the point, and under the overhang, and bring up Adam's body. That beautiful, damaged boy. That difficult, infuriating, extraordinary, complicated man. My friend.

After that, there was clattering and shouting and crashing – later I learnt they pumped his chest – and the whirr of a circling helicopter overhead and finally, down on the beach, another boat: the clank and creak of a different, bigger anchor. More voices: Greek this time. I was aware that Rey was here and, with the confidence of a man who had no enemies he couldn't deal with, was taking over the scene, ordering a blanket for Celia, speaking to the police, telling people what to do, where to go.

No one came near me. I was useless. I thought I would never stop weeping. I wanted to die up there on that rock, for worms to eat me and birds to peck out my eyes.

30

In that first week, while Adam's body lay in the morgue at Kalamata, Celia agitated to know it had been sudden, that he'd died instantly, that he hadn't suffered. She asked it over and over, and it was all I could do not to scream. The house was full of people – milling and crying, picking things up and putting them down, aimlessly cleaning – and everyone gave the same unqualified (both senses) reassurance: '*Of course.*' But her brother John, someone who'd never been much of a fan of Adam, muttered while we were emptying the bins that he thought it couldn't have been instant: bodies that enter face first usually float because the air inside the lungs has no chance to escape, maintaining buoyancy. He squished the black bag down. 'And he'd sunk, hadn't he?'

I nodded.

'So he had water in his lungs; he'd have breathed in after he hit his head. It's drowning that will have killed him – so not technically instant.'

I thought how much I hated this man with his pious ear-hairs and his overlong fingernails, his half knowledge hewn from Sunday-night television dramas.

He said, 'Mind you, even so it would still have been pretty quick. Sorry.' Noticing my expression, he put his hand on my wrist. 'He's at peace now.'

I let his loathsome hand rest for a moment before I flicked it off.

I'd been with Celia for the formal identification, and he hadn't looked at peace. They'd closed his eyes and put a cloth over the top of his forehead, but he was still a brutal sight. I was going to write unrecognisable, though of course he was, that was the point. But the livid colour and bulbous texture of the skin on his arms, and neck, and upper torso – the bits above the sheet anyway – were no colours or textures he'd ever had in life. He was battered, marbled, speckled with nicks and abrasions; though, as I told Celia, his spirit had left before the damage. It was just the sea, and the grip of those strong men, Rey's men, when they'd hoisted him on to the boat. It was just his body, I said to be clear. His soul was with the Lord.

Her knees buckled at the mention of Rey. I lifted her up off the floor and carried her to a chair in the next-door room. Whether she listened, or absorbed anything I said, I'm not sure, but I hope my voice was soothing. All that mattered to me – in that weird, agonising period of waiting – was to protect her.

Who knew if what I said helped? Was heaven a comfort to her? Or was it a torment? Did she believe God was waiting for Adam with open arms? Was the dark part of her grief not just guilt, but terror? Was this God's punishment? Did she feel *seen*?

The police came but nobody probed – not yet. The assumptions were too obvious, too tempting. The state of Adam's body – the catastrophic head injury – was consistent with a misjudged dive. No obvious enemies. Suicide was unthinkable; he wasn't 'the type'. (People kept saying that, as if there *was* a type.) He was in his swim trunks, and that pile of seaweed I'd noticed on the other side of the cove turned out to be his things: a towel, a box of sugary *loukoumia*, half eaten, and an almost empty thermos of coffee: two cups. (Was one of them for me? *Had he been expecting me?*) And if there was no witness to the event, there was a witness to a pattern of behaviour.

'I knew this would happen,' Celia kept saying. 'I warned him over and over again. But he wouldn't listen. I *told* him.'

I held my breath, my nerve. This strange semi-life wouldn't last. At some point, a medical examiner would distinguish between injuries received before and after death; suspicions would be raised. A head injury sustained by an impact with a hard object, while standing, would present differently to one sustained after travelling upside down through air. I knew from my recent research that submersion in water corrupted evidence, but defence wounds? Skin under the nails? Blood splatter patterns? Eventually, questions would be asked, and

I'd tell them what I knew, that Rey had surprised Adam on the beach. Maybe they'd argued, or maybe Rey had approached Adam from behind, maybe even as he prepared to dive, and hit him with a rock: one with a flat surface matching the submerged rocks where the body was found. He'll have hurled the rock to join a million other rocks at the bottom of the sea and thrown Adam's body head first down after it. It was in many ways 'the perfect crime'. I should know because it was in my screenplay, the one only Rey had read.

I waited and said nothing. I'm trying to remember if I was scared – whether I worried that, if I said too much, Rey would come for me. It's odd, but I was more scared of Celia, of the ugliness of her grief, of needing to protect her from knowing she had played any part in Adam's death. Better she discovered when she was calmer, to reach that knowledge by degrees. Though, even as I write this, I'm aware I'm trying to twist my motivation to paint myself in a better light. *I* felt guilty. *I* felt implicated. I'd lied to Rey three times. Firstly, that Adam had raped his sister when there was no real evidence that he had; secondly, that Adam had beaten me up because he thought I was sleeping with Celia; and thirdly, that Celia had told him everything about her affair with Rey. I'd consciously fanned the flames of Rey's fear and resentment. You could argue, and I did long into the night, that I'd driven him to it.

Rey steered clear of both of us. He was there that first day – I remember catching him coming down the stairs from her room. After that he knew to stay away. It was over between them; of course it was. Categorically over – even before his arrest, and God only knew how Celia would respond to that when it happened. For now, it was all about Adam. She lay curled on her bed, talking about him incessantly: what a wonderful father he was; that time he took her to Rome and they threw coins in the Trevi fountain; how he often said he knew he wanted to marry her the first day they met. He was a man resurrected; we'd borne the cross for him and now he reigned above us, arms outstretched.

My role was as holy spirit: invisible, unmistakable, indispensable. I stayed at Celia's side, listening, prompting, agreeing. I added myself to the insurance for the Beetle and did the shopping and took the recycling to the village bins. In that first week, I cooked all their meals; I ferried people to and from the airport, including Jasmine who had quickly booked an easyJet flight home. My godson James arrived back – to support Celia, I suppose, though I found his presence more of a hindrance than a help. More mouths to feed; plus neither James nor Lydia, who had delayed her return to school, seemed to know what to do with themselves; they spent as much time sunbathing as crying. Still, I did what I could to counsel and comfort and support. 'Thanks, man,' James said after one of my Adam-centred anecdotes. 'Good to know.' Next to me on the sofa, woozy after a bottle of wine, Celia rested her head on my shoulder.

She couldn't bear to be alone, and at night, I lay next to her on their bed: her under the sheet; me, fully clothed, on top. It was at her request. She said she needed the presence of another 'living human'. I thought back to what the priest had said about dead humans haunting the people they loved for forty days and wondered if Adam was there on the bed between us. She slept fitfully, and I stayed awake as much as I could, listening out for the change in her breathing. When she woke, which she did every hour or two, the shock of remembering would hit her as if for the first time, and I held her while she sobbed.

The hardest thing was keeping my own grief to myself.

At the end of that week, the first week of September, everything changed. The first disruption was the arrival of Celia's friend Mary, a snobbish, bustling woman with thick blunt fingers and bushy iron hair, who, like many plain people, put value in efficiency above charm. She'd changed the sheets and was unpacking her own things when I first came upon her – laying out a huge navy nightdress on the pillow where I'd slept. Seeing me in the doorway, she came towards me. 'Ah, you must be the lodger,' she said. 'Don't forget this.' She was holding my toothbrush between her finger and thumb, letting it dangle, like something that repelled her.

She seemed determined to get rid of me, or at least to usurp me. She hired her own car and did fresh shopping – throwing away my tinned fish and bags of economy pasta and filling the fridge with parcels of raw meat, obscenely swollen aubergine and great crates of Diet Coke (an addiction that seems to afflict many who struggle with their weight).

She took over the kitchen entirely – within hours cooking

a quiche with her own pastry and a complicated moussaka, cleaning each utensil after she'd used it. 'We need to keep her fed,' she said, as if Celia were a caged animal. She cleared away my tea mug when I was still drinking from it. She forgot to lay a place for me at lunch. Stumbling upon me sobbing under the loggia, she said, 'Come on now, Matthew, pull yourself together. This is helping nobody.'

I refused to budge and, that afternoon, I perched on the end of Celia's sunbed as she lay there in her fugue state. Her eyes followed Mary as she swept the terrace, or folded towels. 'Mary,' she cried fretfully, 'is there any cold water in the fridge?' Later, 'Mary, have you got one of your magic pills?' And Mary would bring one or other to her and lay her palm against her forehead and rearrange her pillow and tell her she was being 'a brilliantly brave girl'.

At one point, I said, 'You don't have to be brilliant, you know. You're allowed to be fucking sad.'

Celia recoiled slightly. 'Oh Matt. Please don't.'

That first night, back in the hut in my single bed, I didn't sleep at all, so alert was I to the silence, like a soldier feeling pain in a missing limb. I knew I should sleep – it was my chance to catch up, to be strong for whatever task, emotional or physical, I was needed for the following day – but the pressure, the ensuing panic, made it even harder. I began to think I would go mad for lack of sleep. I went outside and filled my lungs and looked up at the sky, at all those bright puncture marks. Distant dogs barked. A pilot owl let out its beeping cry. I didn't think it could be true that Adam was revisiting places he knew and loved. I felt my friend's absence acutely: an empty void, a space that should have been filled with his noise and body, his bullying exuberance. If he *were* walking the earth, he wouldn't be able to resist making his presence felt. And I couldn't feel it. All I could feel was a yawning hole.

31

I hadn't been worried when, by the end of the first week, no update had been issued by the police. In Greece a post-mortem is mandatory after any violent or sudden death. It was just a matter of time.

Week two the silence began to niggle; I hated keeping quiet. But still I assumed the delay was all part of due process.

And then one morning towards the end of that week, having overslept, I arrived later than usual at Villa Mimosa. A delivery van was leaving, which I thought nothing of (people constantly sent things: fruit, flowers, bath oils). A couple of new parcels were sitting in the hall, and Mary was in the kitchen trying to wrangle an enormous bunch of flowers – bright orchid-like blooms amid palm-like foliage – into a glass jug. Acres of ribbon and cellophane covered the island top and, with the pretence of clearing up, I took a look at the card. To my horror, it read simply: 'All my love, Rey'.

I scrunched up the card and took a step towards Mary. I wanted to take the jug of flowers from her. I wanted to smash it to the floor, to stamp on the petals; anything to stop Celia from seeing them. Why was Rey making contact? What was he *doing*? Mary tried to get around me to reach into the cupboard for a different vessel – the one she'd chosen was too small. I smelt the heat on her.

'*More* flowers,' I said.

'I know. Aren't they lovely? So extravagant. I bet they cost an actual bomb.'

'I'm not sure,' I said. 'Bit vulgar for my taste.'

She laughed, not particularly kindly, and said, 'Lucky they're not for you then.'

She found a pottery urn and took it to the tap and filled it with water. She took a while sorting the stems. I was still holding Rey's card. When she had considered her arrangement from various angles and seemed happy, she put the urn on the table and said: 'Listen, Matthew, I know you've been an absolute godsend, but as they're heading home soon it might be better to give them a bit of space.' She wrinkled her nose, sympathetic but firm. 'Let them come together as a family.'

'Celia says she's not going home until they release his body,' I said, moving away from her, 'and that won't be for some time yet. She's going to need a lot of support when that happens, so I think I'll hang around for now.' I smiled. 'Thanks all the same.'

She put her hands on her waist. 'No,' she said. 'They're releasing the body on Monday. Thank God, because this limbo's no good to anyone.'

'They can't release the body,' I said patiently. 'There has to be a post-mortem.'

'There *has* been a post-mortem,' she said even more patiently. 'It happened this week.'

'No, it hasn't.'

She sighed, her tight smile indicating I was straining her nerves. 'Yes, it has. And that is why they are releasing the body. Now, you get out of my way; I want to get lunch on.'

I quickly went upstairs – Celia generally lay in until midday – but the bedroom was empty. She'd been there recently; it smelt sour; flies circled in the slow waft of the fan; tissues were balled on the floor. Mary, I was sure, had got it wrong. I plumped the wrinkled pillows, picked up wet towels, smoothed the covers. I opened the windows – the big one facing across to Arcadia first and then the smaller one, which looked down over the garden. James was in the pool and Lydia was on a sunbed reading a magazine.

Back downstairs, I looked in the drawing room, and out the front, and took the side path round to the pool – avoiding Mary.

Lydia looked up when she saw me. Her eyes were red in the corners, and her lips looked chafed and sore. 'Matt,' she said. 'You look like you're having a bad day too. It keeps hitting you, doesn't it?'

I told her it did; and had she seen her mother?

'She went for a walk earlier. I think she's up there now.'

She pointed up the steps to the loggia – a place Celia had, until now, avoided because of the steep drop to the rocks: the reminder.

The cicadas were quieter up there; the sea murmured. Insects clung to the underside of white trumpet-like flowers.

I saw her before she saw me. She was sitting at the table, staring out at the horizon. She'd washed her hair – the first time in days – and she was wearing that blue kaftan with the pink tassels. She pressed her palm into her chest where the skin was wrinkled brown and rubbed it back and forth; then closed her eyes and tipped back her head.

Abruptly, she opened them. 'Matt. Don't creep up on me like that. You made me jump.'

'Sorry,' I said, sitting next to her. 'Just checking you're OK.'

'I'm OK,' she said, but sighed in a shuddering way.

I said it was nice to see her getting some air, and she said she'd needed to get out of the house, that Mary could be 'a lot'. I agreed and suggested she dropped hints about feeling claustrophobic, wanting her own space, to which she nodded and said, 'Thing is, she means well. You all do.'

I didn't *love* that, and I let it sit with me for a minute, before I said, 'Listen, Mary seems to think they're about to release Adam's body.'

'Yes. Next Monday, I think.'

'How do you know?' I felt I was talking gently, like to a child. 'Who told you?'

'I spoke to, you know, whatshisname.'

'Who?'

She pressed her palm to her forehead as if it was irritating of me to make her think this hard. 'The officer who came to the house.'

'Christos.'

'Yes, that's it. He said the next few days.'

'What about the *autopsy*?'

She edged a bit away, twisting to look at me from a greater distance. 'Matt. Can you not be so intense? It's good that it's over. We can get on with everything.'

'But have they actually done an autopsy?'

'I assume so. Accidental death.'

It came out as a cry. 'No.'

She jerked her head in alarm. 'What? Why's that a problem. Rey said it was never going to be anything else.'

'Rey?' I said. 'You've spoken to Rey?'

'Yes. He came up this morning. Don't look at me like that. He hasn't been replying to my texts because he lost his phone. But he's got a new one now. Did you see the flowers he gave me? They're amazing.'

She read something in my face, because she added, 'What, Matt?'

'And Rey said there had been an autopsy?'

'Yes. He said it was only paperwork left now. He took me out for a walk – such a good idea. He's not sleeping either. It was lovely to be out – the sun was coming up. It was good to remember that it still does, that there is still beauty in the world.'

'I'm sure.'

'Which is why, after he left, I came to look at this view. You know, I've been feeling so angry about it – hating it because of what happened. But Adam loved it here, didn't he, Matt? He loved it.'

I nodded. 'He loved this view.'

'And I was thinking maybe we should scatter his ashes here. You know. After all.'

'His *ashes*? What do you mean? You want to cremate him?'

Over previous days, with her brother and the children, we had talked about the funeral. The readings and the hymns were still to be finalised, but the funeral itself was set in stone: the private chapel in Norfolk, the burial in the family plot.

'I've just been talking to Rey. He reminded me Adam called this his spiritual home.'

I wasn't sure what to do with my face. I wanted to be sick. I managed to say, 'A cremation's not very Catholic.'

'Adam wasn't very Catholic,' she countered.

'You must do what you see fit.'

'What's the matter with you? Why are you being all weird?'

'I don't think you should be taking Rey's advice on this. I don't think you should be talking to him.'

'Surely we can be friends.'

'He doesn't want to be your *friend*, Celia.'

'I know.' She smiled sadly. 'He says he'll wait for me when – if – I'm ready. Next year, the year after.' She lifted one shoulder, almost coyly.

'Celia,' I said. I was finding it hard not to get up and scream.

'Just be nice, Matt.'

'I *am* nice.'

She looked at me for a beat. 'Look, life goes on. We will feel better one day. Both of us. It seems impossible now, but we will.'

I nodded.

She added, 'By the way, Rey says he's longing to get back to work with you on your screenplay when life goes back to normal.'

32

I couldn't think straight when I got back to the cottage. My brain was all over the place, the panic of the powerless, the surging injustice of the ineffectual. Rey had bought his way out of Adam's death, just as he'd bought his way out of Marc Ashley's death. His wealth removed normal restraints. Of course he'd push for a cremation. Incineration would destroy all evidence of foul play. Celia had agreed because, despite Adam's dreadful death, she was still in Rey's thrall.

I'd wanted to stay back, to wait for the police to sort it out. I'd wanted to stay neutral. No one likes a messenger. But sometimes in life you have to get off the fence. *Even if someone is offering to make a film of your screenplay.* Sometimes you have put your neck on the line. Sometimes you have to take a risk.

I rang the police station at Aetolia, and held for a long time before I was finally connected to someone who told me they could neither confirm nor deny that an autopsy had taken place. It was not information that could be given out freely. 'I'm a journalist,' I said, which was a mistake because I was put through to some central press office manned by a voice recorder. I left a message saying I had important information, asking for someone to ring me back.

I ate a sandwich while I waited, after which I felt more myself. I made a plan.

First of all, I rang the mobile number I had for Amira; she was at home at her mum's. I'd rung her after Adam died – I didn't want her to find out about it on social media – and we'd spoken for quite a long time. She got it into her head that it was her fault somehow, that he'd 'passed', as the young seem to want to put it, out of guilt and self-reproach. It took a lot to persuade her it wasn't suicide. This time, she sounded more herself. I asked if she'd made up her mind about the PGCE she'd been considering and told her again how I thought she'd make a good teacher and she said, 'Thanks, Matt,' and, 'You're very kind.' I asked if I could ask her a few questions about Rey and quote her and she agreed; I pressed record on my phone.

After that, I opened a new file on my laptop.

Why a full and thorough post-mortem is needed into the death of Adam Murphy

Adam Murphy's death has been deemed 'accidental', that he hit his head on a rock while diving into the sea at the beach below his house, Villa Mimosa. It should be noted that Adam spent two months of every summer at Villa Mimosa, that he had been coming for his entire married life, and that he had therefore dived into the sea at that exact spot approximately 2,000 times. It would be accurate to say that by now he 'had his eye in'.

It is the author of this paper's contention that he was murdered by Reynash de Souza.

1)   Motive

Reynash de Souza had a history of resentment towards Adam Murphy who had bullied him at school. He had recently become convinced of the fact that, during that period, Murphy had raped his sister and was responsible for her suicide. He was in love with Murphy's wife Celia for whom, for religious reasons, divorce was out of the question. Only death would 'free' her. He had become increasingly paranoid that Murphy was on to him and intended to do him harm.

2)   Opportunity and witness

De Souza was seen by the author swimming across the bay towards the beach the morning of Murphy's accident. Contrary to common belief, de Souza was a strong swimmer (he had played water polo at university level), but had concealed this fact as a means of getting closer to the family. This suggests long-term, and short-term duplicity.

3) *Fake alibi and evidence*

Matt Grimshawe (the author of this document) has been bribed, with the promise of a lucrative television deal, to provide de Souza with an alibi for the day of Murphy's death. Grimshawe (author, as above) witnessed the aforementioned swim, and took a video on his phone as evidence.*

4) *Character witnesses*

Amira Bakshi, who stayed with de Souza this summer as a house guest, has provided verbal corroboration of the fact that de Souza 'hated Adam'. He once urged her 'to ruin him', and said he was 'scum who deserved everything that was coming to him'. **

5) *Previous behaviour*

The circumstances surrounding the death of de Souza's business associate Marc Ashley remain suspicious. De Souza had admitted to concealing evidence – Ashley's trainers as well as other running clothes – and it is strongly to the belief of this document's author that he brought in favours to fake alibis and witnesses the morning of Ashley's 'disappearance'. It would be worth investigating whether any bribery of officials has taken place with regard to both the Ashley investigation and the inquiry into Murphy's death. Also worth searching Arcadia for the trainers and running clothes, last seen in an upstairs cupboard (though these may have since been destroyed).

*Attached

**Full transcript attached

I wasn't thrilled with the tone – I'd aimed for businesslike, and it came across as pompous – but it would do. I forwarded the file to the Lieutenant General of the Hellenic Police in Athens; the chief at Aetolia; Dave Baxter, my former colleague, now at the BBC; and the press office at Scotland Yard.

33

They came for me first. A few days later, early in the morning, crashing outside the cottage, fists banging on the door.

I didn't know the men who stood there, but I tried to speak to them with the Greek I'd learnt as they led me up the path to the vehicle that was waiting on the main road. Celia's friend Mary was standing at the entrance to Villa Mimosa, swigging from a can of Diet Coke. I called out – 'Tell Celia it's OK' – but she didn't answer. Just stared. And swigged.

The drive to Aetolia seemed longer than when I'd hitched – maybe they took a different route. I thought we passed the village where the poisoner had lived, and I started talking, because I was nervous. I said I had sympathy for the poor woman – having partial paralysis and feeling ignored by everyone. The officer next to me, in his twenties with a shaved head, said, 'It's hard to be ignored.' I told him about the conversation I'd had on the bus with her 'niece'; how it was the first time I'd heard suspicions against de Souza. The officer looked sceptical. 'People make a lot of things up,' he said, 'for notoriety.' The car went quiet for a moment, and I said I could imagine, that it must be an occupational hazard. I looked up the word for 'time waster' on Google Translate but I don't think it was a good match, because they laughed.

Coincidentally, Andrea, my good friend from the grocery shop, was coming through the rotating doors of the station as they led me up the steps. She stopped and asked if I was OK. The officer who was holding my elbow tried to steer me towards the door, but she put up her hand. 'This is a good man,' she said to him in Greek. 'You look after him.' Her tone was quite firm, and he loosened his grip like a small boy admonished by his grandmother.

There were a lot of people in the waiting room and in the corridors; it was brightly lit and I lost my sense of direction. But it was definitely a different room from before, on a lower floor. This one was larger, with noisy air con and a mirror across one wall, which I knew meant someone was watching. The two officers from the car reassured me one too many times that it was just a casual conversation. Did I want a lawyer, one of them asked. I said no, of course I didn't. I was aware of my own breathing. I was wearing my best shirt, and I loosened it at the collar; the fabric was damp; sweat was collecting in my armpits.

They left me for what felt a long time. I worried about Celia while I sat there; I thought she would ring or text. I kept checking my phone but there was nothing. I wondered what Mary had told her; what she and Celia were saying about me. The door opened and a slim young man with a receding hairline entered; I recognised him as the officer I'd spoken to when I'd first come in to report my concerns about Marc Ashley. He shook my hand and, with a very small smile, said, 'Nice to see you again, Mr Grimshawe. We all appreciate your police work on our behalf.'

I asked him if he was being facetious, which he didn't understand. So I said, 'I expect you are suspicious of people who push themselves into the centre of an investigation. But it's different in this case, because I know what I'm talking about. I've been doing research on the subject for a creative project. It's important to me that the details are factually correct.'

I repeated the information I'd discovered that water-based murders were proportionally under-prosecuted, in the States at least; that it was hard to distinguish between post- and pre-mortem injuries, and between homicidal and accidental drowning. Salt, I added, can interfere with DNA. 'Most people if they intend to murder want to get away with it and sea water is a good place to start. That and animals – if you've got pigs handy to eat a corpse, that's even better.'

He watched me carefully and I knew I should stop but I couldn't. I said I realised retrieving the murder weapon would be close to impossible, but were they confident the shape of the wound matched the shape of the submerged rock on which Adam had supposedly hit his head? Had they looked at debris under the nails? Had they checked for scuff marks on the cliff? The contents of his lungs? 'I don't know who did the autopsy,' I said, 'but they were obviously not up to the job.'

He shook his head, repressing annoyance, and said further investigations were under way and he was not in a position to share their findings.

I said I was very sorry, but there was one thing I felt guilty about; I thought I might have given the murderer the idea. I explained the plot of my screenplay, maybe in too much detail, because his eyes glazed over. He twirled his fingers. 'Yes, well, I doubt that's relevant.'

He told me to wait and he left the room. He was gone only a few minutes. When he came back, he had another man with him – this one in ordinary clothes: a pair of cargo pants and a white T-shirt. Neatly cropped hair, closely trimmed facial hair and a signet ring he spun as he introduced himself: Lieutenant Kouros. There was something knowing in his manner, and I wondered if he had been behind the mirror, listening the whole time.

Once more I was asked if I wanted a lawyer, and once more I declined. He nodded, moving a muscle in his jaw as though he were chewing.

He asked why I was so convinced my friend's death was not an accident and I said, with some frustration, that I had just explained. He nodded. (So he *had* been listening.)

'And Mr de Souza is, in your eyes, responsible?'

I tried to measure his tone, but it was hard, implacable, so I said, 'Yes.'

'And you believe this is as revenge for behaviours Adam Murphy exhibited in the past – towards de Souza at school, and towards de Souza's sister? Or is your theory that he was motivated by fear, that the "murder" was self-defence?'

'Look, all I know is that he wanted to destroy Adam. He bought a house here. He was in love with Adam's wife – though I must admit at one point I thought he was making up to her in order to freak me out. He was obsessed.'

'Obsessed? I see.' Lieutenant Kouros nodded thoughtfully. He glanced towards the mirror and then back at me. He said, 'Could you tell us your movements please, between eight a.m. and four p.m. on the day of Adam Murphy's death?'

I had been expecting the question and I listed the places I'd been, beginning with my early-morning trip to the bakery where I'd bought the baklava, and ending with my conversation with the priest up at the church. Kouros had been writing notes, but he looked up at that. 'Presbyter Nikolaos?' he said.

'Yes,' I agreed (though he hadn't given me his name). 'He blessed me.'

'It is useful to be blessed,' Kouros said. 'Just in case.'

I laughed, which was a mistake because he didn't. He templed his fingers together and said, 'And you are quite sure that you were at Arcadia that morning?'

I said I was 100 per cent sure.

'Only Mr de Souza, whom we have spoken to and who has been very helpful – in fact he has funded a reward for more information—'

'Yes, he always does that,' I snapped.

He blinked slowly. 'Mr de Souza says you were not at Arcadia, that you have never been to Arcadia . . .'

'He's lying.'

He once again spun his signet ring, and then continued as if I hadn't spoken. 'Mr de Souza says you have never been to Arcadia at his *invitation*. But that you have shown up several times, uninvited.' He flicked through to his notebook. 'You swam once across the bay and walked up to the pool from his private beach and drank from his bar; you gatecrashed his birthday party; and you swam up to his yacht and insisted on coming aboard.' He smiled faintly. 'Like a pirate. It is his contention that *you* are the one in the grip of an obsession – with his wealth maybe – and that you have demonstrated unbalanced behaviour in relation to people around him.'

'That's not true.'

'Ms Sara Ashley, for example. How well do you know her?'

'Not very well. We met here this summer.'

'Ms Ashley has expressed anxieties to Mr de Souza about your unwanted attentions. You rang her repeatedly? You followed her to her hotel?'

'Her Airbnb.'

'And you returned to the UK specifically to visit her at her place of work in the south of England in the town of Lewes?'

'It wasn't *specifically*. I was in the country anyway. I wanted to *talk* to her.'

'I also understand you have recently been blackmailed with

regard to sending and soliciting indecent material.' He raised both palms.

'Who told you that? Was it Rey? It's a lie. It wasn't me,' I said. 'I was protecting a friend. *Adam.* I was protecting Adam.' The sweat was running off my face now and the first officer handed me a paper handkerchief which I am afraid in my frustration I thrust back at him.

'I *was* at Arcadia,' I said. 'Rey is lying to protect himself. And I have proof. You know I have.' I got out my phone and brought up the video of Rey swimming across the bay. We watched it together. It was less recognisably him now I looked at it again. In fact, it could have been anyone. I felt my confidence slip.

'Am I under arrest?' I said.

Lieutenant Kouros leant back in his chair; he clasped his hands against his chest. 'As yet there is no crime,' he said. 'But in the event that a crime is deemed to have taken place – have no doubt, we will be in touch.'

I stood up quickly and walked to the door. I turned the handle, but it was locked. The younger officer stood up and made a gesture and, after a click, the door opened.

Lieutenant Kouros walked behind me up the stairs and, when I went a bit wrong, guided me through to reception. I could hear him still behind me at the swing doors, and at the last minute I turned, and said, 'It's hard knowing how to live a good life, you know, working out what the right thing to do is. You think I'm interfering, but I'm only trying to do what's best.'

'Goodbye, Mr Grimshawe,' he said. 'Maybe we will meet again.'

34

After that, things happened quickly. Celia rang the same evening to say the body hadn't been released after all and to ask what the police had wanted – 'Background,' I said, 'nothing important' – and the following morning, she was on the phone again to say a new coroner had ordered a fresh autopsy. She was crying. She said she didn't want Adam's poor beautiful body poked about any more than it already had been; Rey had intervened on her behalf but had got nowhere. 'It was an accident,' she sobbed. 'How can it be anything but?'

I went straight up to Villa Mimosa and persuaded her out for a walk. Careful to avoid the bay, I took a different route, following the path that wound out of the other side of the olive groves. The way was choked with boulders and cacti and prickly pear; loose stones rattled away in miniature landslides, and we walked mainly in single file. It was very hot and insecty. My ankles were getting scratched. When we passed the ruined house where I had seen her and Rey kiss, she paused. The story was, she said, a young married couple had been murdered there after an argument over a dowry; their spirits were said still to pound the shoreline, looking for revenge.

'God,' I said. 'Grim.'

'All because of money. People are awful.'

'It's never really about money,' I said. 'It'll have been about something personal – a resentment, a betrayal, a heartbreak.'

'Do you think?' She let out a shuddering sigh. 'Oh Matt.'

We'd started walking again when she said, 'If only the girls and I hadn't gone out that day. If only we'd been here. Or if only you'd done as you said and gone for a swim with him. I've replayed it and replayed it in my head. I can't bear it. I dream about it every night. If only one thing had happened differently, he would still be here.'

'You can't think like that,' I said. 'You'll go mad if you let yourself.'

I walked ahead then, taking the lead, ignoring the track that led to the road and choosing the one that dipped ahead of us and then rose. Cypresses and poplars fluttered as we climbed. The air was changing. Thunder was in the air.

'Why do they need a second autopsy?' she said. 'Why can't they let it lie?'

I said they had to do what they had to do.

'But why, Matt? You spoke to them yesterday – what did they want?'

We were reaching a crest; the path was dry and stony and steep. I felt breathless not so much because of the exertion but because I knew I had to say something; that now was the time.

'You have to prepare yourself,' I said. 'I think they're beginning to think it might not have been an accident.'

She stopped short. Small stones clattered away. 'He wouldn't,' she said. 'Adam just wouldn't. He loved life too much.'

I stared at her in appeal, and slightly shook my head.

'What else, Matt? What else could it be? I don't understand.'

'Someone might have wanted to hurt him,' I said.

She started walking again, picking up the pace. 'What? Why? *Who? Who* would want to hurt Adam?'

I'd misjudged our route and we'd roamed too high. Ahead was a sudden cleft of bay, an irregular blue triangle under a drift of mackerel sky. The water below Villa Mimosa churned with small dark shapes: boats, divers. I stopped so she would look away and face me. I didn't answer immediately – I thought my expression would tell her what she needed to know – and she looked into my eyes for what felt like a long time before she said, very calmly, 'Was it you? Did you push him?'

'Me? *Celia.*'

'I'd always suspected you hated him.'

'I loved him.'

She laughed and said in a strange voice, 'It's all sort of the same.'

'How can you say that?' I said. 'How could you think it

even for a minute? Of course I didn't. I swear – not to God obviously, but on everything I hold true.'

I expected her to apologise but she started walking again. Was she thinking about Rey? Surely, now, she was – unless the implications were too awful. It put her at the centre of it. Of course it would feel better if it wasn't him, but me.

After a few minutes, I said, 'Would you forgive me, if I had? As a good Catholic?'

'God would,' she said, not missing a beat, 'as long as you placed your faith in Him.'

'But what about you?'

She didn't answer. I could feel the forces fighting within her.

'Well, it doesn't matter,' I said, 'because I didn't.'

35

Microscopic drops of Adam's DNA were detected on the rocks above sea level: blood spatter indicative of a head injury having taken place before, not *after*, his body entered the water. The flat shape of the wound did actually match the flat surface of the submerged rock. However, particles of matter embedded within it bore traces not of algae, as you'd expect from an underwater collision, but fragments that had been exposed to the outside air: grass seed, guano from seagulls and *Massospora cicadina*, an airborne fungus that infects some cicadas.

Debris, as yet unidentified, was removed from under Adam's nails.

Chlorine was also found in Adam's stomach. Salt residue in the thermos and one of the coffee cups suggested both had been washed out with sea water. The quantity of chlorine might not have been enough to kill him, the coroner concluded – it was difficult to say – but it explained blisters on his tongue, and damage to his cornea. He would have been dizzy, disorientated, his vision blurred. Diving under those physical conditions, had he still thought of doing so, would have been extremely dangerous.

Rey was taken in for questioning on 20 September, a week and a bit after I'd sent my email. I was in Celia's kitchen when the news came through. I held her while she wailed – the depth of her horror was a shock even to me. Mary watched on. Celia asked me to go upstairs with her and said, 'You promise no one knows about him and me?' I promised. (It was true: I'd been careful to refer to an infatuation not an affair.) 'We were very discreet,' she said, 'no one ever saw us,' and I nodded, thinking of the photo, the two of them kissing, on my phone. 'He dazzled me,' she railed. 'I was blinded.' I listened, and held her, a flood of relief coursing through my veins. Money and influence were nothing, it turned out, next to patience and hard work.

The relief was short-lived. They kept him in for *two hours* – less time than I'd spent at the police station myself.

And then once more they came for me.

It was worse this time. Celia and I had gone down to Kardamos for a change of scene. The weather was breaking; the air full of tiny flies, black clouds gathering and swelling, spots of rain darkening the tarmac. We were at Dimitri's, forcing down beer. She was talking about Rey, asking why he'd been released. What did I think? Was it all a mistake? I was trying to calm her when I saw Christos walking next to the harbour wall towards us. He was very polite, but his fingers dug into my arm as he led me away.

Rey had counter-attacked. It didn't matter how many people there were back in that room at the police station – Kouros and Christos and whoever else was lined up behind the two-way mirror watching the interrogation. It was between Rey and me.

Kouros told me de Souza had denied being in love with Celia; there was no evidence of any affair. Mrs Murphy herself had said the idea was ridiculous; they were 'just friends'. I was the one, de Souza had said, who was obsessed with her.

I stayed calm. I didn't want to show the photo of them kissing unless it was absolutely necessary. 'It's not true.'

I was bitterly jealous of Adam – both personally and professionally.

'Not true,' I said again.

'You mentioned to us Mr de Souza finding inspiration in a screenplay you've written. Mr de Souza says as a favour to Celia, who felt sorry for you, he agreed to read it. And that he found the content disturbing – a warped fantasy, a trial run for a murder that he believes you committed yourself. Is that true? Did you kill Adam Murphy?'

'No. I did not.'

'Even after Mr Murphy beat you to a pulp?'

He continued to stare at me, and at my cheek where the bruising had faded but was still evident.

'Even after then,' I said.

Hours passed. They asked me again about Amira and the whole dirty pics/blackmailing thing – which I once more rebuffed – and also my 'stalking' of Sara Ashley. They had contacted her, Kouros told me, and she said she'd been scared of me initially, but she'd realised in the end that I was just 'a bit sad'.

'Well, "a bit sad" doesn't hit their best friend over the head with a rock,' I said. 'Not last time I looked.'

They left me alone and when they came back they asked again if I wanted a lawyer. Without wavering, I said no. 'Tell Rey to get a lawyer,' I said. 'I'm not the one who needs a lawyer. He does.'

It became hotter in the room – maybe they switched off the air con. I asked for water and Kouros waited until I'd finished the glass.

'Could you please tell us your movements between nine a.m. and eleven a.m. on the day in question,' he said.

'So, you've narrowed down time of death,' I said. 'Is that because of the temperature of the coffee in the thermos? Oh no, he tampered with that. Was it the eyes – the vitreous membrane? Or was the skin wrinkled – had the dermis and epidermis begun to separate?'

Kouros pulled down his chin. He probably didn't have the information in front of him. He was going with what he'd been told.

I sighed heavily; there was a forty-five minute period just after 9 a.m. I couldn't account for. I hoped he wouldn't notice.

'OK. Anyway. I went to the shop in the village to buy pastries – ask Andrea, she'll remember me being there. We talked about her father. After that, I went straight to Arcadia. I was at the door, as I've told you before, at about ten a.m.'

'Mr de Souza says not. It's your word against his.'

'It's not just my word. There was a woman there – she brought me coffee – he'll have paid her to stay quiet.' I could feel frustration rising. 'Talk to her. I brought the tray down to the kitchen. Ask her if she remembers.'

I remembered the video of the swim. They'd taken my phone off me, but I told them to look again. 'Even if he's not identifiable, can't you see from my location that I was where I said I was?'

And then, finally, I mentioned Rey's phone. 'I don't know if he told you that he lost it that day. Anyway, Celia told me that he did. Have you thoroughly searched the rocks where he pushed Adam? My assumption would be he dropped it in the struggle.'

It was a dirty trick. Just as poking the phone into a crevasse in the first place had been – though it was panic at the time. My only defence: saving my own skin.

They did find his phone – not that anyone thanked me.

In the end it was the microscopic fibres under Adam's fingernails that were to prove most damning for Rey. It took time but they turned out to be fragments of fine brown 'jacquard-shell' polyamide. Jacquard is particularly distinctive as it is made on a loom machine in which complex patterns are woven directly into the material. In lightweight 'shell' form jacquard has a subtle sheen and was found to match a clothing line released earlier that year by Gucci, specifically swim shorts, a pair of which was removed, under warrant, from Arcadia. The police also found chlorine tablets in the pool-maintenance hut.

They charged Rey finally in the middle of October and he was taken before the Public Prosecutor twenty-four hours later. The investigative judge who brought the case against him claimed it was a premeditated crime, that Rey had swum across the bay with the intention of murdering Adam. He had secreted the chlorine – waterproof-wrapped, taped to his shorts – into Adam's cup of coffee. The two men had talked for a while. Rey had waited for the poison to take effect before making his move. Adam fought back but, weakened by the poison, was easily overcome by the smaller man, who hit him with a rock he later hurled into the sea, before dropping him head first after it.

Rey was refused bail – on the grounds that his private jet and extreme wealth made him too much of a flight risk – and to await trial he was transferred to Korydallos, a high-security facility in a western suburb of Athens. Due to severe overcrowding, he was put up in a single room in the women's wing.

Even there his money helped. Money always did.

36

Adam's body was repatriated in November and Celia accompanied it home, heading straight to Norfolk to organise the funeral (there'd been no further mention of cremation). The family house was full and, not wanting to press myself on them, I booked an Airbnb in the village. I saw her as much as I could in that period, finding her surprisingly calm – though she was biting her nails again. I only once saw a chink in her armour. We were walking, the two of us alone, in the garden and she stopped alongside the tennis court, where the net was sagging, and asked me intently if I thought 'the silly business' between her and Rey might now come out. I thought for a moment, and then said that as far as I was aware, only the three of us knew. Rey's defence would rest on denying it, and she could of course depend on me. She didn't mention it again.

Dead Heat

At the funeral, she wore a black dress and a black veil that had belonged to her grandmother; her family clung to her like bodyguards. It was a full Catholic mass – no eulogy, but prayers, the promise of resurrection, communion. I didn't go up to take the host, though I was tempted – if only to get closer to her. I'd been seated back in the seventh row. Her eyes searched the congregation when they filed out; I hoped she was looking for me, but when she saw me she didn't even smile, just nodded as though I were some distant relation. The churchyard was full of leaves – they'd come down overnight – and the way they rushed and tumbled around the grave and the mourners gave the final proceedings a wildness that felt right.

I didn't see Celia at all over Christmas – I spent it in Manchester with my sister – but in early January she rang to ask if I would travel back to Greece with her for the trial. She said she'd told the children to stay away, and she couldn't think who else to ask.

There were no direct flights to Kalamata at that time of year so we flew out to Athens where a driver met us at the airport. When we arrived at Villa Mimosa it was raining. A bitter wind swept off the sea, bent back the shrubs, puckered the leaf-strewn surface of the pool. We had separate rooms – I slept in Lydia's bed under a panoply of fairy lights (on a timer; hard to switch off). We ate scrambled eggs and sat by the fire, playing what I called Pairs and Celia called Pelmanism, and in the morning, I drove her in Daisy, the draughty Beetle, across the mountains to Sparta where the trial was taking place. The courtroom was packed – a lot of Rey's 'trusted friends', providing support, and a lot of journalists, none of whom I recognised, wanting the dirt. It was hot and claustrophobic, with constant pauses for translation.

The first day was a bit of a blur – interviews with various officers of the law, a lot of waiting around. Celia held my hand when we were in session, keeping her eyes on the ground. As far as I was aware she didn't once look at Rey, down there in the dock, though his eyes were often on her.

She gave her evidence on the third day. She spoke clearly but quietly. Yes, she had got to know Reynash de Souza quite well over the summer. It had started with swimming lessons and progressed from there. No, she hadn't been aware that Adam had bullied him at school, but Rey had asked her lots of questions about Adam's past. 'And I was beginning to realise his attitude towards him wasn't very charitable. He definitely held a grudge.'

She wept when asked if there had been more to her relationship with Rey than friendship. Someone bought her a tissue and, after a bit of delicate nose blowing, she pulled herself together and said that she would have to admit, as she was under oath, that she had been flattered by Rey's attentions and by the presents – various pieces of expensive swimwear – but that nothing improper had happened between them. 'He turned my head, I admit to that, but I loved my husband very much.' She made a quick cross. 'I *love* my husband very much.'

The lawyer, who'd been addressing her in English, either didn't understand what she had said or pretended not to. 'So you and Reynash de Souza were in a relationship,' he said, frowning slightly. 'He "turned your head", you say. You were having an affair.'

'No.' Her voice sounded shrill then and for the first time her eyes went to Rey. 'There was no affair.'

The whole thing took it out of her and we agreed, once her evidence was completed, that the journey to Sparta was really too much. It would be better, we decided, if, from then on, I went alone. Thank God, really, because my own stint under cross-examination was quite rocky – the defence went hard for my credibility – mainly the stuff I'd already encountered from the police: obsession with Rey, obsession with Celia, obsession with Adam. But there was a new strain, too – that I'd purposefully misled Rey.

'You maliciously led him to believe Adam was the man who had raped his sister.' I wasn't prepared for that and I felt my face burn because it was true. It hit me how much I *had* actually wanted Adam dead, not always but for that short period, those hours after I'd kissed him, and how I had willed that animus on to Rey. I'd wanted Rey to think of Adam as violent and unhinged. I'd wanted him to *hate* him, to feel the force of it, because to do so made me feel better. And that was a terrible thing. I looked at each of the three judges, each of the four jurors in turn, and for a moment I wavered . . . but, in the end, I said yes, I knew. I was sorry. It *was* malicious. I regretted it deeply. It had been evil of me. I used the Greek word, *kakos*, which translates as mean and ugly, but also worthless.

I just think it's best to be honest.

In the end, it was honesty that did for Rey. The defence

called several character witnesses, including someone called Phil Cohen, a friend of Rey's I vaguely recognised from the party (the one, in fact, who thought he'd recognised me: 'he knows how to birthday'). He took the stand and most of his testimony was along the lines of what a great guy Rey was, how understated and kind. 'He'd do anything for you. I'd do anything for him. Anything at all.'

Quick as a flash, came the cross-examination: 'So you'd lie for him?'

Phil Cohen floundered. 'No, of course not.'

'So you've never lied for him? Not even when you told the police you saw Marc Ashley set out on a run? Because you didn't, did you? You were seen by a fisherman on a jet ski at the time you claimed to be in the house.'

He tried to bluff it out and the evidence from the fisherman was ultimately deemed inadmissible, but the damage was done. There were fewer people in court the following day – all that loyalty wavered when the tide turned – so not many of his friends saw his maid confess he had paid her to lie about not having seen me the morning of Adam's murder. She admitted that I had been in the house. She had brought me coffee and I had brought baklava and then later I'd taken the tray downstairs – none of his other guests had ever bothered to bring down a tray. I'd even, she said, offered to fill the dishwasher. She was sorry to have caused me a problem. Turned out, I discovered, she was Andrea from the shop's niece. ('You ever need a favour,' Andrea once said, 'you come to me.')

Rey's fate was sealed even before he changed his story and

admitted he had swum across but only to talk to Adam and that when he'd got there, he'd found him already dead. It was the last hurrah of a desperate man. The answer is always the most obvious. Occam's razor. When you hear hoofbeats, think horses not zebras. Think man who admits to being there not mystery assailant.

Sara Ashley approached me in the foyer when court finished that day. Until that point, I'd seen her but steered clear. 'You were right,' she said. 'If only I'd listened. You just don't want to believe the worst of people, do you?' It was too late, she thought, to open the inquiry into her brother; Rey had paid for the funeral, cremation included. But she'd been looking into the sale of AdVent; she'd found papers and printouts of WhatsApp messages in her brother's effects.

I left her talking to a reporter from *Le Monde*.

On the first Tuesday in March, the Spartan Court of First Instance found Reynash de Souza guilty of the murder of Adam Murphy. When you're up against normal people, with mortgages and bills, money means nothing. In fact, you could say it counts against you, that what counts for you is evidence, painstaking research, and small acts of kindness: taking down a tray, being friendly to people in shops.

37

We took a taxi to Islington from the airport and I helped her in. It's horrid going home when you've been away for a long time: piles of post, mainly flyers, and a cold hall, the kitchen filthy – Lydia and her friends had pretty well had the run of the place. I cleaned up and lit a fire and went to Tesco Metro for a Charlie Bigham's fish pie. I put it in the Aga, laid the kitchen table for two, and brought a Campari and soda up to the drawing room where I'd settled her. Celia was holding a framed picture when I walked in – it was of Adam in black tie at some TV award. I made a joke about her expression – she was studying it fiercely – and she told me she had a headache. Lydia was playing Taylor Swift loudly in her bedroom and I suggested I went up and asked her to turn it down. She smiled, but said, 'Darling Matt, I think I'll be better *toute seule*, if that's all right,' so I kissed her forehead, told her to sleep well, and went out into the night.

Down the steps, into the square, huge naked plane trees towering, I was about to turn right into the road that led to Upper Street when I saw a young girl coming towards me: bare legs, chunky trainers and an Afghan coat. As she got closer, I realised it was Jasmine. She smiled, vaguely, not sure who I was, until I said, 'Jasmine. It's me, Matt.'

She stopped then and said, 'Yes, of course.' Her hair was different – smoothed back away from her face. She was paler and wearing more make-up. I asked after her mother and she said she was OK, but her dad's new girlfriend was pregnant, which was rank. She'd got an offer from Newcastle to read Philosophy, thanks for asking, but she wasn't sure – she wanted to stay closer to her mum.

She smiled and seemed to be about to walk on, when she hesitated.

'Oh shit,' she said, opening her eyes startlingly wide. 'You gave me twenty euros to spend at the airport. And I never gave it back.'

'It's fine.'

'No. I feel bad. I feel bad about everything.'

I told her she didn't need to, that neither of us wanted that, and only then did she seem to focus on what I'd been doing there, then, in that particular street. She looked past me. 'Oh shit, is Celia back from Greece? Is she in the house? Oh no.'

Assuming it was the embarrassment of Celia's grief she was keen to avoid, I said encouragingly, 'Best just to go in and behave like normal. She'd love to see you, I know.'

Her eyes swerved away and she shook her head. 'Oh no, Matt. I don't want to see her. And she won't want to see me.' She let out a small groan, and then took out her phone and sent a text. 'I'll meet Lydia at Spoons,' she said and then walked alongside me as I continued away from the house.

I felt something ominous in the heaviness of her steps, the downward tilt of her chin.

'Why don't you want to see Celia?' I asked.

She kept her eyes down. 'She hates me.'

'Don't be silly. Of course she doesn't.'

'Well, she should.'

She was still stroking the railings with one hand. The street light flickered through the bare trees.

'As far as I know she's very fond of you.'

'She didn't speak to me after . . . not once.'

I took my mind back to the days after Adam's death: Jasmine in the kitchen at Villa Mimosa, helping herself to a glass of water, slipping out of the door down to the pool, on her phone. There were snippets: a flick of wet hair, footprints across the tiles, a bowed head, the ripple of shoulder blades. She'd kept a low profile, but then hadn't we all? We'd tried to be supportive without being in the way. It was day three when she came to find me to ask if I would take her to the airport; she'd managed to get on a flight, but she'd had to pay twice – easyJet hadn't refunded her original booking – which was largely why I'd lobbed her a bit of extra cash in the car. She'd been quiet on the drive up. But again, those few days, who *wasn't* quiet?

We reached the lights and splattered frenzy of Upper Street, which had the hysteria of London rush hour in the dark and wet. Cars drove splashily by; cyclists tried to outgun lorries. Being in the middle of urban life, at the edge of a frantic, open thoroughfare, seemed to release something in her, because she stopped walking and looked at me.

She said, with an edge of boldness, 'I wasn't in love with him. I mean he was *old*. It's just . . .'

She wiped her cheeks and dabbed the pads of her fingers beneath her eyes.

My own throat closed. It's a killer, other people crying.

A Deliveroo moped driver bounced on to the pavement and we separated to let him pass. When we came back together, she blinked fiercely: 'It's just, you know.' She lowered her head, thrusting her hands deep into the pockets of her Afghan. The fur at the sleeves at the neck was tatty, matted; it was cheap fake suede. From a charity shop, or Boohoo.

Boo hoo. Adam's voice. His laugh. 'Oh Jasmine,' I said.

She'd started to cry. 'You know, I thought we had something a bit special.'

'Did you?'

'He wasn't like other dads.'

'No. That he wasn't.'

She wiped her eyes and looked away. The traffic lights near us changed to red and the pedestrian crossing bleeped.

'He was always so nice to me – I mean they were both were. Celia too. I can't stand it that she hates me now. But you know, my dad was being such a *shit*, and Adam was, like, interested in what I had to say. We had a lot in common, he said, and he was always telling me how pretty I was; he taught me how to play poker. Like properly, not just taking your clothes off when you get the lowest number. We had a laugh. Until . . . He was a laugh, you know, before—' She broke off with an intake of breath.

'Before what?'

She screwed up her face. 'Before that last afternoon. It was *so* hot. We'd both been drinking. He'd come into my room to try and persuade me to stay behind, you know, not go up for cocktails with Celia's school friend, and I suppose I was teasing him, saying it would be boring, stuck in a house with no pool and an old man for company. We were just fooling around. I'm not like that. I never meant it to happen.'

I didn't need to say anything; just held her gaze. It wasn't a shock; of course it wasn't. The way Adam's eyes had rested on her. His laugh as he'd flicked water on to her back; the little noise he'd let out when she'd walked into the kitchen in her tiny pyjama bottoms, a high whine, like a dog locked out of a room.

But Jasmine. His daughter's friend.

'It was just a kiss,' she said quietly.

'A *kiss*?'

She rubbed her forehead. 'Yeah. Fuck.' She wrinkled her nose, squeamish, repelled even. 'He backed me against the wall, and pushed his tongue against my teeth. And honestly, Matt, I would have told him to fuck off anyway, even if Celia hadn't walked in. I'll never forget her face. It was just like blind fury. She looked devastated. And the worst thing . . .'

I waited.

'The thing I can't bear is that they spent their last night together arguing. Her last memories of him are just shit. And I know they didn't even make up, because in the morning he was in such a state. It took her forever to get organised. She got us up early to go to her friend's hotel but then kept us waiting in the car. It was just chaos.'

I was aware of my heart hammering in my chest. 'What do you mean "chaos"?'

'She said she'd forgotten her sunglasses and she left us there while she fetched them but she was gone ages. When she came back, it wasn't from the house, but up the path. And she was in a state – I think she'd gone to find Adam and they must have been arguing. She was all sweaty and she went in to change – took off the shorts she'd been wearing and put on a dress.'

'What time was this?'

'I can't remember. But we were late getting there. Her friend was cross. But listen, please – if you see her, can you give her a message?' She put her hand on my arm. The paint on her fingernails was chipped. 'Can you tell her I'm sorry that she saw me with Adam and I would do anything for it not to have happened.'

38

Celia was evasive those next few weeks back in London. I left messages on her phone and a care package on her doorstep (a box of those chocolates, John Carey's *100 Poets* and some 'smellies', as she called them, from Space NK). Since I'd lost the Battersea basement to the new au pair, I'd been sofa-surfing – doing everything I could not to wear out the patience of old friends.

She didn't answer the phone, though she texted to thank me for the gifts, said she was taking some 'me' time.

Rey's sentencing was announced for the second week of February and, if it hadn't been for that, I wonder if I would have seen her again. As it was, I told her I planned to attend in order to represent the family, and I suppose it was for appearance's sake that she agreed to accompany me – at least as far as Villa Mimosa; she couldn't face 'going the whole hog'.

We travelled out separately – she flew direct to Athens where she spent a few 'restorative' nights in a boutique hotel; and I flew slowly to Kalamata, a circuitous but cheap route. I arrived in the village six hours before she did, which gave me time, among other things, to visit Branwell and her kittens, now happily ensconced with Andrea. I didn't go straight into Villa Mimosa, but walked down the path to the cove, just as I had the night I arrived the previous summer. It was earlier in the evening when I got there but, being February, just as dark. Black water rolled at my feet as I stared across at Arcadia. How different it was now. No movement, no lights. Just a black hulk. Andrea had told me some of the tiles had come off the roof. Nature claws back. It always does.

At Villa Mimosa, the front door key was hidden under a tarpaulin on the back wheel of the Beetle, and after letting myself in I walked around the house, imagining I owned it, before I began a proper search.

I had supper – stuffed courgettes – and a bottle of wine waiting on the table when her taxi pulled up. I heard the engine purr, and voices, the slam of the door, the rolling clatter of her suitcase (such an annoying noise).

She said, 'Oh, you are precious,' when she saw how much trouble I'd gone to. She took off her coat – sheepskin luxe – and straight away picked up the wine and poured herself a glass. It was one of the bottles Rey had brought to lunch that day – I'd found it among other things on top of the fridge – but I don't think she realised. She asked about my journey, which had involved a seven-hour stopover in Amsterdam. 'Quite the adventure. Dear Matt, you are a brick.' She looked at me directly for the first time. 'Adam would be so grateful.'

It wasn't until she'd started eating that she noticed the manuscript of my screenplay on the table. I saw her eyes alight on it, dart away, and then return. She took a mouthful of courgette before looking back at me. The smallest of questions in her eyes. 'The housekeeper's been then?' she said.

'It certainly seems spick and span in here.'

'That's good. I wasn't sure. She's so unreliable.'

I waited until she had finished eating. It was getting dark and windy; a plant was scratching its nails against the side window. I thought how dismissive she sometimes was about people who worked for her.

'I found it in the drawer of your bedside table.'

She nodded.

'I looked everywhere before but didn't find it. I'd decided Adam must have thrown it away. Did you read it?'

Another nod.

'Any good?'

A non-committal twist of her mouth. 'Maybe stick to the day job?'

I laughed. 'If only I had one of those. I'm running out of savings.'

She let out an amused grunt.

I said, 'Do you think it gave the killer ideas?'

She picked at the side of her mouth. 'You mean, using water to try and cover your tracks, the idea of misdirection, hoping people's assumptions – that it was an accident waiting to happen – would distract them?' She smiled coolly. 'Maybe.'

'Shame Adam never got round to reading it. He might have been prepared.'

The branch scratched once more against the window. Celia was looking at me very directly. She wet her lower lip with her tongue, and then brought her finger there and tapped. 'There's nothing about poison in your script,' she said.

'True.'

'The chlorine in the coffee. I . . .' She looked as if she was struggling to find the right phrasing. Finally, she settled on, 'I've never understood how and when that got there. Would Rey really have smuggled the capsules across the water and then into Adam's coffee, and waited for them to take effect?'

'No,' I agreed. 'It does seem rather more premeditated than the rest of his actions. And, of course, poison is usually a female weapon, though I suppose all the more reason for a man to choose it. The perfect misdirection.' I held her gaze. 'However, it's important to remember the coroner couldn't be sure the chlorine killed Adam. Just weakened him.'

'Maybe enough for a fatal accident,' she countered. 'When "he" put it in his coffee "he" might have thought it would be enough on its own.' She looked at me closely.

'We'll never know.' I lifted one shoulder, a lopsided shrug. 'It's not worth thinking about, Celia. Certainly, the poison wasn't enough for a murder conviction. It was the other evidence that counted, and the head injury that killed him. That, in the end, was the actual murder.'

'Do you think?' she said, staring into what felt like my soul. 'I suppose you would.'

I collected our plates and put them in the dishwasher, and then I picked up the screenplay, shook the sheets together, and stuffed them in the mouth of that awful rusty pedal bin. I returned to the table. She was staring at the piece of brown clothing I'd hidden under the manuscript, now lying there exposed.

'I found these on top of the fridge,' I said. 'I don't know how they got up there.'

She swallowed. 'Oh, Rey's Gucci shorts.'

'Odd because they found those in his house – in order to match the brown threads in the autopsy. But of course, this must be the *other* pair. I remember he had two pairs.'

She cleared her throat. 'Yes. Maybe. I lost the bottoms to my green bikini. I might have worn these instead once or twice.'

I looked at her, smiling. 'Oh. OK. Possibly I even have a photo of you in them. Kissing him down by the ruined house.'

'You have a photo of us?'

I nodded and she lowered her eyes.

Feeling my advantage, I said, 'Do you think we should hang on to them for Lydia? She was always a fan.'

She shook her head.

'Not for eBay or . . .?'

She shook her head again.

'Maybe we should bin them, too,' I said, wrinkling my nose.

A long pause; eventually she nodded.

I busied myself about the kitchen, putting the sheep's milk cheese I'd bought on a plate and chopping up an apple. She liked her apples sliced (tooth still not sorted; a bone graft needed). I left both on the table and turned away to make the coffee; when I came back, she had cut herself a piece of cheese but instead of eating it, she was grinding it with the knife into smaller and smaller pieces on her plate.

I sat down opposite her and bit into an apple – I'd kept mine whole. 'It's so lovely here,' I said when I'd taken a bite. 'Do you mind if I stay for a bit?'

Still looking down, she laughed quietly – or I think it was a laugh. 'Stay as long as you want.'

'Really?'

'Of course.'

She carried on with her destruction of the cheese. I watched her.

'Why didn't you cremate him in the end?' I said.

'The children wouldn't let me.'

It was dark in the kitchen; her face was full of shadows. I should, I thought, put on a light.

I didn't, though.

Finally, I said, 'Have you forgiven him?'

She looked up. 'Who? Rey?'

'No. Adam.'

'For what?'

She stared at me and I looked into her pale eyes, shade and light, and shade again. They narrowed slightly and I thought it best not to push it. I knew by then that she was capable of anything.

Church of Agios Petros

Sparta
February 2025
2.40 p.m.

She isn't outside the courtroom where she said she'd be waiting and I go back to the car in case she's there, but she isn't. I walk around a bit and in the end I go into the church. The moment I push open the heavy doors, I can see her in the front pew, head bowed.

It's lavish in here, gold and velvet, every surface glinting with icons. At the table, I light two candles – one for each dead man – and drop five euros into the box. Is that enough? Rummaging in my pockets, I find a couple of loose coins which I post in too. How much for eternal salvation? I wish I knew.

I walk down the aisle and slip into the row behind her.
She flinches.
I bend my face and murmur in her ear. 'It's done.'
'How long?' Her voice is a whisper; she doesn't turn.

'Twenty-five years.'

Her head drops forward a few inches.

I wait a while for her to process it. Nothing for a murder he committed; twenty-five years for one he didn't. It's longer than either of us thought.

Sick of the church suddenly, I coax her up and escort her along the aisle and out into the open air.

The Taygetus mountains rise in the distance. I think of Patrick Leigh Fermor's description of them as 'a dead, planetary place, a habitat for dragons'.

We walk back towards where I parked the car. Small brown doves, pairs of them, balance on the telegraph wires. Sparrows in our path flutter off and resettle. I feel suddenly the relief of it being over.

I take her hand. It's slack for a moment but after a while her fingers curl and she grips mine back.

She looks up into my face, a bit unsure. 'You're quite something,' she says eventually. 'Quite someone.'

I nod.

'You and me, eh?' she says.

I know what she means, that we're tied together now. Common purpose. She thinks our parts in Adam's death are equal. I'm not sure.

Dead heat? Maybe.

Maybe it doesn't matter.

I smile.

Celia looks at me and smiles uncertainly back.

We're a bit scared of each other this evening, skittish

even. Last night in bed, I'd had to remember her entwined with Adam before I could come. Not a day goes by when I don't imagine I see him: throwing his arms around Dimitri; or recklessly casting himself into the waves, bare-chested, flamboyant, unashamed; or teasing me, barrelling towards me, his face creased with laughter.

Tomorrow she flies home – too cold here, she says, too grim – but I'll stay a bit longer. I love Greece – the birds, the colours, the light. It'll be nice to have Villa Mimosa to myself. I've got an idea for a book, and the drawing room's the perfect place to write. Maybe I'll go to Norfolk next. Play some tennis. I'm in talks with Adam's production company; they're looking for someone to present the Romanovs. I'm not sure I'm the perfect fit, but I'm getting better at taking risks.

So, all good really. It's just—

I must have let out a sigh.

'What?' Celia says. She's still trying to read me.

'Nothing.'

I drop her hand and we walk in silence the rest of the way to the car.

Acknowledgements

Thank you to the brilliant Selina Walker, all one could ask for in an editor, and to the rest of the amazing Century team, most notably Charlotte Bush, Mary Karayel and Laurie Ip Fung Chun. Thank you to Richenda Todd for her close attention to the text. And to Catherine Bennett for all her genius with titles. Thank you as ever to my agent, Judith Murray, and to everybody else at Greene & Heaton, particularly Kate Rizzo, Mia Dakin and Stephanie Cohen.

I am very grateful to Sophie Milner for putting me in touch with Jo Dawkins, lecturer in forensic science at the University of Leicester, whose knowledge, so generously imparted, was invaluable. I don't think it's possible to meet anyone as enthusiastic about bloat.

Thank you to Jessica Cecil for alerting me to the interesting parallels with Mike Lynch long before he hit the headlines.

Acknowledgements

And to Andrew Watson for providing a constant supply of translation, fact and nuance. If it hadn't been for Andrew, the Mani would never have got into my head in the first place.

Lastly, thank you to Barney, Joe and Mabel for putting up with me and to Giles for making everything better.

Bringing a book from manuscript to what you are reading is a team effort, and Penguin Random House would like to thank everyone at Century who helped to publish *Dead Heat*.

PUBLISHER
Selina Walker

EDITORIAL
Laurie Ip Fung Chun
Mary Karayel
Richenda Todd
Mary Chamberlain

DESIGN
Dan Simpkins

PRODUCTION
Helen Wynn-Smith

INVENTORY
Lizzy Moyes

UK SALES
Alice Gomer
Emily Harvey
Rhian Steer
Kirsten Greenwood
Phoenix Curland

INTERNATIONAL SALES
Anna Curvis
Barbora Sabolova

PUBLICITY
Charlotte Bush

MARKETING
Lydia Weigel

AUDIO
James Keyte
Meredith Benson